The Carriage House

THE CARRIAGE HOUSE

A NOVEL

LOUISA HALL

VIKING
an imprint of
PENGUIN BOOKS

VIKING

Published by the Penguin Group
Penguin Books Ltd, 80 Strand, London WC2R 0RL, England
Penguin Group (USA) Inc., 375 Hudson Street, New York, New York 10014, USA
Penguin Group (Canada), 90 Eglinton Avenue East, Suite 700, Toronto, Ontario, Canada M4P 2Y3
(a division of Pearson Penguin Canada Inc.)
Penguin Ireland, 25 St Stephen's Green, Dublin 2, Ireland (a division of Penguin Books Ltd)
Penguin Group (Australia), 707 Collins Street, Melbourne, Victoria 3008, Australia
(a division of Pearson Australia Group Pty Ltd)
Penguin Books India Pvt Ltd, 11 Community Centre, Panchsheel Park, New Delhi – 110 017, India
Penguin Group (NZ), 67 Apollo Drive, Rosedale, Auckland 0632, New Zealand
(a division of Pearson New Zealand Ltd)
Penguin Books (South Africa) (Pty) Ltd, Block D, Rosebank Office Park,
181 Jan Smuts Avenue, Parktown North, Gauteng 2193, South Africa

Penguin Books Ltd, Registered Offices: 80 Strand, London WC2R 0RL, England

www.penguin.com

First published in the United States of America by Scribner, a division of Simon & Schuster, Inc. 2013
First published in Great Britain by Viking 2013
001

Printed in Great Britain by Clays Ltd, St Ives plc

A CIP catalogue record for this book is available from the British Library

HARDBACK ISBN: 978–0–670–92204–8
TRADE PAPERBACK ISBN: 978–0–670–92289–5

www.greenpenguin.co.uk

Penguin Books is committed to a sustainable
future for our business, our readers and our planet.
This book is made from Forest Stewardship
Council™ certified paper.

ALWAYS LEARNING PEARSON

For Ben

· Book I ·

Yes, he had done it. She was in the carriage, and felt that he had placed her there, that his will and his hands had done it, that she owed it to his perception of her fatigue, and his resolution to give her rest.

—Jane Austen, *Persuasion*

Chapter 1

From the time that his daughters could lift their rackets, William had loved nothing more than to watch them play tennis. As soon as the workday ended, he hurried home to get to their afternoon clinics in time. In the winter, he watched them play in the indoor courts, surrounded by echo, reverberation, and the smell of thick tarp and synthetic felt. Later, when they were old enough to compete, William spent his finest weekends at their tournaments, moving between athletic facilities that started, with time, to feel like home. After years of watching them play, he had begun to feel that there was something important—something historically continuous—about the ritual of walking to the club to see them perform.

The occasions for this ritual were less frequent now. Only when Diana came home from Texas for the ladies' club championship did he have the chance to resurrect that feeling. That crisp, fine pride of watching his girls on court. Elizabeth hadn't touched a racket since she took up acting, and now she'd committed herself to yoga, an activity that William could not bring himself to classify as an athletic pursuit. Izzy walked away from tennis for no apparent reason when she was fourteen, and when she did, it was as though William lost a daughter. She shed every ounce of the nimble girl she had been, becoming instead an adult young creature who both saddened and confused him.

But today, the second of June, 2000, he would walk to the courts again. Today, as he used to do so often, he had hurried home from the office, speeding along the treacherous curves of Kennedy Drive, propelled by his desire to see Diana play. He had jogged up the stairs to change into casual clothes, charged with the same excitement that used to thrill him when his girls were in tournaments. As he pulled off his tie, William examined himself in the mirror behind his closet door. He was still a fine-looking man. He had held up well. He hung his coat on a wooden hanger and changed into a yellow polo. He held his breath while he tucked it in, then took stock of himself once more. Diana had played in national tournaments. What was the ladies' club championship compared to that? But still. Once more he would take his place in the lawn chairs behind the outdoor courts. Once more he would bandy jokes with the other members, who would lean against the fence, hoping to catch a glimpse of his Di. Once more her body's expert movements would awe them into silence, and afterward the two of them would walk home together, he and Di, best pals, her racket bag slung across her back.

Complete in his casual clothes, William hurried down the stairs. In the foyer, he stopped and looked out through the living room window to see Margaux planting pachysandra under the third linden tree. She was kneeling with her hands in the soil, her dark hair falling over her shoulders. Beyond her, the carriage house stood ragged against the sky, a ghost of its former glory. In its shadow, Margaux gardened, oblivious to its disrepair. Frustration spread through him. She had not remembered the significance of the day. She would not come with him to see their daughter win the championship match. She would only continue gardening, face forward, as though the world in which William and their daughters lived had disappeared behind her.

In the kitchen, he passed Louise, absorbed in a gossip magazine, both feet up on a chair. William sometimes wondered whether he had accidentally hired her to lounge full-time in his kitchen, rather than to care for his wife. "Hello, Louise," he said pointedly, and she uttered something incomprehensibly Australian without looking up from her page. "Goodbye, Louise," he said, amused with himself, then took an apple for the road and stepped outside into the fading afternoon.

It was a perfect time of day. He had the sense that a net of light had fallen over the world. He crossed his yard and moved out onto the golf course that stretched behind the houses of Little Lane, smelling the grass beneath his feet, luxuriating in the give of the soil. He, William Adair, moved easily against the resisting force of the world. He was a presence, walking across the golf course in his yellow polo shirt. This knowledge expanded him. He didn't turn to dwell on the carriage house; instead, he moved forward, passing his neighbors' backyards. So generous did he feel, so vast, that he waved at Mrs. Cheshire, who was taking her laundry off the line. He wasn't annoyed by the flock of pink plastic flamingos that Sheldon Ball's kook of a mother had planted in their backyard and that Sheldon had failed to remove since her death. It was a pleasant sensation to lift so high above the issue of the flamingos, to ascend over the carriage house. He even waved at the Muslim man who'd moved in at the corner of Little Lane and Clubhouse Road. Uzmani stood up from whatever surreptitious hole he was digging in his yard. He glanced over his shoulder, turned back with a confused look, then lifted his hand toward William. William shook his head at his own high spirits.

The clubhouse rose before him: redbrick facade supported by white columns, settled between two magnolia trees. The symmetries of its architecture buoyed him; William was a man who appreciated columns. Rather than moving straight through the clubhouse, he took his usual detour down the back hall, lined with wooden plaques commemorating club tennis champions back to 1892. Under Men's Club Champion, his own name—William Adair—appeared in gold paint seven times, from 1967 to 1974. Henry, his brother, won it from 1963 to 1965, before he went to war. Their father's name appeared six times, in the span between 1941 and 1951, when his famous rivalry with George Legg drew spectators from as far as Delaware. And on the ladies' plaque, William's girls. Despite their mother's genes, they were each born with enormous potential. Elizabeth was club champion from 1981 to 1983. At twelve years old, she beat Mrs. Weld, with her stolid thighs and her passive-aggressive pacifism in neighborhood association meetings. With her sunny collusions during the carriage house coup d'état. That was one of the best days of William's life. If only he could once more see Elizabeth running up to volley, staring across the net with such intensity that Mrs. Weld started cranking framers up onto the clubhouse roof, he would die a happy man.

And then. From 1984 to 1999 Diana reigned. What a satisfying thing it was to see, that column of Diana Adairs. Fourteen of them lined up, interrupted only by those two disappointing years. No one at the club could match that. Not Jack and Elaine Weld, with their simpering daughter. Certainly not that Cheshire girl. No, the clubhouse plaques belonged to the Adairs.

Only Izzy was absent. There were, of course, a couple of Isabelle

Adairs on the Girls' Club Championship plaque, from the years before she quit. But she was the most talented of them all. William considered the carpet beneath his feet. It was more threadbare than he'd appreciated before: he would have to speak to the committee about recarpeting. The awareness that his clubhouse was fading lodged a quick pain behind his left ribs. His left hand involuntarily twitched; he clenched it into a fist. If only she would play again! Everything could be righted. If Izzy would walk back out on court, her limbs swinging, the racket precise in her knowledgeable hands. Even Elizabeth could return to the game, now that she was back from L.A. and her children were both in school.

This prospect soothed him. His granddaughters, young as they were, already showed promise. The pain had passed in his rib cage, although his head had started to ache. William knew he shouldn't dwell on old defeats. It was enough that Diana still played, enough that he still could make the walk for the Championship Match. She wasn't finished yet. He'd picked her up from the airport three days ago, and when he saw her waiting on the curb, tears came to his eyes. She was standing, as she always had, with her racket bag slung over her shoulder, her hair in that familiar ponytail. When he pulled up, she swung the bag into the backseat, and it was such a familiar gesture that it pierced him to the core. His athletic girl. Every year she came back for the championship. She knew it made him proud.

Beyond the clubhouse veranda, the grass tennis courts stretched their backs beneath the sun until they reached the line of chestnut trees that bordered Breacon Avenue. The chestnuts bent their heads in the breeze. William breathed; the smell of early-summer foliage produced in him a vivid recollection of bringing his young family to the club when they first joined. His little tribe, the family he'd made for himself. As clear as day, William saw Izzy as a baby in her mother's arms, the afternoon light across Margaux's face, the way Margaux seemed to look past the visible world of tennis courts and trees, an explorer scanning for islands. He saw Diana and Elizabeth as they once were, running out to the grass to turn cartwheels. Diana, ten years old and already more coordinated than any of the girls her age, outstripping Elizabeth, vaulting across the green. And Elizabeth right behind her, a show-off at fourteen, aware that she had her mother's looks. A friend of William's complimented her hair once, and she agreed with him: "Spun gold," she said, then twirled. Such brilliant girls. From the moment he'd seen them, his heart had pummeled him with pride.

In the stands behind court eight, Adelia had already found a place. She shaded her eyes with her hand and waved to him. William closed the space between them. "Miss Lively," he said, taking her hand, playing a Victorian gentleman. She grinned the dear old grin. "Sir William Adair," she said. "Of the Breacon Adairs. A pleasure, as always." She made a place for him at her side. It was comforting to sit with her. The pink cardigan she was wearing reminded him of the outfit she hated having to wear to church when she was nine years old, and the feel of her shoulder was as angularly girlish as it was when they played tennis on these very courts.

Beyond the bleachers, Diana was warming up against Abby Weld. Her body was loose; she jogged in place between shots, as she had since she started competing. She'd grown up jogging in place between shots. He hated to see her in that knee brace, but everything else about her movement had the particular sureness that only truly gifted athletes possess. She would have no trouble in this match. Elaine Weld boasted about how happy it made her daughter to play: "As long as Abigail's happy, we're happy," she liked to say with that ostentatiously shy smile. "Varsity at

Amherst is plenty good enough for us." But it was all baloney. What child is happy when she's losing? Not simpering Abigail Weld, with her mother's thighs and her tearfulness. Twice in the club championships, William had seen Abigail Weld break down and cry. She was not a happy girl, and furthermore she had a weak backhand and Diana would clobber her.

Diana warming up was a thing to see. There was a fluidity to her game, a perfection of technique, that made him relax into his seat beside Adelia Lively and feel the orchestra of his emotions tuning itself into a better harmony. The first game began and Diana served: up the ball rose, up to its highest point, and Diana unfurled her body. Liquid and matter at once, both feet lifting off the ground. She was still great. She won points tidily, as neatly as the little scoop of her leg and racket with which she picked up stray balls.

Of course, at twenty-eight she was no longer a prodigy. William watched her, contemplating this fact. When she came up to the net to take a sip out of her water bottle, he was surprised to realize that she was getting older. One does not expect one's children to age. She glanced over in his direction. She always found him in the crowd, even during her biggest matches. All her coaches had attempted to train this out of her. For years she had to give them a dollar every time she searched for William in the crowd. They worried that it broke her focus, but William understood what she was looking for. He pumped his fist in her direction; she nodded, returning to herself, then walked back out on court. There was the slight limp she had never shaken after knee surgery.

She wasn't the same after that injury. The year she was hurt, William continued flying to Texas for her team's biggest matches, but after a while it was just too grim, watching her sitting on the bench with that enormous knee brace, crutches by her side, when she was supposed to be number one on the team. When she came back for summer break, she'd changed. His Diana, who had always been so sure. Adelia tried to help, God knows, but despite their efforts, Diana had lost something. And where had it gone? Where do these parts of our children fly off to?

Diana was returning serve now, swaying low with the sun in her eyes. She was squinting. Elizabeth would have stared straight through it, no matter how bright. But not Diana. William could see her wavering, and it pained him. She was so good-looking once, quick and blond in her pleated tennis skirts. Since then her hair had gotten darker. Today she'd drawn it back in a limp ponytail. It was the club championship, after all; William wished she'd presented herself with a bit more pride. He reminded himself to have Adelia speak to her about that. Four years in graduate school was too much. Particularly for his Di, who had always loved to play outdoors. He had never imagined her as an architect. He understood—respected, even—her desire to choose the family profession; he himself had become an architect because it was an honor to inherit his grandfather's firm. There was no dignity in breaking roughly with the past. And yet this was not the family tradition William had hoped his Diana would follow. Architecture had fallen so far from the days when his grandfather built his legacy. No, William had never dreamed his Di would spend her gifted life hunched over the plans for someone else's parking garage.

Texas, in general, hadn't been kind to Diana. The architecture was abysmal, and the cement dragged on and on. He blamed those hard courts for the problems with her knee. He should have encouraged her to come back home as soon as she had that injury; he should have insisted on it, architecture school be damned. Considering this, William felt himself growing out of tune. Out of tune and helpless, watching his daughter play in a way that struck him as hopelessly old.

Beside him, Adelia squeezed his hand. "If only Margaux could be here to see this," she said. It was a silly thing to say, uncharacteristic of Adelia. William examined her profile. When she came back to Breacon, she seemed no older than the days when they played tennis after school. Then and now, people thought Adelia's looks were hard, but to William she had always been beautiful. Her eyelashes and eyebrows were so blond that her blue eyes seemed uncurtained. Her cheekbones were a warrior's: they deserved a streak of wet black paint. As Margaux faded, Adelia grew more fierce. And yet she, too, was growing old.

And where was Elizabeth? And Izzy? Over her second bowl of cereal that morning, Izzy had made a sound that William had interpreted as assent when he asked her to please support her sister. It was not as though she had anything else to do on a Friday afternoon. With all the scorn that an eighteen-year-old can summon, she had joined a sum total of zero scholastic activities. She had challenged herself only enough to get in to Ohio University, of all incomprehensible places, and they had considered themselves lucky at that. She, of all the Adairs, had time to watch Diana.

His daughters' absence darkened William's mood enough that he couldn't afford a false smile when Jack Weld trotted out from the clubhouse to sit beside Adelia. "William!" Weld said, grinning excessively across the line of her shoulder. He was the kind of man who sheathed his calculating nature in an overabundance of cheer, the type of enthusiastic spirit who might stab you in the back and pretend he was just playing tag. William did not return the greeting; Weld's presence revived his headache. "This should be a great match," Weld was saying, but it would not be a great match. Abigail Weld was not even remotely in the same league as Diana. Weld stretched his legs. They were clothed in khaki shorts, culminating in a pair of weathered boat shoes. No socks. William hated sockless men in general, and in this case there was something particularly infuriating about the coiled athleticism of Weld's bare calves. "What a day for a match!" he said. Neither William nor Adelia was responding to him; he was engaged in a conversation with himself, forcing them to listen in. "Listen, William! I'm glad I ran into you here. I've been meaning to talk to you. I wanted to say that I'm sorry about the way things worked out with the carriage house petition. I find Anita Schmidt as odious as you do. But it looks like people are just ready to let it go."

"That's fine, Jack," William said, although it certainly was not fine. He refused to look at Weld. He wanted to be alone with Adelia. There was a clarity to her presence that he needed. She was so intently focused on the match that her nails had dug eight red crescents into her palms.

"Look, William," Weld continued. "Don't get me wrong. I'm with you. I understand the value of history on Little Lane. We have a past, and it wouldn't be right to let it go like that, with the snap of a finger. It will break my heart to see that carriage house torn down. But we have systems in place. Rules for governance. We can't just ignore the vote of everyone else on the street."

Adelia put one hand on William's thigh. "What a point!" she said. "Focus, William, she's playing, you've got to watch this."

But William couldn't focus. His eyes were losing their grip on the match. An image of his carriage house, decaying in Anita Schmidt's backyard, rose in his mind. It was a beautiful building once. Designed by his own grandfather, described in the papers as one of the foremost examples of shingle architecture in the United States. While other men of his generation dreamed of making their fortunes in industry, William's grandfather dreamed of perfect spaces, of rooms designed so that within their walls you became a better version of yourself, more capable and brave. That was the kind of blood that ran in William's veins. Inside the carriage house, there was one cavernous room and a loft under thick cedar beams. Encompassed by slabs of hewn wood, the air was hushed. It held promise. One corner was rounded into a turret shape; the roof was a series of intersecting gambrels, one for the turret, one for the carriage room, one for the owl's nest that peeked up over the loft. Outside, the shingles were white on the siding, dove gray on the roof, weathered by decades of wind. It was the kind of house that belonged on a windswept beach, confronting the tumult. When William was a boy, there was a telescope in the owl's nest, pointed out over the downhill slope of Little Lane. As children, he and Adelia, best friends by proximity, played pirates in the loft, surveying the houses beneath them and crying out their barbaric yawps. What she lacked in gender and years, Adelia made up for with ferocity. One evening she very nearly cut off her finger for the sake of a complicated escape; William had to hold her hand above her head, in the cathedral light that filtered through the owl's nest, in order to prevent catastrophe. That carriage house, as it was maintained in those days, inspired William to go to architecture school. It was all that remained on Little Lane of his grandfather's craft. The main house was rebuilt after a lightning fire, and since the subdivision, neighborhood covenants had all but required the construction of stucco faux-colonials. The subdivision, sloppily executed by William's father, so that the carriage house fell on Anita Schmidt's plot of land. And now the carriage house, too, had been sacrificed by the neighborhood association in their crusade for democratic mediocrity. How far it had fallen from its original form! His children had never known it as it once was. For them, it was a collapsing relic, rodent-infested, the window in the owl's nest shattered and never replaced.

William closed his eyes. He felt the crisp lines of his structure dissolving. "Weld," he said, summoning his reserves, "I will say this once, and then I will watch my daughter play. My grandfather built that carriage house. If Anita Schmidt would let me on her property, I'd take care of the rodent problem. It's a goddamn shame. That carriage house is my family. It's history."

"Of course it's history," Weld said. "But it's not actually historical, according to the county historical society." He lifted his palms, innocent as a murderous boy. "I'm with you, but as president of the neighborhood association, I can't just ignore the petition."

William's headache had escalated. It struck him that what Weld was doing amounted to aggravated assault. There were arrows of pain lancing the base of his skull, spots in the field of his vision. He pressed his temples between his thumb and middle finger, then tried focusing on Weld for one final word.

"I won't talk about the goddamn carriage house," he said. "My daughter is playing tennis. If you will, I'm going to focus on that."

Upon uttering this, he turned back to watch Diana, and his face went entirely numb.

Chapter 2

Before the doctor ushered the girls into William's room, he held a brief consultation in the waiting room. "Your father's condition is stable," he reported, holding his face mask politely folded in one hand. "Fortunately, the stroke was a minor one. It was lucky that Dr. Weld recognized its symptoms early." He oriented his body toward the girls. Off to the side, excluded by their closeness, Adelia stood by herself. A woman not his wife, dressed foolishly in a pink cardigan with pearl buttons. But none of them had even been born when she and William stood poised on the brink of their lives, next-door neighbors on a crucially important street, their bodies thrumming with the voltage of all their potential. None of them knew. To them she was only a faded woman, dressed in a cardigan she'd chosen because it seemed cheerful, but in which now she felt childish and absurd, standing on her corner of hospital linoleum, watching William's daughters experience a grief that rightfully belonged to them.

The doctor consulted his clipboard. He puzzled for a moment, as if considering an allergy. "Adelia?" he finally asked, looking up from his notes.

The girls turned toward her, and Adelia stood straighter to withstand their collective scrutiny. Diana was still dressed in her tennis clothes. *Come stand with me,* Adelia wanted to beg her. It would have helped her hold up to Isabelle, tall and polished, her face framed by long hair. To the scrutiny of a teenage girl, that particularly terrifying kind. But Diana only looked away, and even Elizabeth withheld herself, despite the bond Adelia dared to imagine they'd built this year. Elizabeth held her daughters by their shoulders, radiating such motherly authority that her sisters could scarcely help but be drawn to her side. Adelia had rarely seen them standing so close. In the moment of William's weakness, a new intimacy emerged. Normally, they orbited around their father like planets in separate spheres; now Elizabeth filled the role of matriarch. All year she had floundered, lacking a role. Here, of all places, she'd hit a certain stride. Her gestures had taken on new breadth. She offered her sisters long embraces. A head or two beneath the level of their elders, Lucy and Caroline stood as guarantee of their mother's maternal substance, clinging to her closely, moving with her as she surged into position at the family's helm.

And off to the side, shriveled Adelia, childless. The doctor had summoned her into sight, and the girls remembered this woman who had entered their lives ten years ago and persisted in clinging to them, an enormous burr. If they only knew that she, too, was once a girl their age. But how could they know? They took the luxury of staying young, these children of William's. When Adelia was a girl, you couldn't linger in your endless childhood. William asked her to marry him after his first year of college, and that was reasonable at the time. She was seventeen. Her family was moving to a suburb in Connecticut. When she told him on their way to the club, he shrugged: *Then let's get married now.*

She was younger than Isabelle, with no idea what it meant to be married. *We'll wait until after college,* he said when he saw the terror on her face. Not terror at the idea of spending her life with him, just terror that they couldn't be children forever. Even now the word "woman" made Adelia cringe. But then! At seventeen years old! When he asked her, she challenged him to a game of left-handed tennis: *If you beat me, I'll marry you.* And then she creamed him, because she hoped they could stay as they were forever, through to the end of time. But he went back to college angry, and she moved to Connecticut. She wrote him letters, but his replies were curt: to one he answered, "These are things you'll understand when you're not a little girl." It hurt her feelings. "I'm dating a senior," she lied the next time she wrote. She hoped that would slow things down. Or else she was proving herself, a crafty competitive child. He never wrote back. After his senior year, he married Margaux and left late-blooming Adelia behind.

Adelia averted her eyes from Elizabeth to focus on the grandkids: Caroline with her pink plastic glasses, squinting upward as if they hadn't gotten the prescription right; Lucy glaring sideways at her older sister with that feasting expression that sometimes took hold of her face. Adelia wanted to go kneel beside them, to escape to their height. Normally, she felt antagonized by children, but these girls were different, these children of William's blood. Adelia slipped into their company easily. If she could go to them now, the three of them could speak a language of their own, like dolphins or whales, beyond the radar of their sharp-eared mother or their complicated aunts.

Lucy and Caroline, like her, were children of Little Lane. They came to be taken care of on weekends when Elizabeth had to work at the studio. When they did, Adelia walked over from her house on Mather Street and imagined that they were her own. Sometimes, in William's kitchen, she tried to bake them cakes. She'd never had an instinct for baking, and the cakes were always flattened on one or all sides, but even so, the girls could be counted on to eat, and if Lucy wasn't pouting, she'd ask Adelia to tell them about William when he was a little boy. Then Adelia would close her eyes and remember the sheen of his fair hair under the sun, the way he moved on court, the expression on his face as if he were just about to laugh, even when he was sprawling out for a drop shot. She'd point out the house where she lived as a little girl, across the street, with the long screened-in porch where she used to sit and wait for William to appear. She'd tell them stories about the carriage house, where she and William played games of pirate in the loft beneath its rafters. How their friendship ceased when he was eleven and she was eight—when those ages seemed too distant to cross—and resumed again in high school when he saw her playing tennis at the club. He leaned on the net post, watching her. *You've gotten pretty good!* he said, and she blushed so deeply that she felt it in the webs of her fingers. She'd tell them about the way she could beat him if they played left-handed, about the way he changed an empty house when he walked through the door and called her name up the stairs. About sitting in the carriage house and planning their lives, their legs swinging off the side of the loft. How, with him, oddly, she could feel new parts of herself: her kneecaps, the arches of her feet, the edges of her shoulder blades when they pressed against the cedar planks of the loft.

These things she told the grandkids, closing her eyes to remember them better, and if she opened her eyes, there was William himself, sitting at the kitchen table or in his reclining chair, watching her above the horizon of his newspaper. He watched, and sometimes he entered the plane of their pretending so that for the length of an entire Saturday, forgetting that Margaux was only upstairs, they played the parts of the family Adelia imagined she might have had if she'd grown up as women are meant to grow.

"Adelia?" the doctor asked again.

"I am Adelia," she heard herself reply, in a language that didn't belong to dolphins or whales but sounded instead like cold fingers tapping against a windowpane.

"Mr. Adair asked to see you along with his children," the doctor said.

They looked at her. Adelia had the strange idea that they might stand there eternally, blocking her way to his room, but already they were moving forward. Of course they wouldn't block her. Not even Izzy would be so cruel. Elizabeth instructed her daughters to wait; they slumped in their shiny plastic seats as the elders filed in. Only Adelia, last in line, gave them a final look before the curtain that smelled of antiseptic parted before her and William appeared.

His lips were dry. His shoulders were bare down to the blue sheet that had been pulled up over his chest. In the hospital's fluorescent light, Adelia could see sad contours in his shoulders that she hadn't noticed before. There were a few white hairs on his sternum, usually hidden by the collars of his polo shirts. His aging skin, his hair. She had somehow never imagined these components of William: he was William, entire, not composed of physical parts. Adelia could feel herself blinking rapidly to tamp down the emotion that was rising in her.

In front of her, the girls each went to him.

"Dad," Diana whispered, leaning over him. She kissed him and he turned away. "Oh, thank *God,*" Elizabeth said, taking her father's hand, shouldering her way to his side. "Thank *God* you're okay." William received her attentions; he seemed to be exercising fortitude. Isabelle's kiss was briefer. She swept in and withdrew, sparing in her effusions. And then the three of them stood by his side.

It would have been unimaginable, ten years ago, to see them in this state. When Adelia came back to Breacon after the second divorce, she saw them first at the country club Easter brunch. She knew she'd see them eventually; she'd come back for them, after all. For years she watched them growing up in Christmas cards; twenty-three cards were pinned with magnets to the refrigerator in her Brooklyn Heights apartment. The first one arrived just after her first divorce. She was living alone, twenty-six years old, starting her first year of law school. She'd dropped out of college and quit the tennis team to marry Ed in the middle of her senior year. She told herself she was staying on schedule and managed to feel proud. Two years later, she found herself crying over a fallen spinach soufflé: "I wanted more for myself," she told him. He had only just gotten home from the office; he was wearing his suit, and in one hand he held a fresh glass of Scotch. "Then we'll have children," he told her, attempting to touch her with his empty hand. Her laugh sounded like a dropped glass breaking. And so she divorced him, Adelia the Brave. She found the Brooklyn apartment. From her window she could see barges passing slowly under the bridge. She finished her college credits and applied for law school. She wore knee-high rubber boots when she trudged through the snow to her classes; her hood had a fur lining.

In December, she opened a Christmas card to find a photo of William with his wife and their baby, Elizabeth. She kept it on the refrigerator all that year out of loyalty, though catching a glimpse of it felt like swallowing a rock. Every night when she got home from studying in the library, she took her cottage cheese and olives out of the refrigerator and considered the surprised smile on Margaux's face, the baby's pale hair. She saw them once a year, so they changed dramatically each time. As she watched, Adelia's jealousy shifted, and she became attached to them in her way. Five years after Elizabeth, Diana appeared, squinting and bald. Later there was one of Diana and Elizabeth dressed as crabs, crouched on the beach. Adelia could see William's shadow on the sand beside them, cast from where he stood behind the camera. In an abstract sense, she started to imagine that she was their banished mother. It was easier with Diana, who had none of Margaux's looks. She was fair, like William, broad-shouldered and strong. For a long time she had a page-boy haircut and the straight lines of a tomboy. She was the kind of girl Adelia imagined she could raise.

In the same Brooklyn Heights apartment, with the Adairs pinned to her refrigerator, Adelia graduated law school and went to work at a firm. Her hours got longer. She had no family of her own and didn't necessarily regret this until, at the age of thirty-six, she received the card with baby Isabelle. When she pinned that card up, Adelia understood that she was ready to have a child. She was ready to hold that baby in her arms. She felt it with a ferocity that nearly knocked her over. She had to kneel down on the kitchen floor and place her forehead on the vinyl tiles to steady herself, drawing deep breaths into the great empty pit of her stomach.

The next morning she set about the task of finding a husband. What she ended up finding was Peter Magnusson, a lawyer three years her junior whom she met at a conference on tax reform. During their initial outings, he seemed sensitive and tidy enough to fit into her life without excessive disruption; it was possible, however, that her judgment was not performing at peak capacity. She was so blinded by her desire to have a child like Isabelle that homeless men started to look like they were a single shower away from paternal possibility. That spring she asked Peter Magnusson to marry her, and two weeks later they arrived at the courthouse to undergo a civil ceremony with a judge whose uncompromising stance on tax fraud Adelia particularly admired. That night she and Peter crossed the threshold of her apartment and she dreamed vivid dreams of immediate conception.

Peter, as it turned out, was shy about anything that occurred in the bedroom and avoided it assiduously. In every other regard, he was careful of her feelings. He cooked her elaborate dinners, and she grew to love the sandalwood smell of the pomade he combed into his hair in the morning. But his excuses for sexual avoidance were manifold and increasingly embarrassing. For three years Adelia crafted various strategies for entrapment. Still, they never conceived. Dreams of immediate conception became dreams of immaculate conception. Peter's presence was a constant apologetic hovering. They attempted in vitro fertilization. Despite the insane expense of the procedure, it failed to produce a blastocyst for Adelia to nurture. The doctor informed her that it was possible she had a "hostile womb." That was something Adelia had suspected of herself for some time, but to hear a professional tell her as much made her cry in his office as if he'd told her that all the world's children would die. By her side, Peter patted her hostile hand.

After drying her tears, Adelia fired the doctor. The next ob-gyn was a fresh-faced woman in her prime childbearing years. She assured Adelia that there was no such thing as a hostile womb and proposed a second go at IVF. Peter seemed crestfallen at the news, yet determined Adelia forged ahead with her plans. On the day of the appointment, Peter accompanied her as far as the doctor's waiting room and then stood and left the building. Two days later he reappeared in their apartment and told her he wasn't sure he wanted a baby. A wave of exhaustion hit her and she slept for two days, which accounted for the only two sick days she'd ever had an occasion to take. After she finally got up, she walked over to the refrigerator, looked at William's family, and started to cry. She was forty years old. In her first marriage, she missed the chance to play tennis as she might have played. In her second marriage, she missed the chance to have a family. And years ago, in ancient history, before she even understood that chances could be lost, she missed the chance to live with William and be his wife.

Peter agreed to move out with an unconcealed relief that hurt Adelia to the center of her unwifely core. Injured Adelia returned to her routines. The smell of sandalwood started to fade. At night, after work, she ate her cottage cheese and olives, alone at the table that faced out over the East River toward the lights of Manhattan. In the morning she ate a bowl of muesli while standing up in the kitchen, perusing her gallery of Margaux's girls. All these routines she performed without hope of a child. She felt this loss, strangely enough, in her gums, which became painfully sensitive to all temperatures. She started brushing with Sensodyne. She was given a promotion at the firm, and she underwent two periodontal surgeries. She took up Pilates at her local gym. Obedient Adelia was attentive to all her Pilates instructor's instructions, and she improved quickly. Sometimes she surprised herself in the mirror, after she had showered in the ladies' locker room. She looked like a woman young enough to have a child. But.

On her refrigerator, Adelia collected three more years of Christmas cards, and then one arrived with a note from William. *Adelia,* it said. *I've been reading the paper all these years in the hopes of finding your name in the Wimbledon finals. To no avail! Still, the Cheshires tell me they saw you on Montague Street and that you're a partner at a law firm. I expected no less. Things here are fine. So many of the old families have moved away. I reminisce sometimes. It would be nice to have a friend from the neighborhood to talk to. Margaux has little patience for it; she's always lived in her own world. But I do have tragic news. Anita Schmidt has taken the carriage house hostage. You remember the carriage house, don't you? Dread Pirate Wendy's Lair? Well, according to His Highness the County Commissioner it now belongs to Anita Schmidt. An error in the subdivision proposal that my father drew up. Nobody caught it until Anita took it upon herself to study the original plan. Anyway, we're fighting it tooth and nail in the neighborhood association, but unfortunately many of the neighbors are assholes, as you may remember. She won't even let me paint it. You remember how white it always was? It's getting dingy now and there's a crack in the owl's nest window. You have no idea how it pains me to see. One of the foremost examples of shingle architecture in the United States! But I'm rambling. I'm sure you have little time for this kind of thing. I think of you often; I thought you should know. I hope you'll come visit sometime. Work is blah but the girls are beautiful, and Diana has the kind of talent that hasn't been matched on the eastern seaboard since the Adelia Lively Era. I'm attaching a clipping about her performance at this year's junior nationals: third in the nation! She reminds me of a girl I knew when I was a kid. I send my love and I remain, Yours, William.*

Adelia pinned the card—and the clipping—to the refrigerator. In a week she'd memorized the note. After that week, she initiated divorce proceedings against her willing and helpful husband. She tried not to blame him for her losses. It was she, Adelia, who had always arrived too late. Instead, she set her mind to finding a way to relocate to the firm's office in Philadelphia. By March she was back in Breacon, moving the furniture from her apartment into the gaping spaces of the house on Mather Street. She reassembled her gallery of Christmas cards on the new refrigerator door. She established routines that were sharpened this time by the knowledge that she might run into Margaux at the grocery store, Diana at the gym, William as he made his familiar way over the green to the courts.

But to see them in the flesh at Easter brunch was something else. It took her breath away to find them there together, gathered around a table, eating a communal meal. They were like a still life: *Family Gathered at the Easter Table*. Margaux was there. She still went out with them at that time. She was the picture of a mother, with her dancer's posture and otherworldly poise, her dark hair coiled at the nape of her neck. Elizabeth, seated at Margaux's side, was just out of college, in full possession of the confidence that only a twenty-one-year-old actress can possess. She was wearing a cowl-neck sweater and her lips were dramatically red. At her side, Diana: broader-shouldered than she seemed in her pictures, entertaining the compliments of club members. And on Margaux's other side, little Isabelle. Her plate was littered with cracker crumbs, and in the wake of that destruction she was drinking a Shirley Temple, lost in a dream world that Adelia saw and immediately wanted to enter. She approached them, and William stood up with such energy that the silverware rattled.

"Adelia Lively!" he said, and she couldn't answer because something was stuck in her throat. "I can't believe it. Adelia! You look exactly the same as when I saw you last." She hugged him awkwardly; they had never offered each other such a formal embrace.

"Adelia," Margaux murmured, smiling. Without the slightest trace of jealousy. But what did she have to be jealous of? Adelia and William had loved each other as children; Margaux was a mother, his wife, a person beyond. Adelia could only try to make her smile look less skeletal.

"This is my family," William said. He gestured to them. "My girls." And how could they have been anything other than complete, backed by his pride? How could they have failed to become the talented creatures they were? She could feel William's tenacity across every inch of her skin; the hairs stood up on her arms. It was this that made her love him first. *You could be a Wimbledon champion one day,* he told her when she was sixteen, the summer before he went off to college. He wasn't even joking, just planning for the future. No one else believed in her like that. With him, a sense of her potential took shape. Her promise had texture and weight. With everyone else, she was only a girl. Her father called her Dee-Dee and bought her pearl-button cardigans from Bendel's for Christmas. But William believed she'd be a champion, and two divorces later, having twice come up against all that she'd never accomplish, she'd returned to Breacon to find that his children had inherited the gift of his belief. She could see it in the way he looked at them, and she couldn't help but envy them their luck.

"How do you do," she said, regretting at once the old-fashioned awkwardness of the expression. They returned her greeting impeccably, unaware that she'd come home out of ancient love for their father. And then William turned to her again. She could feel his eyes on her; it was a sensation so old, so nearly forgotten, that she reached for a chair to keep herself steady. "Adelia Lively!" he said. "It's been so long. What brings you back to the old stomping grounds?"

She concocted something about missing the smell of tennis courts. He beamed. "Do you still play?"

She forced herself to be honest. "I haven't for something like ten years." She registered his disappointment and took a breath before diving back in. "But I'm back for a while now, and I'd love to pick it up again."

And now, in William's hospital room, those children stood

by his bedside in three states of fallen grace. Isabelle, her thin shoulders thrown back, hostile and defiant. Elizabeth, washed up, playing the role of daughter as if it were her comeback to the stage. And Diana, holding the broken center, no more than a shadow of the girl she was when she was playing her sport. They were not what they used to be. Though this might have caused Adelia to pity them, it only made her angry. They should have held up better for his sake. They had allowed themselves such depths of suffering. While he summoned all the reserves of his confidence, they had done nothing but practice the art of slow drowning. Drowning and waving. Dramatically drowning. Time after time, William with his fine athlete's shoulders dove in after them, and now, when he needed them, they came before him in this state, waiting to be saved.

"I don't feel very strong," was what he finally said, and Adelia heard herself emit a sound like air hissing out of a punctured can. All three girls looked at her. She composed herself again. "I don't feel very strong, and I don't want to talk much right now," he said, repeating himself. "I've had to think about whether to say anything at all, because I know what I'm going to say will be hurtful. But I've been thinking maybe I've damaged them more by refusing to see the truth." He paused to collect himself before continuing. "And the truth is, I'm disappointed in you. You've disappointed me."

"Dad," Diana said, and Adelia looked away. Never in the past had she imagined such a thing. When he refused to acknowledge their failure, Adelia had acknowledged it for him.

"Let me finish," he said. "I want to say this while I can. You should know that the two of you—Isabelle and Diana—have broken my heart. You had all the potential in the world. You could have been so much."

The color washed out of Diana's face, but she remained still, prepared to face the bald truth of her sentence. Elizabeth, absolved, flushed in a way that made Adelia want to exile her from the room. She had done no better than her sisters; she had not confirmed William's consequence. Her only triumph had been that of bringing her children back home so that William could think of them as his own. In that one act she'd renewed her promise, but it was not for her to flush with exception. She'd fared no better than either one of her sisters.

"I'm not sure how this happened," William continued. He peered at Isabelle, as though hoping she might supply an answer. "Isabelle, for the life of me, I can't say. What happened? What happened to make you change as much as you did?" Isabelle watched him. Her expression was flat beneath the arches of her eyebrows. He waited for her to answer him for a long time, then turned away and lifted a hand to his eye. His wrist was encircled by a blue hospital band. There was an IV tube hanging out of his vein. Adelia noticed for the first time that his eyebrows were disheveled.

"And Diana," he said. "For years you've persisted in suffering. Since the day you quit tennis, you've chosen over and over again to struggle." He stopped and swallowed. "I'm not sure what it is in you. You should have *seen* yourself as a girl on that court. Everyone at the club would stop what they were doing and turn. They'd ask who that girl was, that brilliant girl. It breaks my heart to see what you've become." He licked his lips. The vein in his arm that held the IV needle was purple under the skin.

Adelia knew she was blinking too rapidly. The stillness was ruining her; if only they could move. If they could run, or swing, they would become themselves again. William would remember himself. She took a step forward, but as soon as she moved, Elizabeth swept over him. An exotic bird of prey, all feather and excessive wing. "Daddy," she said, "you're tired. Please. You should rest."

Isabelle surveyed her father, composed as a cruel priestess. "Dad," she said, "that's unfair to Diana. The only thing she ever quit was tennis, and no one can play tennis forever."

William focused on Adelia. "Tell them it's time for them to leave," he said to her.

She shook her head, helpless and numb.

"You're the one who won't let it go," Isabelle continued. "You had one dream for her, and you won't let it go. What was she supposed to do, play tennis until she died? Was that what you had planned?"

"You don't know what you're saying," William said. "I'm not feeling well. I'd like to be alone now. Adelia, tell them to leave."

Diana hovered, caught between apology and retreat. *You're better than this,* Adelia wanted to tell Diana, but she and Isabelle were already moving out of the room.

"Me, too, Daddy?" Elizabeth asked.

"Yes, Lizzie," William said. "I'd like to speak with Adelia."

Elizabeth kissed him on the cheek and stood. She held herself regally. "I'll wait with Lucy and Caroline. They love you, Daddy."

"Tell them I'm proud of them," William said. "I'm as proud of them as a person can be."

And then Adelia was alone with him, with William, whom she had loved from the time she was a little girl without knowing it was love. Without knowing that the end of such love was marriage. William, with whom she had played pirate in the carriage house, dressed in a Tanner of North Carolina dress she pulled behind her bike for miles to get it bedraggled enough. For which act of rebellion she was later spanked, but did not weep, because One-Eyed Pirate Wendy never cried. Her ship was the Carriage House Loft; William battled his way up the stairs with a toy sword his father brought back from a trip to Mexico. "I've got you, wench!" he said, and she: "You're mine, slave!" And all around them light streamed in from the owl's nest, so that they were suspended in its glow, weightless like the dust motes that swirled in the cedary air. He played with her after he was too old to be playing pirate in the carriage house; he kept pretending because he wouldn't let her go. Now, in his hospital bed, she went and knelt at his side, pressing her cheek against his palm.

"You're fine," she said.

"No, Adelia, I woke up lost," he said. "I'm lost."

"You're right here," said Adelia. "Nothing has changed."

He closed his eyes. "Does Margaux know?"

"I spoke with her, but I'm not sure how much she understood. She tried to comfort me. Louise said she wasn't clear enough today to come to the hospital, unless it's important to you."

"It's fine," he said. "It doesn't matter anymore."

Adelia stood before him in her cardigan. There was no place for her hands. This was not as it should be. She had hoped for this disloyalty so long, and to receive it in this state, with his forearm mapped by purple veins, his pale chest showing over his sheet.

"I didn't feel old," he finally said. "I didn't think that they were getting old."

"You're still young," she said. "Nothing's changed. We're all exactly the same."

"But they've sabotaged themselves."

"They'll be fine," she told him. "The girls are going to be fine."

"They could have been so much."

"They will be."

"It's too late. They're not children anymore."

"You're wrong, William. It's not too late."

"I've made so many mistakes."

"We all do."

"I should have married you."

Childless Adelia stared, clutching the sleeves of her cardigan in her own curled fists.

"Move in with me," he said.

She caught her breath too sharply. "Wait, William. Wait before you say that. There are the girls, and Margaux. Don't say such a thing too quickly." He set his jaw. Because he wasn't answering, because perhaps the idea would slink away to the place from which it came, Adelia heard herself chattering on. "You should think about this more. You might regret it. There are the girls to think about, and Izzy's still at the house." Adelia was ticking things off with her fingers. "We're not children anymore. And there's Elizabeth's divorce, and Margaux, and the carriage house."

"Stop," he said. "Stop." Adelia stopped. The skin beneath his eyes looked bruised, and an unshaved spot of white stubble remained on his jaw. This was her William, after all these years. "Say you'll live with me," he said. "Just for a while. Just while I get my strength, and then you can go. But I will not go back to that house without you in it."

Because she was feeling too much, because there was nothing else to say and nowhere else to go, Adelia climbed into the bed with him. Her hands found him with relief. She was careful of the IV needle, careful with the contour of his body on the hospital cot. It was the first time she had lain in a bed by his side. So often, as children, they'd lain beneath the cedar beams of the carriage house. She remembered him smelling like grass. And now!

How many years had passed, and only now could Adelia Lively climb into the bed of William Adair. Beside his body, pale in the hospital sheets. So much was fading around her. It was the saddest thing in the world. Blinking this away, she lay close to him, close to his face. She kissed the stubble of his hair. She kissed his eyebrows, his antiseptic shoulders. She kissed the wisps of hair on his chest and laid her head there, listening for the sureness of his brave competitor's heart.

"Is it too late?" he asked. Adelia blinked, blinked, blinked. She could feel his chest against her lashes as they moved. The chest of William Adair.

"No, William. It's not too late for anything at all."

Chapter 3

Louise Wilson was expiring in Breacon. The boredom was literally killing her. She had applied for a job with the Philadelphia agency on a whim, after her boyfriend-if-you-can-call-it-that broke up with her and she decided it was time to get out of New York. The boyfriend, if you are calling him that, was an idiot named Bradley who did monkey work in the back office of an investment bank and dreamed of becoming a trader. The end of the relationship arrived when Brad procured himself a blond girlfriend who worked in fashion marketing. This circumstance shouldn't have been as devastating as it was. Louise was sick of going to Irish pubs with him when all around her New York gleamed. But when he broke up with *her,* rather than the other way around, she found herself in the midst of a drunken tailspin that resulted in, among other things: a) a chipped tooth; b) a single night in which she was twice mistaken for a prostitute; c) the intensely regrettable decision to shag some poor girl's boyfriend while the girl cried in the next room over; and d) the even more regrettable decision to alert her shipping-magnate boss to the fact that his mother was not actually senile but simply had no interest in his life. And so Louise was in need of a new position. Furthermore, as she was no longer in possession of her comfortable room in the shipping magnate's Carlyle penthouse, she figured she might as well try a new city while she reorganized her life.

She remembered Philadelphia from a course she took in American history, which goes to show that it's not always wise to take your cues from history. Now she was stuck day in and day out in a suburb so boring she sometimes thought the sheer tedium would cause her to vomit. At first Louise was dutiful in every aspect of her job. She went around labeling kitchen drawers with her professional label maker, at which point Margaux stopped coming down to the kitchen. She accompanied Margaux on her walks, at which point Margaux abruptly stopped walking, choosing to go out to the garden. After several months of scurrying around, trying to find tasks that she could perform, attempting to remind Margaux of things she should not fail to remember, and sensing Margaux's distinct and rational-seeming frustration with her every effort, Louise finally became exasperated enough to confront the situation head-on. "Listen, Mrs. Adair, let's be straight," she said. "I get the feeling that you'd rather I wasn't around."

"I'm sorry?" Margaux asked, looking off into the distance. She had what people call the lion's face, the expression that Alzheimer's patients develop sometimes, when they seem to be forever gazing out over the Serengeti, blinking at the prospect of blankness. Louise repeated herself, and Margaux finally focused on the person in front of her.

"I'm sorry, but do I know you?" she asked. Louise waited, unwilling to back down. Margaux heaved a sigh. "I don't mean to be rude, but I'd like to be alone right now."

"I'm only here to help," Louise said, parroting the dialogue she had been given in training. "I'm here to help because your husband was worried. You were getting lost on your walks. He hired me to help you remember things, so that you can continue living your life as normally as possible."

"That was kind of him," Margaux said. "But I'd like to be alone now. If I forget, I forget. All this insistence on constant remembering," she added, then stopped. Margaux rarely seemed to feel the requirement to finish her sentences. "And the inability to be alone . . ." She trailed off, her eyes going distant again.

"Point taken," Louise told her, and relocated to the kitchen for the rest of the day. As Margaux declined, Louise told herself, she'd take a more active caretaking role. For now Margaux seemed capable enough to float around on her own, unburdened by constant remembering. Never acknowledging Louise's presence, she moved between her third-floor studio-bedroom and the garden. She ate alone in her room. She slept often. Louise sat in the kitchen sometimes, the second-floor guest room other times, and if it was warm enough, she occasionally would lie out on a chaise longue on the patio. From time to time she was asked to run to the grocery store, or to find a lost shoe, or to drive to doctors' appointments, since Margaux's license had lapsed and no one in the family felt it was safe for her to renew it. Margaux tolerated these services, and Louise provided them without expecting gratitude; she was used to moving around in other people's houses as inconspicuously as possible.

Other than these small chores, the day was a vast unoccupied expanse. Unfortunately, this allowed her to engage in marathon text conversations with Brad, which wreaked havoc on her commitment to forget he'd ever existed. She was able to take holidays off, during which spans of time she visited New York and inevitably ended up sleeping over in his sloppy apartment, then talking casually about his new girlfriend over postcoital coffee in the morning. Back in Breacon, she began to nurse a tabloid addiction. In the absence of other forms of mental stimulation, she looked forward to trips to CVS as though it were a veritable Mecca of eternal life and beauty. She considered moving back to Melbourne to finish her communications degree, but she loathed the idea of admitting defeat to her mother, who would blow on her tea and stir the soup and only partially disguise her triumph at having been vindicated in the lifelong quest to lower Louise's expectations. And then one day Brad texted Louise to let her know that he and his blond girlfriend were getting married, and that he was coming to Philadelphia on business in two weeks and could he stay with her, wink-wink, and Louise found herself in the Adair kitchen, fluctuating between the desire to cry over the loss of a person she didn't even like and the competing urge to plot a complicated revenge.

Revenge won out—Louise Wilson had never been one to succumb to sentiment—and the plan she settled on was as close to perfect as revenge plots ever get. She would a) never talk to Brad again, and b) write a novel that would be published to much acclaim, thereby causing Brad to seethe with regret that he had not plucked her up while he had the chance. Because the thing that most devastated Louise about the Bradley debacle was the fact that he had decided the blond girl was a surer key to success. Louise knew this because she understood the sad creature that was Bradley Barlow. It was clear that he had chosen the blond girl—with her fashionable shoes, her conspiratorial niceness, and her palatable job—because she exuded whatever it is that successful people exude.

Therein lay the problem. Louise had always imagined, with utter confidence, that *she* would be a success. She never knew exactly how, but from the time she was a child in Catholic school, she was aware that she was charming and clever. This awareness gave her confidence. She never worried about speaking up, in class or otherwise. There was no reason she should *not* succeed. That Brad chose someone *else* to help him achieve the success he so desperately desired was a blow that Louise was finding it difficult to recover from. And so she would write a novel that would allow her to attend glamorous book parties in New York, to which she would wear ridiculously attractive outfits, and maybe she would run into Brad on his way to some Irish pub and she would brush him off by saying, "Oh, I'm just in town for my book signing, yes, it's getting made into a movie, sorry I can't stay and talk, I'm just devastatingly busy this trip, maybe next time, you moronic wanker."

Louise was excited about this idea until she realized she would have to come up with a topic for her novel. It was skull-splitting work. She allowed herself a new *Us Weekly* magazine as a reward if she put in a solid hour of thought. As a result, her novel ideas tended toward the fantastic: Actor falls for his costar and splits from his wife of nine years! Child star divorces her mother, then falls for her manager! Each of these ideas sparkled for several hours, then fell depressingly flat. And then, like a vision, Adelia Lively marched into the kitchen while William was in the hospital and announced that she would be moving in to help with his recovery. Louise could do nothing more noteworthy than sit back down in her chair. She took a deep breath. Her subject had been sitting under her nose the entire time, only she'd been too bored to notice. The tagline appeared to her whole: Husband of Alzheimer's-afflicted wife reunites with his high school lover, and right beneath the wife's afflicted nose, the two fall madly in love while all around them snooty neighbors and spoiled children ball up their fists and howl. The novel lifted its head and roared.

She began to take notes in a spiral notebook she purchased at CVS, along with a new pack of Crest Whitestrips. The next week, from Margaux's upstairs window, Louise observed Adelia as she helped William—back from the hospital—out of her Acura. Later, coming down the stairs with a hastily assembled load of Margaux's laundry, Louise took note of William's humbled state. She stayed an unprecedented hour late to fold the laundry so she could eavesdrop on the family meeting that Adelia convened. The daughters' reactions were muted. They rolled over when Adelia announced she was moving in, which was odd. Louise was expecting some fireworks from Elizabeth, some levelheaded reasoning from bland Diana. She had hoped for more vitriol from Isabelle. But there was no grand display. As one demented family unit, they moved right on to the issue of the carriage house.

Tying Margaux's socks into loose knots, Louise wondered at people's appetite for defeat. They pretend they're avoiding it their whole lives, but when it finally arrives at their front door, they fall into its arms with gratitude, allow it to shag them for a year, then watch in horror when it leaves them for a blond girl with a marketing degree. When the kitchen-table meeting was adjourned, Louise carried her laundry basket up to Margaux's room. Her charge was preoccupied with painting a pale pink streak in a landscape of gray wisps and white space. Louise set the basket down noisily, hoping to attract some attention. Margaux ignored her. Louise rattled the glass of ice water on the bedside table. Still nothing. Finally, she sat down on the bed and jumped right in. "Are you angry that Adelia's moving in?" she asked.

Margaux heaved a sigh and turned to address her interlocutor. She looked tired but present. In fact, the sharpness of her presence seemed almost uncomfortable to her. She winced slightly, peering out at Louise. "I'm sorry?" she asked. There were shadows under her eyes.

"Adelia," Louise repeated. "Are you angry she's moving in?"

"Adelia?" Margaux asked. As soon as she said the name, her expression began to recede. Louise watched each step of its steady retreat. Her face relaxed, and the Serengeti started to shimmer around her. "She's a friend of his," she finally said from somewhere off in the distance, then turned back to her canvas and resumed painting.

"But they're not little kids," Louise insisted. "It's not a sleepover." Louise knew she was breaking cardinal rules for interacting with delusional patients but now she was no longer Louise the Caretaker but Louise the Artist, Louise the Seeker After Novelistic Truth.

Margaux sighed. "No," she said, agreeing mildly. "No, it's not."

"The point is, you still think of William as your husband, don't you? You remember that, don't you? That he is your husband?"

Margaux stopped painting. Her brush hovered an inch away from the canvas. Louise wondered if she was angry for once. Some Alzheimer's patients are aggressive, disturbed by all the unrecognizable people who keep intruding in their lives, but Margaux was never violent. She floated around serenely. Still, could she really remain calm while Adelia moved into her house, down the hall from her husband, one floor beneath the bedroom of her youngest girl? Louise watched Margaux's frozen hand, holding her breath, waiting for a response.

"For God's sake," Margaux finally said. "Let it be. You're a stranger in this house." And then she returned to her canvas, looping the pink streak around a new blank space.

From that day on, Louise kept herself busy with taking note of everything. In the grocery store later that week, she ran into Beebee Cheshire from the house next door. Casually, while pretending to test the ripeness of peaches, Beebee asked whether Adelia's car in the driveway suggested perhaps that she was living with the Adairs.

"She is," Louise said, watching Mrs. Cheshire for material.

A peach was bruised in the spirit of victory, then replaced and passed over. "That's shocking," Mrs. Cheshire said. "Don't you think?"

"Well, it's not really any of my business, is it?"

"To just swoop in," Mrs. Cheshire continued. "I never put this past her, of course. I'm only disappointed in William." The neighbors had always hated Adelia. Ostensibly, the reason was some altercation that took place between Adelia and Mrs. Cheshire's overweight son, but Louise suspected it had more to do with Adelia's successful career, which functionally undermined the importance of their housewifely routines. Louise had always felt for Adelia, if only because she fit so poorly into the schedule of grocery shopping and lasagna trading that held the women of Little Lane in its death grip. The petty triumph that a woman such as Mrs. Cheshire felt upon discovering that Adelia had disgraced herself irritated Louise, and she renewed her commitment to depicting Adelia as a complicated and at least partly sympathetic villain. Mrs. Cheshire should be the worse of the two. Louise reminded herself to describe the precise stiffness of Mrs. Cheshire's anachronistic beehive hairdo, and the waxy permanence of her magenta lipstick, both of which caused her to resemble a well-off zombie sent from the American suburbs of 1959.

"Listen, Louise," the beehive continued, "do you mind if I ask a personal question? Is Adelia staying with him, in the bedroom?"

Louise feigned a shock of morality. "No, Mrs. Cheshire, of course not. She's moved her things into the guest room."

"I see." Mrs. Cheshire's eyes gleamed. This was the neighborhood gossip event of the century. She was damaging swathes of peaches in her excitement. "Well, give my best to Margaux," she said, and Louise agreed to do so, although she would not, because the last time she carted Mrs. Cheshire's greetings to Margaux, Margaux murmured, "She always frightened me," and Louise could see her point.

Back at the house, Louise started surreptitiously snooping. While Margaux was out in the garden, she rummaged through various desk drawers and made the following list in her CVS notebook: *Margaux's Desk Drawer Contents: a) tiny red paper clips; b) oil paintbrushes, uncleaned, well ruined now; c) unpaid bills (tell William to call credit card company; you should have caught this earlier, you fuckwit, Louise); d) photos of Margaux with her girls when they were little babies, dressed in costumes and other such heartbreaking stuff; e) silver box with mother-of-pearl-clasp, full of broken glass.*

And then, in the bottom left-hand drawer, Louise found a pile of notebooks. They were unmarked, but it was clear they had been well used. Louise reached down for the top notebook and changed her mind, going for the bottom of the stack. As soon as she opened it, she knew from the elegance of the cursive with which Margaux had filled its pale blue lines that she had found something important. In the back of her brain, she began to hear the buzz of a book party, and she imagined that Bradley would understand, forever and for always, that his bland blond wife was no match for the fascinating woman he'd left behind. Attempting to temper the increasingly noisy chatter of her daydreams, Louise took a deep breath, smoothed down a crease in the binding, and plunged.

March 14, 1988

I remembered yesterday that my mother kept a memory book. The idea of it intrigued me and I told myself to get one next time I went to the store. When I went, I remembered this notebook but forgot to buy apples and tonic water. William will be frustrated and Izzy will have to go without fruit in her lunch bag. Still, I'm happy to have remembered this, at least. There's so much I'd like to write down.

For starters, there is this: I have suspected for six years that I would develop my mother's illness. The feeling came first when I was pregnant with Isabelle. I was trying to remember how my mother looked when I was a child, and suddenly I thought, "I can't be a mother for another little girl." The idea of it sickened me. I tried to tell William, but he was too happy to listen. He is deafened by excitement sometimes. Later, when Izzy was born, I wished I had never seen her face so that I could never forget it.

The first real symptoms started this year. I sometimes go out on my walks and forget what I've gone out for. When I find my way back, I open the door to this house and think, "This place is meant to feel like home," but I can't remember why, or if it ever did. I see my children, even, and I know I'm meant to feel like their mother, but there are days when I can't feel it. Days when I feel like a person who has somehow wandered into another family's house. Mostly I feel stuck in a younger version of myself. I remember baking bread with my mother on the farm, and I feel so strongly that I am that child. And then a daughter of mine walks in and I can only think, "Who does that girl belong to?"

Other days I wander around the house and think, "This place reminds me so clearly of him," but it's not William I'm thinking of. It's someone I knew in a past life whose name I've long since forgotten, and yet I miss him in a way that makes me want to lie down on the floor and cry until the world is swept away by my tears.

But it was William that I married. I first saw him in art history class. I remember watching him from the back. The way he laughed with his friends, the way he whispered during the slide shows. He was so handsome that I blushed when he answered questions in class. After two weeks he left his friends and sat next to me. It was only us in the row. I felt so shy I couldn't even look at him. He asked for a pencil and I gave it to him. I'd unwrapped my lunch at my desk and felt embarrassed to be eating with him sitting so close. I was ashamed of my hard-boiled egg and the napkin I'd unfolded in my lap. The egg smelled awfully sharp. I started to wrap it up so that I could eat it later, when I was alone, but he said, "Don't stop eating for my sake," so I had to eat, miserable and ashamed. That I remember. He continued to sit with me all through the rest of the year. I was still shy, and I couldn't pay attention when he was sitting so close, but I felt privileged that he chose me. I wasn't a popular girl. My mother was getting sick, and I was too often alone. There was something strange about me. I knew I was different from the other college girls. And he was so confident. I remember how lucky I felt to be seen at his side. But I can't remember why he married me. I didn't even hesitate when I told him yes, I'd be his wife, of course. I couldn't imagine it, but I didn't hesitate. I can't remember why. I know I felt lucky that he came to sit at my side.

Later the wrongness seeped in. I recognized it first as the desire to be alone. Every conversation felt uncomfortable. An unnecessary engagement. A scrimmage from which I emerged a little more shaken. I couldn't get alone enough, and the houses we lived in never felt like my own. He laughed when I tried to tell him. His careless laugh: "Margaux, you strange creature." I'd hate him for laughing, but later I'd feel lucky again that someone like him would choose me. It's a gift to have a place made for you by someone like him. Someone so buoyant. In exchange, I tried to fill our houses with beautiful things—the little nouns, my discoveries, that I'd kept with me since

I was a girl—but he called them trinkets and laughed as though they were habits I ought to shake off. As the children grew up, they broke so many that I finally packed them up and stored them away in the attic.

Our children were so rough. Strong girls, different from me. When they were babies, I dreamed they'd grow up quiet. There were so many stories that I wanted to tell them. I dreamed they'd play piano, imagined teaching them about the way to choose a vase for a flower arrangement. But instead they played sports. They became less comprehensible to me. Like William, they never let me go off on my own. They needed my company so much. Elizabeth laughed as he did, in the same sharp way, when I tried to explain the importance of my trinkets. For her sake I was happy she resembled him, and hoped it would last. Diana was different. She listened to my stories with that solemn expression. But her body was strong, like his. By the time Izzy was born, Diana was so tall and athletic, I couldn't imagine she was mine. The house was so noisy by then.

Here is a memory: two years ago, maybe more, Diana running through the house with her tennis bag across her back. She knocked my collection of small glass horses off the bookshelf. All seven of them shattered. A family of glass horses. When I was alone—when William was at work and the girls were at school and I could finally breathe—I would look at them and wonder that they could remain perfect when everything else had fallen off-kilter somehow. After Diana broke them, I ran to kneel beside them, crying. It was the only time I had cried in front of the children. Then Elizabeth didn't laugh. She came in from the dining room and knelt with me, trying to pick up the pieces. Their shattered glass bones. But I didn't want her to touch them. I slapped her hands away and only later, when I stood and turned, I saw that she was holding Diana, both of them down on their knees. I knew I shouldn't have cried. It was unmotherly. They were only things. But I was hurt, and they were both strong girls. They were his daughters; I knew they'd be fine. I went upstairs and buried the shards of my horses in a silver box. As I did, I could feel their worry spreading through the house, and I pitied them, but I didn't come down for dinner. They were unusually quiet all night. Diana slid a card beneath my door before she went to sleep.

What a terrible thing to remember. I should have gone to her and made her know I'd survive. I should have reassured her that the horses were only glass. They weren't real; she hadn't ruined anything. I don't know why I didn't. It wasn't right to leave them there downstairs, to wait until their father came home. But something was wrong with me. It was already there, biding its time, secretive as an egg, eaten alone.

I want to be strong for my girls. I won't tell them I'm sick till Diana's finished with school. My mother waited that long for me; I can do the same for Diana. But I won't be able to wait for Isabelle. One day soon the disease will have a life of its own.

Already I feel myself slipping away, and here is a secret I'd like to remember: in truth it's not too bad. I'm scared, but only in the way you are before you dive beneath a wave. Once you've dived, there's nothing but cool darkness and the tumbling into something that was part of you from before you were born.

At the end of the entry, Louise closed the notebook. She wanted to read more but forced herself to stop, one hand on its cover. The room she was sitting in was silent. More silent than any empty room in any empty house she'd ever wandered through before. She listened to herself breathing, the sound of it magnified. She was completely alone. So often when she was sitting in the empty houses of her employers, she found herself in conversation with some invisible person: Bradley, mostly, but her mother also, and old friends from school. She complained to these people about her boredom in Breacon, and about the insufferable routines of the people she loathed. But at some point while she was reading, her crowd of listeners had exited. Even Margaux was gone.

Louise was alone, and although this was slightly disturbing, she understood that she was no longer bored. The painting on the easel looked different in this light, clearer somehow, and in the end Bradley Barlow didn't matter at all. Margaux's notebook described a kind of world that a person such as Bradley couldn't dream of. The world of a person as she slowly forgot, as the characters around her exited the stage. As her whole life narrowed to the edge of a single pellucid moment. Bradley was too stupid to imagine such a thing. He'd never be this lonely, but that was his loss. Some people never look back long enough to know there's nothing there anymore.

Chapter 4

On Saturday night, after the Horrifying Woman brought William back from the hospital and put him to bed in his room, her first move was to call an emergency summit. The sisters gathered around the kitchen table promptly, good peons that they were. Adelia pulled out the legal pad on which she had outlined her strategy, then cleared her throat to make an announcement: she would be moving in to help take care of William as he convalesced. A silence ensued. Something resembling excitement stirred in Isabelle's stomach. The silence widened, delicious and hovering, but before anyone could fill it, Adelia jumped in again to specify that she would, of course, be staying in the guest room. This superfluous detail only caused Isabelle to imagine Adelia hiking up her J. Crew skirt and climbing aboard their father with a determined look in her eyes. In reality, there had never been any evidence of shenanigans between William and the Horrifying Woman. Plus, the idea of them having an affair was the least of Izzy's concerns.

The problem was the finality of the thing. For years the Horrifying Woman had approached, moving closer and closer to the inner room of the Adair family, left vacant by Margaux so many years ago. Izzy harbored the suspicion that once the room was occupied by a woman as staunch as Adelia, there would be no going back. Margaux couldn't return, and the house would never be what it was when Izzy was small and the family was complete.

Izzy looked across the table at her sisters to see if they registered the threat. This had been coming for years, but only Isabelle had been home to measure its approach. Elizabeth and Diana were already gone by the time Margaux was diagnosed. They were consumed by their own dilemmas. Only Izzy was left at home. Only Izzy was expected, without actually being asked, to think of Adelia as a second mother. Neither of her sisters had faced the daily chore of having dinner with William and Adelia, while Margaux ate leftovers upstairs, staring at the empty spaces on her canvases. By the time Isabelle got to high school, William and Adelia were sharing driving duties, which left Isabelle with no option but to initiate flirtation with her art teacher so that he, rather than Adelia, could drive her home from school. Fortunately, Izzy turned sixteen shortly after commencing the ordeal with Mr. Knapp, so she was able to terminate their relationship before things got out of hand. Thus, her fellow students were denied further grounds for gossip, and Adelia was denied cause for an awkward lecture on the value of innocence, delivered after manifold prerequisites such as "I know I'm not your mother and I have no right to tell you this." Unfortunately, the incident with Mr. Knapp made it uncomfortable for Isabelle to spend time in the art room. Free periods became wastelands dedicated mainly to avoiding contact with other kids her age. She blamed Adelia for this.

Throughout all these developments, Diana and Elizabeth were gone. They missed Margaux's still-present absence. They weren't privy to William acting like a bereft husband, Adelia consoling him, both of them treating Margaux like a benign Mrs. Rochester locked away in her painting studio. They never caught the neighbors watching through their blinds for Adelia's car in the driveway, or pretending to water their prefabricated gardens while spying on the Fallen Adairs. They missed the bond between Adelia and William as it deepened through early-morning jogs, skirmishes with neighborhood association foes, and regular takeout dinners at the kitchen table, to which Margaux was always invited but never attended.

Izzy moved around the edges of these scenes. Much as William and Adelia tried to include her, she had no place in the new family eating at that table. She envied them their homey happiness, but she wasn't ready to abandon the dream of her old family. Only after Adelia made the Big Push to include Izzy in their fight for the carriage house did Izzy comprehend how little she wanted to join them in their tribal allegiances, around which the rest of the world dropped away. Then her sadness was replaced with scorn, which was subsequently replaced with the desire to get as far away as possible from Little Lane.

Her sisters had been spared all this. Once, Izzy called Elizabeth in L.A. to ask if she could move there to escape the Horrifying Woman. Elizabeth, dripping with self-pity as always, said, "At least with Adelia you have *some* sort of mother. Mom was just *absent* most of the time."

When Elizabeth came back to Breacon after the divorce, Izzy expected her to express some kind of indignation at how comfortable Adelia had made herself in their house. But Elizabeth was so wrapped up in her narcissistic disappointment that she could barely put one foot in front of the other, let alone examine the situation on Little Lane with any sort of clarity. In fact, Adelia fawned over her so excessively that Elizabeth seemed to be growing attached to the Horrifying Woman. It was Adelia, after all, who encouraged William to invest in Elizabeth's yoga studio, who treated the whole dumb scheme as if teaching yoga were not a hideous cliché for a washed-up actress and young divorcée. Three times a week, Adelia attended Elizabeth's yoga classes, staking out a place in the center of the front row so she could glare at herself in the mirror. Once Izzy accompanied Adelia to a Wednesday-evening class, just to see what it was like. When the class began, it was clear that the entire world had dropped away from Adelia. Between Adelia and her reflection, a battle to the death had commenced that devoured all the air in the room. There was something startling, even frightening, about her focus as she bent her leg back into dancer's pose. Watching her, you had the sense that she would never find her way back into the world. Afterward, in the changing room, Izzy overheard two girls whispering. "That horrifying woman was at it again," one said, giggling, and Izzy immediately knew she was referring to Adelia. She felt an unavoidable stab of pity for ragged Adelia, but the phrase stuck. Back at the front desk, Adelia was telling Elizabeth that she had both Charisma and Charm. Elizabeth was acting bashful, Adelia was repeating herself, and Izzy thought, *That Horrifying Woman! She loves us so much, she'd eat us alive, then howl at the moon in her loneliness.*

Izzy's sisters were unperturbed by such images. Elizabeth was grateful for Adelia's confidence, and when Diana came to visit, she was too tattered to notice. She was like a dragon on its last legs, once fierce but now so sad and bedraggled that you wished it would lift its head and incinerate the whole damn town. For years Izzy had hoped that her older sisters would return and confront the degenerating state of affairs, but she had at last grasped the fact that they were too far gone to help. Now, as Adelia made her final approach, they were as absent as they'd been when they were living on opposite sides of the country.

When Adelia called the summit and announced that she would be moving into the guest room, neither Diana nor Elizabeth refused. "You're much too kind," Elizabeth told her, and Diana wondered if they should change the sheets on the bed. Isabelle turned away from her sisters toward the ghost of her own face in the window glass. She could only marvel at Adelia's tactical prowess. It was such a tidy little invasion. She had been baby-stepping her way into the family home for years, so that now, when the royal heirs were distracted by other concerns, she had only to open the door and walk in. Izzy swallowed. They had reached the end of the line.

"Mom should be here," Izzy said. Diana winced, and Isabelle immediately regretted having taken the opportunity to strike.

"I've already spoken to her," Adelia said. "In the garden this morning. We agreed that this was the best." She blinked so hard, Isabelle thought she could hear the click of her eyelids hitting each other.

The sisters consulted their consciences. Isabelle waited and watched. What would Margaux think about Adelia moving in? Of all of them, Isabelle was least likely to know. She was only ten when their mother was diagnosed, and even before that, most of her memories consisted of Margaux brushing past, always just leaving. Only her flowers remained. Sometimes Izzy would open her history textbook in school and find one stalk of delphinium pressed between the pages. On good nights, when she went to sleep, she found a bouquet on her bedside table, ferns and white stephanotis and anemones with deep blue centers. These she took in place of the other things a mother is supposed to give. If she asked for more—if she pressed her mother for an opinion, for comfort, for guidance—she was forced to remember again the expression of vague politeness that fell across Margaux's face. If she were to go to her now and say, "Adelia's in love with Dad," Margaux would force herself to look up from her painting and smile courteously. "That's nice . . ." she might say, then trail off.

But despite all this, it was hard for Izzy to believe that Margaux couldn't remember that she, not Adelia, was William's wife and her children's mother. It wasn't as if she'd forgotten how to dress herself for the day. Her memory of the fundamental facts was strong. It was more like she'd forgotten how she was supposed to feel. She knew each of her daughters by proper name, but she couldn't remember how she was meant to relate to them. It was an illness, of course. It was no one's fault. But it was difficult for Isabelle not to be hurt by the nature of her mother's forgetting. They probably did have a talk in the garden, Adelia and Margaux, the least likely allies in the land. Adelia probably proposed her solution as if she were proposing it to her own reflection in the yoga studio mirror. And Margaux probably agreed, her mind already twisting toward the sweet autumn clematis, newly trellised on the eastern wall of the house.

"What about Louise?" Elizabeth asked. "Couldn't Louise help out?"

"She's busy with your mother," Adelia said.

"Well, I can help as much as possible," Elizabeth continued, which was kind of her considering that William was paying nearly half of the mortgage on the "cottage" on Wimberlyn Street that Elizabeth insisted on buying when she moved the grandkids back from L.A. "The girls are off from school, and I'm working full-time, but I'll steal away as much as I can."

"Thank you, Elizabeth."

"I can help, too," Diana said. "I'm not going back to Texas."

Everyone turned to look at her.

"I don't need to go back. I'm not in school, anyway."

"What are you talking about?" Elizabeth asked.

"I dropped out. Last fall." For some reason, she chose to focus on Isabelle while she made the announcement. Isabelle looked away. This was Diana, whose matches Izzy used to watch in awe, twisting a visitor's badge between two fingers, sitting courtside while the cameras flashed. Then Diana never flinched; her court face was stony. Now her lower lip was quivering with the difficulty of admitting this most recent failure. "I had my final defense in November, and I didn't show up. My project wasn't finished."

"What have you been doing since then?" Adelia asked.

"House-sitting," Diana said, getting control of her trembling lip. She became oddly expressionless. "Trying to finish my thesis design. I was almost there, and then I lost my blueprints. I left them on the bus, I think, and it's been hard to find the energy to start over from scratch. I told them I needed some time." She stopped talking, aware that she hadn't fully explained herself, and no one came to her aid. Isabelle would have liked to—she was searching for things she could say that would help Diana glide past this incident with the least possible friction—but the strangeness of her sister's paralysis silenced her. "I'm almost there," Diana said. "And my adviser said once I've finished, I can come back and re-enroll and defend at any point."

"I didn't think it worked like that," Adelia said. She was as compulsively honest as an X-ray.

"Within a year," Diana murmured.

"Why didn't you tell us?" Elizabeth asked.

"I didn't want to disappoint you. I was hoping to finish soon."

Adelia consulted her legal pad. Isabelle looked out, past her sisters' profiles, toward the blackness of the night that was smacking against the windowpane. She could see moths flocking around the outdoor lights above the patio. She didn't want to look at Di. She didn't want to look at Elizabeth. She wanted to fly through the glass and hover over the garden, her wings whirring in the thick darkness.

"Well," Adelia said. "It's sweet of you to offer. We could use your help around the house while your father's recovering."

Thus with a single "we"—what sleights of tongue are used in the most sweeping invasions—negotiations were completed, and the groundwork was laid for the Horrifying Woman's relocation to Little Lane. The second item on Adelia's agenda was to make a declaration of war. "Anita Schmidt is not going to win this fight," she said, flipping the page on her pad. "We can't underestimate how much the stress of the carriage house situation has affected your father. His grandfather designed that house. It was part of his childhood. This whole thing with the neighborhood association has been an attack on everything he holds dear. Do you understand? Your father has been fighting for his life ever since Anita Schmidt discovered that subdivision mistake. She essentially, if not legally, kidnapped the carriage house. That was one thing. But for the neighborhood association to deny that the building is historical is quite another. For them to sign a petition demanding its demolition. It undermines your father's sense of self. His sense of his family's history. You girls may not understand why he values it so much, but he does, and it would mean the world to him if you rallied to save it in his name."

So there would be another battle. Izzy remembered the last one. After Margaux's diagnosis, when Diana started her inexplicable failure to produce quantifiable results, when the carriage house battle was raging and Elizabeth's marriage was failing, William entered a period of minor depression that caused Adelia concern. Izzy was recruited. "You have no idea how happy your tennis makes him," Adelia told her. Izzy was sitting at the kitchen island, eating a toasted peanut butter sandwich. Up to this point, the youngest by far and the child of a defected mother, Isabelle had operated mostly on her own, unmonitored by the authorities, lost in a world of her own elaborate imagination. Now Adelia was reeling her in. "If we could just jolt him out of this," Adelia murmured, passing Izzy a napkin. After which there had been no more secretly believing Izzy was a rabbit like the ones she watched in her mother's garden. She became fully human. There were tennis tournaments and William telling her how beautifully she'd performed. There were matches played while William pumped his fist and Adelia stared with her lidless eyes. Izzy became an efficient performer. She was known on the local junior circuit for keeping her cool, but in truth she felt brittle and overconcerned, aware that her father's well-being hung in the balance. Each time she walked on court, she girded herself for battle, telling herself how little she cared, so that she could play in front of a crowd and feel nothing but movement.

And now, at Adelia's belligerent behest, the sound of axes rang in the kitchen again. "We understand," said Elizabeth, speaking for all of them in a dramatic tone that ought to have been magnified by a sound track. "What can we do to help?"

Adelia was prepared. "Anita Schmidt is dictatorial and mean," she announced. "She is a bully in the worst possible way. Believe me when I tell you that your father has attempted to be diplomatic. After the injunction didn't go through, he tried to persuade them. These are good friends of his, keep in mind. Ted Cheshire. Jack Weld. In return, they signed a petition rushing the demolition. These people are ruthless."

Izzy was aware that Adelia was propagandizing, but still, she felt it. For Jack Weld to be involved. For him to have refused her father something as simple as an ancient carriage house that stood—for William only, but still, for William!—as a guarantee of his place in the world. Jack Weld had taken enough from William already. He had witnessed William's losses. He had lurked in the background, grinning, while Izzy refused to become the girl her father had hoped she'd become. Jack had watched as she hollowed herself out, and that had been a triumph for him. It was almost enough to make Izzy want to join Adelia's war, if only to spite Jack. But then there was Adelia, excessively intense of eye, continuing to rally her troops. "The fact," she said, her lips thinning, "that the injunction didn't go through was a catastrophe. But the petition was more than a catastrophe: it was a personal assault. You've seen what it's done to your father. He's not himself. Diana, Isabelle, I'm sure you're hurt by what happened in the hospital, but he's not himself right now. So. What I am saying is that I can't overemphasize the importance of regaining the carriage house. If we could only do that for him, I feel confident that he would recover. But if he wakes up one day and sees that Anita Schmidt and her cronies have bulldozed the carriage house, it will destroy him completely."

"I agree," Elizabeth said. "I couldn't agree more. We have to save that carriage house."

"Good. I need to know you girls are with me. I don't want to do it without you. Your father wouldn't want me to do it without you."

"Okay," Diana said, obliging minion that she was. "Okay, what do we do?"

"I've drawn up a plan. The first step is to halt the demolition. Without a court order, it will have to be a matter of persuasion."

"Winning the hearts and minds," Izzy said.

"You're being sarcastic, Isabelle, but it is true. If any of this is to work, we'll have to get the neighbors to understand that blocking the demolition is a categorical imperative."

"What happens if we stop it?" Diana asked. She was listening as carefully as she could, straight-backed, so alert she might as well have been pinning little flags to a map.

"Then we move the carriage house onto your father's land."

All three of the sisters stared.

"We can do that?" Elizabeth asked.

"Yes. It's an iffy procedure, especially in the case of the carriage house, because of its condition. But it is possible."

"If Mrs. Schmidt wouldn't let Dad onto her property to make repairs, will she allow him onto the property with bulldozers or whatever to relocate the carriage house?"

"Jacks and timbers," Adelia corrected her. "The process requires jacks and timbers. And I can't necessarily speak to Anita Schmidt's reaction. Anita Schmidt is a pill, and I can't predict which way her pill of a mind will turn on this issue. If she's opposed, I'm not above just taking it. It's a quick procedure. I don't see an enormous objection on the part of the neighbors."

And thus, Izzy thought, the tribal wars of American suburbs commence.

"When do we start?" Elizabeth asked, trigger-happy and emboldened.

"Tomorrow morning. None of the wives work, so they'll all be home. And we can't waste any time. The demolition is scheduled for Thursday. It was supposed to be the week after next, but Jack Weld called an emergency meeting—while your father was in the hospital, of all things—which resulted in a date change."

"He's a terrible person," Izzy heard herself saying.

"Yes, he is." Adelia watched her for an extra moment, and Izzy wondered, as she always had, how much Adelia knew. Isabelle glared at her until she looked away.

"How could he *do* that?" Elizabeth asked. "How could he call it an e*mer*gency?"

"Because of the rodent problem," Adelia said, flipping through her plans.

"There's a *rodent* problem?"

"Yes, Elizabeth, there is a rodent problem. Because Mrs. Schmidt would rather let it be overrun by rats than allow your father onto her property to make the appropriate repairs."

"So tomorrow we go to the neighbors to ask for a stay."

"Yes."

"How are we doing this?" Izzy asked. "Divide and conquer?"

"Yes. I imagine that's the best way. Izzy, you and I will go together. We'll head left, toward the club. We'll speak to Ted and Mary Cheshire, Sheldon Ball, and Yusuf Uzmani. Elizabeth and Diana, you'll speak with Jack and Elaine Weld and Suzanne Legg. And I'd like you to speak with Anita Schmidt."

"The very Heart of Darkness itself," Izzy said.

"We need to propose the idea of removal," Adelia went on, ignoring Izzy. "I don't believe it will go over well, coming from me."

"We can do that," Elizabeth said, without consulting Diana.

"You might not get Anita herself. She's been sick: she had a tumor, or something awful like that. We sent her a beautiful bouquet of flowers, though little good that did. Her grandson is taking care of her. What is his name again?" Adelia pinched the bridge of her nose, attempting to remember. "I'm blanking on his name right now. Anyway, he's the one you'll speak to, most likely. What is his name, Di?"

Izzy watched Diana. She was sitting even straighter, focusing on Adelia's battle plan, but Izzy could see that a faint flush had risen to her cheeks. *Arthur,* Izzy wanted to say. Arthur was the name of Anita Schmidt's grandson, whom Diana was in love with once.

"Oh, God," said Elizabeth. "*God,* what is his *name*? Di, you dated him, didn't you?"

"Arthur," Di said. She was a good soldier. "It's Arthur."

"Yes, of course," Adelia said. There was an almost wistful tone to her voice. She made a note. "Anyway, Arthur has been caring for her for several months now. I imagine he can be talked to about these things." She considered her pad, blinking more deliberately than usual. A surprising softness spread momentarily over her face. "He's improved, you know," she said. "Since he was younger. He seems more confident. He grew out of that little slouch he used to have."

Diana sat very still.

"I saw him at the supermarket the other day," Elizabeth said, as though she had produced a crucial piece of evidence. "He's grown into his face. I think he owns a restaurant in New York. Maybe even two; I think he's opening a new one. Addie Ball told me it got excellent reviews. She went on and on about the pork ribs. But anyway, I saw Arthur at the supermarket. Mrs. Cheshire was telling him how to pick good eggplants, and he was listening as if he didn't own a *restaurant*. It was sort of adorable. I remember I used to think he was arrogant, for a kid who wasn't overly impressive, but he was definitely different."

"Still," Adelia said, calling her minions back into order. "We have to remember that he is his grandmother's child. He will not contradict her orders. If we're going to build an alliance with him, it will be a delicate one. He clearly loves Anita, hard as that may be to believe."

"She raised him, didn't she, Di?" Elizabeth asked.

Diana nodded, her flush deepening.

Adelia sallied forth. "Anyway, I'd like to gauge whether he'll be amenable to the relocation. But more immediately, we need him to agree to delay the demolition."

"How long do we need?" Elizabeth asked.

"As long as possible. But worst-case scenario? A month. I have contacts who will help us get a building contract quickly. After that, it's a matter of pouring the foundation and moving the structure. I've spoken to the contractor your father was thinking about. Wayne Construction. They have a highly advanced lifting system. They'll need a day to survey the structure and measure the footings. Some time to prepare the machinery. Another day to dig the whole thing up."

Izzy wanted distance from the kitchen table so she could think. She had begun to feel an unbidden desire to help. To get the carriage house for William as a tangible sign of his family's importance. To give him one solid thing to hold before she went away to college and left this hideous town forever. One step backward so that she could move forward again. But in proportion with this desire to help, there was the sense of herself getting lost, as it had the other time. Her boundaries felt tenuous, sitting with her sisters, hatching another plan with Adelia. "We understand," she said, wanting to leave. "We have our orders. Permission to go to bed now, Sergeant Lively."

"Isabelle, you can do whatever you like in this house." Adelia sighed. "I'm only trying to help."

Elizabeth gathered her bags; Diana excused herself to go outside for a walk. Adelia remained, pencil alert, at her post. And Izzy, as she had done each night since she could remember, walked up two flights of stairs to her bedroom across from Margaux's studio. The darkness in her bedroom enveloped her. She was alone with the forms of the furniture, dark, hulking shapes that scared her when she was a little girl because she imagined them coming to life. Beside them, she felt hollow and small. A vision of William as he used to be—vibrant, sitting in her chair and reading a story about enchanted mice or families of rabbits—made her want to cry. Izzy lifted her finger to her sharp, infinitely human nose. William's face in the hospital had looked like a paper mask. The image of that mask was more painful than the memory of him asking what had happened to her, why she had changed. To be honest, those questions, mean as they were, came as no surprise. Something *had* happened to her. She had gotten misplaced. He was as much at fault as she was, but it was too late for blame. The hopelessness of his paper face was worse. As though he were finished with fighting for the daughters he'd lost. When he came home from the hospital, he'd gotten out of the car and looked up at the house as if he didn't recognize it. They were all adrift, the Adairs. The house was at sea, with only Adelia's hand on the tiller.

For a while longer Isabelle sat in her desk chair, pressing the tip of her nose with her pointer finger, listening to nothing moving around her. When the stillness started to swim, she walked across the hall to her mother's studio. "Mom?" she whispered.

There was a silence. Then, finally, a wary voice: "Come in."

Isabelle opened the door a crack. A stripe of her mother revealed itself. Her dark hair, streaked with silver, was pulled back into a loose coil; she was facing her easel. The chair where Louise usually sat, absorbed in some crappy magazine, had been vacated for the night. Beyond the easel, the window was open wide: Isabelle caught the smell of new leaves from the yard. To the right, the single bed was neatly made, its deep red spread folded over pink floral sheets. Beside the bed was a vase of purple iris. Long ago Izzy had strung a train of paper lanterns between two corners of the room; Margaux sat beneath them, swaying gently before her wide and almost empty easel. She was like Switzerland up here, a one-woman nation of alpine air, refusing to take part in the wars. Behind her, pressed against the frame of the door, Isabelle felt bellicose and sharp. She considered stepping into the room and wondered, if she did, whether the softness of her mother would sweep up over her and settle all the edges of her bristling heart.

"I just wanted to say good night," Isabelle said, standing outside the door.

Margaux turned. Izzy thought she could detect warmth in her mother's face, and she was almost tempted to go sit beside her, but the expression faded to blankness.

"Good night, Mama," Izzy said, and then gently, trying not to make too sharp a sound, closed the door again. In her own bedroom, she checked her bedside table: there was a new vase under her lamp. She touched the petals of the clematis that her mother had cut, but something in their thinness made her chest ache, so she moved over to the window that was brushed by the canopy of her coeval tree. It was a yellowwood, planted just a week after they brought her home from the hospital. Now its crown reached up to the third floor, whispering all night long in the wind. The leaves were dark green shapes rustling the blackness like moths. Through them she could see Margaux's garden, and beyond, the rotting carriage house. Between the garden and the house, there was the shape of Diana moving forward through the night. Poor obedient Di. Izzy closed her eyes and imagined herself floating in the midst of the yellowwood leaves, a shape of cut-out cloth, brushing the darkness. She felt the sweep of leaves on her cheeks. And then there was the rasp of a branch scraping her windowpane, and Izzy opened her eyes, jagged again. She reached forward and switched on her desk lamp, and in its angry glare the outside world went blank.

Chapter 5

Diana slid through the kitchen door and moved over the patio, past the fishpond and the rings of her mother's garden. So Arthur was only the length of a yard away. One light in the Schmidt house was on, in the kitchen, and she could see the form of a table and the cabinets beyond it. She shivered. All around her, Margaux's irises bloomed, purple ghosts hovering in the darkness.

Past the pond, past the irises, there was the stretch of lawn that led to the Schmidts' fence. She climbed the stack of bricks that had been hidden behind the compost pile since she was in high school and swung one leg over. Staying close to the periphery, so that no one in the Schmidt house could see, she moved toward the carriage house. The door creaked when she pushed it open: inside, the quality of darkness was different. The empty space practically dripped, as though inside its old warped beams the night had been compressed into liquefaction by the pressure of uninterrupted years. She didn't dare climb the rotten stairs; she sat on the lowest step, feeling the wood bend and settle beneath her.

She couldn't blame them for not remembering his name or what he meant to her. It was so long ago. Isabelle was only eight when they started dating. Adelia had just moved to Breacon, and Elizabeth was preoccupied by her dramatically hasty marriage. And anyway, even while she and Arthur were together, Diana didn't talk to her family about him much. It was a thing she kept for herself. Now so many years had passed. Of course her connection to Arthur was less than vivid in their minds. She was probably the only remaining person who believed it was real, not some figment of adolescent imagination. When children fall in love, adults imagine that the end will be like a shed skin. Each childish breakup is meant to be a sloughing off of another potential self until the most desirable version can emerge. That had not been Diana's experience, but her family couldn't be expected to understand that. They couldn't possibly know how often she still thought of him.

The thing between them lasted two short years. Their senior year of high school and her freshman year of college. In their junior year of high school, he arrived in Breacon to live with Anita. His mother had moved to Paris and left him behind. They met for the first time in the driveway, as Diana was leaving for tennis practice and Arthur was taking out the trash; when Arthur explained the story of his mother's departure, he shrugged and squinted up toward the sky. He didn't know, or he was waiting for rain.

When William learned that there was a boy living with Anita Schmidt, he invited him over for dinner. They ate a thawed lasagna. When William asked where Arthur intended to apply to college, Arthur explained that he wasn't sure he would. This produced a furrow of consternation in William's forehead. When asked what sports he played, Arthur announced that he didn't.

Conversation dried up quickly. But Arthur had a way of sitting there at the dinner table. He was sure in the shape of his frame despite its slight slouch. There was confidence in his hands as he lifted forkfuls of lasagna to his mouth.

From the start, Diana had the sense that her success didn't impress him. He didn't particularly care about tennis. The fact that she was class president made him laugh, without derision, but with something else that Diana couldn't completely comprehend. Her 5 on the Calculus AP had no meaning to him. At first her inability to impress this directionless kid from across the lawn annoyed her. What had he done that was so terribly great? He had merely arrived and stayed. Then it started to fluster her. She searched around for an arrow in her distinguished quiver that would make him understand her unique impressiveness. When this failed, she settled in to watch him. He ate quietly. He asked William about architecture, to which William swatted his hands and muttered, "It's not what it once was, I'll tell you that. It's a fallen discipline." Arthur asked more questions. "Architects were once Great Men," William explained, jabbing the air with his fork. "They built cities. They laid the bedrock of civilization. My grandfather built this town. Now we work on commission. The art of it has gotten small." Diana watched Arthur engaging her father as though William Adair was just another man, curious and cramped.

Arthur wasn't handsome, but he had a look that drew Diana to him. His eyes were the greenish-slate color of old hard courts. This was what Diana remembered. Other than his eyes, the details of Arthur's face had become less clear as the years passed. Diana couldn't remember the particular shape of his nose. At UT, during that first year when they were together, Diana fell asleep every night by imagining his face beside her, watching her as she drifted off. Even after they'd broken up, she kept imagining this. Even when they hadn't spoken in months. One night, after a year or so, she realized that she couldn't remember his face anymore. She couldn't sleep. She spent the whole night feeling as though she were falling, slowly, off a steep precipice.

But if she closed her eyes, here in this house where they spent so much time, she could feel the shape of his jaw in her hand.

Something scurried somewhere off in the darkness. She opened her eyes again. She was getting accustomed to the dark. She could make out the wide cement panels on the floor, the wood slats of the inside wall, the gambrel ceiling with its cedar beams. Above her was the loft, encircling three walls of the house, the place where she and Arthur had accumulated the trappings of a bedroom. She brought books; he brought an air mattress and a heap of blankets that smelled like mothballs. She brought a space heater; he brought wooden whiskey crates to use as furniture. For two years they kept a secret world up there. It was the only thing about her life that no one knew. When, after her freshman year of college, in the filtered light of the loft, Arthur asked her to marry him, it seemed completely natural. In the secret world of the carriage house, they'd been living together a long time, alone in their private universe. He bought her a slim gold ring with money from the construction job he'd worked all year. She slipped it on, and in the surge of excitement that followed the gesture, she bit his hand so hard she left a red semicircle on the web between his index finger and his thumb.

As soon as she stepped out onto the lawn wearing the ring on her wedding finger, she became aware that there would be problems. Though William knew that Diana and Arthur were dating, he was confident that Di would move on in college. Because of this, he could temper his disapproval. If asked about Arthur, he'd say, "He has no direction." Or, more thoughtfully, "It's not his fault, he can't help the family he has. But he has no sense of his consequence." Her mother wouldn't care: she and Arthur had spent time together in the garden, and he had helped plant her bulbs. Oddly, it had seemed like the two of them got along in a way Diana couldn't entirely understand. She'd watched them from the stone bench by the pond, their white hands darting in and out of the soil. She'd been curious about the easy way they knelt together side by side. Even before her diagnosis, Margaux seemed lost when it came to advising her children. She had ceded this ground to William long before she got sick. No, the more important thing was that William wouldn't approve. His disapprobation would be compounded by the issue of Elizabeth's pending marriage to Mark. After college, Elizabeth had moved out to L.A., and when she came back for Thanksgiving, she announced that she was engaged to a successful character actor who lived in Los Feliz. It took William a couple of days to recover from the shock. They'd never even met him, and William hadn't been asked for his blessing. He had to mentally redefine the engagement as a move that was good for her career. "Things are different out there in L.A.," he said to Diana, trying to arrange his surprise into a useful system. He sliced the air into vertical segments with his hand. "Your sister has always been smart. I'm sure what she's doing is good for her career." By the time Arthur gave Diana the ring, Elizabeth was three months pregnant with Caroline, and William was struggling to understand how children had become a part of Elizabeth's plan. Diana felt his disappointment, thick and awful because he was always so proud of his girls.

That was what she was thinking about as she walked across the lawn with Arthur's ring on her finger. William had only just wrapped his head around the idea of Elizabeth's marriage, and now his middle girl had gotten engaged before she was twenty. There was no pride, Diana told herself, in breaking your father's heart. He had given them so much; she would not add to his disappointment. She took the ring off before she reached the patio and put it in the pocket of her jeans. When she walked through the kitchen door, William looked up from his paper and asked how physical therapy had gone. She kissed him on the cheek before going up to her room, where she put the ring on a chain that she could wear around her neck, hidden under her clothes.

Only a week later, Margaux announced that she'd been diagnosed with early-onset Alzheimer's. She was only forty-seven at the time. Precisely forty-seven, because it was her birthday when she told them. Izzy had planned a party, with Japanese lanterns and angel food cake. Adelia was there, new to Breacon but already a regular presence in the house. On the night of the party, she exuded a fever of gratitude for having been invited. At the head of the table, Margaux wore a pink crown cut out of construction paper. She made the announcement with a placid expression, right before she blew out the candles that Izzy had arranged on her cake. There was an enchanted glow to the whole suspended moment. Margaux in her pink paper crown, the girls, William, and bright-faced Adelia. They all hovered at the cusp of something, and even as the announcement unfolded, Diana somehow imagined Margaux was going to give them good news.

Once she finished talking, she closed her eyes and leaned forward to blow out the candles. Her long hair dipped so close to the flames that Diana imagined her head engulfed in a fiery halo. Izzy stuck her knife through one of the paper lanterns. Ever so slowly, it sighed and collapsed. "Are they sure?" William asked. Through lingering smoke, Margaux nodded. "Oh, Margaux," Adelia said, and Izzy stood up and punctured every other lantern on the chain. They deflated slowly. "I should go upstairs," Margaux said. "I'm sorry to have ruined the party." And then she left, and Izzy ran off somewhere, and the rest of the family, including Adelia, picked up the tinselly mess left in her wake.

After they all moved into the kitchen, Diana watched William washing the silverware, and she could see that he was perplexed but not upset. It was comforting, in one sense, to have a concrete medical excuse for the many ways that Margaux had left them all behind. It was good to know that they weren't imagining the ebbing they'd felt for years. At the same time, Diana experienced a quickening of the fear that had been building in her throughout the year, while she was injured and anxious about her tennis career. In Texas, far away from William and Arthur and the town where she'd been a great champion, Diana felt the boundaries of herself beginning to blur. There were other athletes at UT more impressive than she. She could not define herself as the most athletic girl in her class. She was sidelined after her injury, and without matches to prove herself, she had little else of substance to produce. She struggled with sleeplessness, and only during Arthur's visits, when she fell asleep anchored to his physical closeness, did she feel rested enough to imagine a comeback. Since returning to Breacon for summer vacation, she'd felt infinitely surer about herself. But Margaux's announcement made her worry again about something lurking in her genes. A shortwindedness. As she dried the silverware that William passed her, Diana remembered those sleepless nights at UT, listening to doors slamming shut throughout the recesses of the athletes' dorm, and she felt as though a destroyer angel had swept past at some point and marked her forehead with its thumb.

The announcement offered new proof for the things that Diana had started suspecting existed in herself. Afterward, aspects of her daily life in Breacon came to stand as proof of the propensity for early decline. Even the carriage house, with Arthur, started to seem like evidence of a Mom-ish desire to shrink off into dark recesses, leaving a former, more successful self behind. It was these doubts that caused her to tell Elizabeth about the engagement. Elizabeth told William; William told Adelia. Elizabeth's disapproval wouldn't have bothered Diana much, as she was clearly preoccupied with her own romantic drama. Even William's disapproval, Diana could have handled. There were techniques she could have used to avoid breaking his heart. She could have promised him that she would wait until she'd finished with school. She could have assured him that it would not affect her tennis, and she could have proven that to him on court. But the talk with Adelia shifted something in her.

In a short period of time, Diana had come to cherish her relationship with Adelia, this woman who had come back to her childhood home, single, with a successful career at a law firm downtown. She swept into Breacon just as Margaux was getting more distant, and she attached herself to the Adairs—to William and Diana in particular—with an enthusiasm that felt like a life raft. William admired her; by extension, Diana hoped to impress her. In a short time, Di came to want to please Adelia almost as much as she had always hoped to make her father proud.

"Di, I know I'm not your mother," Adelia said after she found out. "And I know I have no right to talk to you about these things. But I have some experience with marriage. I've been through it twice. When I was young, all women *did* was get married. It was the only ambition we were given." But Adelia was an athlete. She dreamed of playing in Wimbledon. She was college champion. And when she was twenty, in her senior year, because everyone around her was getting married and she thought she was running out of time, she married her husband and dropped out of school. Every night for a year she made him a different dinner out of *The Joy of Cooking,* and then one night, over a fallen soufflé, she started to cry. She wanted to *become* something. He never understood. He couldn't imagine that, in marrying him, she had not become the thing she dreamed of, that every day she spent in his house, she was moving farther away from herself. That she had finally come so far, she feared she would never get back to the person she'd hoped to become. After the first divorce, she returned to school, but it was too late for her tennis career. Billie Jean King was winning Wimbledon. Adelia might never have gotten quite so good as that, but she regretted her whole life not having given it more of a try. "You have so much potential," Adelia told Diana. "I couldn't bear to see you lose that."

They were sitting at the same glass table on the patio where Margaux had made her announcement. Beyond them, the sound of the pond, trickling. And beyond that, the rows of Margaux's garden, meticulous and opulent. And then Adelia said the thing that most clinched Diana's mind. "I say this for the sake of Arthur, too. If you marry him now, your life will be settled. That's a wonderful feeling. Safe. But it wouldn't be fair to him. To ask him to settle before he's had a chance to dream of the person he'd like to become. He's working construction, but he should be more. He must want more than that for himself." "He's going to own a restaurant," Di murmured without meeting Adelia's eye. "That's exactly what I mean," Adelia agreed, although from the sound of her voice, it was clear that she wasn't certain that owning a restaurant was a big enough ambition for the man Diana would marry. "A bigger ambition, like owning a restaurant, or whatever else he decides on. He needs time to pursue that on his own. If you get married, he'll have everything he wants. But now is the time for him to want more." She gave Diana a moment to contemplate the possibilities she'd take from Arthur if she were to marry him now. When Adelia spoke again, she leaned forward as if sharing a secret from her life that no one else could know. "And Di, listen, if you two are meant to be, you'll end up back together in the end."

After that talk, Diana spent the rest of the summer meeting Arthur in the carriage house, pressing her face against the slope of his pale shoulders. He knew she was wearing the ring hidden, but he never pressed her about it. He must have trusted that she was only taking her time. Without telling him the truth, she clung to her final days with him, watching shadows pass across his half-hidden eyes. Treasuring the secrets of their private life in the loft. In the last week of the summer, she told him they needed to fulfill their promise before they could end up together.

"I don't know what you mean. What is this 'promise'? We promised to get married. What other kind of promise do you mean?"

Diana's confidence faltered. "I just mean there are things we should accomplish before we end up together."

"We will accomplish things. I'm not worried about it."

"But we should accomplish things for ourselves before we've settled down." She could feel her logic becoming less clear, but she remembered the certainty in Adelia's voice.

Arthur watched her stumbling. "Do you want to date other people?" he asked.

Diana hadn't even considered that. "No, Arthur, it's just I have this feeling that we're both becoming different versions of ourselves, and we have to finish that before we marry each other."

"What is this different version you want to be?"

"I don't really know," Diana said. She was getting flustered. "I want to win the NCAAs. I want to do well in school. I want to be an architect or a politician."

"An architect or a politician?" he repeated, and Diana felt his scorn.

"Arthur," she said, "I don't know what I'm going to become, but I want to become something before we settle down."

And so, with Adelia's advice echoing in her ears, Diana continued holding on to the familiar shape of his body, aching from head to toe. Finally, exhausted, she told him goodbye, left the ring in his palm, and walked back over the lawn to the house.

The next day she went back to Texas, to the flat, glassy heat of the tennis courts in August. She stood there, alone on the bare expanse of exposed concrete, under the full stands, and only then did she know how much she'd given up. Sleeping got harder. She tried to date other boys, but no one was as good as Arthur. Her knee never fully recovered, or at least that was what she told herself, because something changed about her game. She couldn't perform as she once had. Tennis was no longer simple. It was an effort that involved her entire body and her entire mind. It became exhausting. She had a bad season, and the next year a new recruit from Florida assumed her spot at number one.

And she lost Arthur for good. He wouldn't return her calls. There was no "for now" in his mind. His mind had comprehended the concept of forever and didn't adjust itself back to the level of now. He spent another year working construction, then went out west somewhere for school. She heard he was paying his own way by working in a restaurant, and she tried to call him to offer congratulations—she had never done something so independent or self-directed in her whole small life—but his number had changed.

Now he was here, only a yard behind her, so close that the feel of his jaw in her hand had returned. He was here, and the span of time when Adelia had been so sure Diana would find herself had passed, and there had been no flowering of her potential. She had faded, and that was all. She was pursuing a discipline that didn't make her father proud, and she wasn't pursuing it well. For Diana Adair—class president, acer of math and science APs, class pet of the shop teacher with his sawdusty mustache and his missing thumb—architecture school ought to have been a breeze. But she applied three times and was rejected twice. After she was finally accepted, only she, of all her cohort, failed to graduate on time. She left her flawed blueprints on the bus rather than have to defend them. Diana had practiced the art of failure and no longer remembered what it was like to be the successful girl she was when she gave Arthur back his ring.

Tomorrow she would see him. At twenty-seven, she wasn't as pretty as she was when he met her at seventeen. He had become everything he hoped, and she couldn't remember how her confident seventeen-year-old self once talked. Restless, Diana stood up. She tested the second step with her foot. She placed half her weight on it, then all. It shifted beneath her. It wouldn't be safe to try. They'd had a ladder when they slept up there; even then the stairs weren't safe. She backed down to the floor and considered those sagging stairs. If only she could climb back up to the loft. She wondered whether anything remained up there: the space heater, a blanket, some books. She had no idea. She'd stayed away from the carriage because Arthur wouldn't talk to her. Without him, she hadn't wanted to spend time inside.

And now it was going to be demolished unless Adelia's wild scheme to move it could work. The desire to succeed in the relocation flooded her. She did not want to lose this place. If they could get it onto the Adair property, a renovation could work. She could even help. The structure could be saved, the materials preserved. The idea animated her. She walked out of the carriage house and circled it once. Tomorrow she would talk to the contractors. There were things she could do. Encouraged, she walked back through the garden into the house and climbed the stairs. On the second floor, before she turned in to her bedroom, she caught sight of Adelia walking out of the bathroom. Her hair was tousled, and she was wearing a floor-length white nightgown. The sight of her startled Diana. Adelia was generally so composed. She wore sweater sets and capri pants. There were always earrings in her ears and clips in her neat blond bob. To see her in a nightgown like that, blurry-visioned without her contacts, was somehow upsetting.

"We're going to get that house back," Di said, as though to offer strength.

Adelia straightened some, and her eyes came into focus. "Yes," she said. "Yes, we will." She reached out and took Diana's hand. "We'll get it back, sweet Di."

Chapter 6

Monday morning was chaos. From the time they woke up to the time they tumbled into the car, the girls were a nightmare to corral, Caroline having left her tennis racket at science camp and Lucy insisting that she had flown on her way down the stairs to breakfast and would they please just come and watch, and Caroline reminding her that flying was impossible for Homo sapiens because of gravity and winglessness and the lack of evolutionary need, and both of them evading their toast with a slipperiness that was incomprehensible to Elizabeth so early in the day. She thought again, with a welling sensation to which she had grown accustomed in the last year and a half, that she was doing all of this all alone, while Mark was probably having morning sex. To settle her nerves, she breathed in through her nose and out through her mouth, then wrapped the toast in foil and gave it to the girls for the road. She was in the process of reminding herself to feel grateful for her blessings, for these little girls who were her own, when she walked out the front door and caught Lucy throwing the remains of her toast into the pachysandra bed, and Elizabeth flew to pieces again.

By the time they got into the car, there was a pit in Elizabeth's stomach, the feeling that she had forgotten something important. This pit welled with anxiety when she found herself stuck driving behind a bulldozer, moving at a speed that could only be described as prehistoric. As a result, the girls would probably be late for the tennis court she had reserved in their name, which had been difficult to procure at that hour in the morning, popular with all the undivorced housewives who were not raising children on their own. She attempted to remain calm as she followed the bulldozer for the entire length of Clubhouse Road, but she found herself beating the steering wheel with her palm when it took a left onto Little Lane. At this point she started to wonder what the bulldozer could be doing on their street, which was a cul-de-sac and could not be used as a throughway. And then her anxiety sharpened into something resembling fear because the bulldozer was turning onto Anita Schmidt's driveway, joining a crane-thing with an actual wrecking ball. She braked in front of the house.

It was Monday. Today was not the day for the demolition. The demolition day was Thursday, was it not? They were meant to have some time to start fighting for neighborhood hearts and minds. Daddy had just had a *stroke*, and that asshole across the street was speeding up the demolition plan? Elizabeth glared at Anita Schmidt's house, which was ugly in an old-person-house way: ranch-style, with pale bricks and orange-brown shutters. It was the ugliest house on the block: the neighbors never should have allowed her to build it. Specifications should have been made about shutter color when Granddaddy subdivided the land.

Two construction workers in hard hats climbed out of their machines. They consulted a clipboard; one of them made a joke and the other one laughed, and in her frustration Elizabeth beat the steering wheel again. Now they were waving their hands, and the machines rumbled and moved out onto the lawn, approaching the carriage house. Elizabeth tried to summon inner calm. She needed to think clearly. She attempted to practice her ujjayi breathing, but as she pulled into the driveway of her childhood home, Lucy let out an earth-shattering screech, followed by "I CAN NOSE-FUCKING FLY IF I WANT TO!" The ujjayi breath went out the window, and all Elizabeth could think was, did Lucy have a cursing problem before the divorce, and why had literal-minded Caroline told her she couldn't fly when it would obviously upset her, and how had Mark left her to do this on her own? But she didn't have time to think about any of these questions with a peaceful mind or an open heart because there was a fucking bulldozer ready to tear down Daddy's carriage house and she had to hustle the girls inside so she and Adelia could strategize.

Inside things weren't less of a wreck. Daddy was sitting at the kitchen table, looking disturbingly discombobulated in an old pair of corduroys and slippers and a patterned sweater. A patterned sweater, of all uncharacteristic things. Elizabeth had never seen him wearing it: he looked like Linus from *Charlie Brown,* defeated and small. And he was just sitting there, looking down at his coffee mug, muttering, "I can't smell it," over and over again. Adelia was there, ignoring Daddy, staring out the window with an intensity that made it seem as though she were preparing to dive through the glass. She was wearing some kind of Gothic floor-length nightgown. Even the girls could sense that something was terribly wrong. They clung to Elizabeth's skirt as though their grandfather were naked and his best friend had transformed overnight into a little vampire girl.

"Shit," Adelia said. "Shit, shit, shit." She abruptly fled the kitchen. Elizabeth wondered if that was where Lucy was getting her cursing, and she reminded herself to talk to Adelia about it, but then she heard Daddy saying, "I cannot smell a thing," so she attempted to focus on her father.

"Daddy," she said, squatting by his side. "Daddy, what do you mean?"

"I cannot smell this coffee," he said. "It tastes like nothing. Do you understand?" Elizabeth was trying to listen to him, but a second later, through the kitchen window, she saw a rock the size of a fist fly through the air and strike the ground a foot away from one of the construction workers. The worker spun around, covering his head with his arms. Elizabeth stood up, speechless. "This coffee tastes like dishwater," Daddy said, and then another rock—this one the size of a sneaker—flew through the air and struck the crane-thing so hard that Elizabeth could hear the clatter from inside. The rock had definitely come from above her.

"Mommy, what's going on?" asked Caroline. Lucy was gone somewhere, striking a tragic pose, most likely, and then another rock flew through the air and landed with a thud between two other hard-hatted workers, who by this time were cowering in the shadow of their machines.

"Stay here, sweetie," Elizabeth said, although she was not entirely confident about leaving Caroline with Daddy in his strange condition. She ran up the stairs and saw Adelia standing at the guest room window, in that Gothic-virginal nightgown, launching rocks at the demolition team. She was pulling the rocks from a threatening stockpile that had somehow accumulated on the guest room carpeting, and while she launched, Diana was sitting there on the guest room bed, watching Adelia without making a single move. Then Izzy was running down the stairs from her little lair up in the attic, and there was a crazed flush on her face. "Is she bombing them?" she asked. "Are those coming from Adelia?"

When she saw that indeed it was Adelia, she started laughing like a keyed-up lunatic before turning and retreating up to her lair.

Elizabeth rushed into the room. "What are you doing, Adelia?" she asked, then noticed that this was where Lucy had run off to. She had wedged herself between the open door and the corner and was watching Adelia with her mouth slightly ajar. "And Di," Elizabeth said, "*what* are you *doing*? Why are you letting Lucy *watch* this?" Di, startled, looked back at her with a brand of vague guiltiness that evaporated the last vestiges of Elizabeth's inner calm. It was unfair for Elizabeth to have to be the voice of reason in this mess. She was only thirty-two, and yet she was as old as if she had lived for a thousand years. That was the saddest thing about being a mother: you gave up your right to youngness forever. She would have liked to run laughing up to her room. Or to sit on the bed and watch the show unfold. But she was a mother. She had to act adult, and here was Adelia, almost fifty-five, pelting rocks out of the window in a nightgown. And where was Margaux? After years of therapy, Elizabeth had learned to stop asking that question, and yet now she wanted to go knock on her mother's door, to plead with her, "Please just take care of this chaos in your house, I'm so tired of dealing with it all." But first she had to get Lucy out of there. She took her by the wrist and literally dragged her up to Izzy's room, where Izzy was sitting at the desk, peering out the window like a cat watching a bunch of crippled canaries. Of all the crazy people in the house, she seemed the least harmful influence at this point, so Elizabeth deposited Lucy there, after which she marched across the hall and took hold of Margaux's doorknob. Then she stopped. It wouldn't help. Instead, Elizabeth ran back down the stairs to deal with Adelia, realizing as she did that she would miss her nine o'clock class and she had not called in for a substitute, and in order to get to the ten-thirty class she would have to leave the girls with one of several lunatics.

By the time she got back to the guest room, Diana was gone. Adelia was still launching projectiles, which, Elizabeth recognized, were the rocks Margaux used to line her iris beds.

"Adelia, *stop,*" she said. But even as she said this, she glanced out the window and saw that the construction workers had taken refuge within their machinery and were backing off the Schmidt lawn, beating a lumbering retreat down the driveway.

Together Elizabeth and Adelia watched the bulldozer and the crane-thing, with its swinging wrecking ball, totter off down Little Lane, away from the carriage house. It was like watching the last two dinosaurs on earth seeking safety in solitude. There was something momentous about the accomplishment. They had vanquished the powerful machines. Elizabeth felt framed by the window, illuminated, caught in a moment that ought to be watched. Adelia was flushed and triumphant in her nightgown. Adelia, Elizabeth realized, had pioneer grit. She was no flabby suburban mother, bent on smoothing rough edges. She thrived at the point of a blade. This incident with the rocks required more courage than any of the women on Little Lane ever could have summoned. Elizabeth enjoyed the understanding for a few minutes, feeling a kinship with Adelia that she had never felt with her mother. They were both women who didn't belong in a town such as this one. She could see herself and Adelia, standing by the window, as the workers must have seen them: two women, one old and one young, both regal in their way, defending their family.

The sweetness of the moment, however, was short-lived, because suddenly, three police cars rounded the corner from Clubhouse Road onto Little Lane, silent but alarming with their rolling red-blue lights. Panicky sensations were unfurling in various parts of Elizabeth's body so intensely that she worried she was having an anxiety attack. She closed her eyes and practiced trataka visualization, but all she could see were the flashing lights of the cop cars, and when she opened her eyes, they were still there, pulling into the driveway.

"Shit," she said. "Shit, Adelia. You should change into some clothes."

Chapter 7

When Isabelle opened the door for the police, she found herself explaining that her mother—who had been suffering from advanced dementia for many years—had thrown the rocks, and that it wouldn't happen again, and that she was very sorry for the disturbance.

This came as a surprise. When she called to report the Little Lane Offensive, she had happily imagined the Horrifying Woman getting carted off in her nightgown, blinking in her lidless way while the cops pushed her head down to avoid the frame of the car. But as Isabelle was making her triumphant way to the door, she passed William, muttering at the open refrigerator. He seemed so small, washed by the false light of the fridge, that Isabelle stopped in her tracks. She wanted to stand beside him and snake her arm around his waist. When he felt her presence, he shut the refrigerator door. "I can't smell anything," he said. It had been a long time since she had felt for him so strongly. The cops were at the front door, Adelia was upstairs with her pile of rocks, and William was looking at Isabelle as if only she could restore his sense of the world.

When she opened the front door, she found that she had turned on her charm. This charm was separate from her; she, Isabelle Adair, was not a charming person. But she did have access to a switch that she had been able to turn on or off ever since she started competing on court. When her charm was on, she entered rooms and people adjusted themselves to orient around the pole of her presence. It was a quality her sisters lacked. Elizabeth had no ability to differentiate between her outer and inner selves, a significant failing for an actress. She was one entity, frantic and agitated, incapable of controlling multiple layers of selfhood despite years of study. Diana was athletic, and that was sometimes attractive to people, but she wasn't charming. Her looks were frank; they seemed to conceal little mystery. No, Isabelle was the most charming Adair. It made her into a powerful secret agent, capable of dangerous missions and covert activities.

As soon as she opened the door, the officer started to stutter. Isabelle acted awed by his presence; she widened her eyes beneath his gaze and awaited his judgment. The officer consoled her; he took full responsibility; he offered to write a letter of apology to the family as a whole. Isabelle accepted this gracefully—no, charmingly—and sent him on his way, waving him off in the driveway.

When the cop cars had receded, she turned the switch off and felt the familiar crumpling that always occurred post-charm, as her veneer faded and she was left alone with whatever existed beneath. By the time she was back in the kitchen, surrounded by her family, she could summon nothing but a dirty bathwater feeling. William had returned to his seat at the table. Adelia was behind him, dressed in a lilac sweater set and capri pants, her hair clipped back like a little girl's. Beside her, William peered at his coffee as though a dead mouse were floating in it. By the refrigerator, Diana gripped a carton of orange juice, and in front of the potted fern in the corner, Elizabeth clutched Lucy and Caroline, two large chickens that she was getting ready to carry down to the market.

"What happened?" Adelia asked, her voice taut as a coiled spring.

"It's fine," Isabelle said. "They think it was Mom. They apologized."

"Oh, Izzy," Adelia said. "Thank you. You're wonderful."

It should be illegal, Isabelle thought, for a grown woman like Adelia to wear two little clips on the sides of her head. It should also be illegal for her to feign innocence or any kind of fragility. Because when all the Adairs had crumbled to dust—when Margaux evaporated into the hazy atmosphere, when Elizabeth combusted and Diana slipped sadly away, when William finally aged in the way he had committed himself not to do, and when Isabelle had found it in herself to cut the remaining threads—Adelia Lively would rise out of the ashes, craggy-browed, the sole survivor of the whole pathetic group. The chance had been there for Isabelle to vanquish her, but she'd chosen not to. Adelia wouldn't have chosen the same.

From the crook of Elizabeth's elbow, Lucy spoke. "We were supposed to play tennis this morning," she said.

Elizabeth freed her chickens in order to raise a dramatic hand to her brow. "Oh my God, they had a tennis court! At ten o'clock. And I have to get to work. And Adelia, Daddy says he can't smell his coffee."

None of the assembled characters responded to this list of grievances. They examined one another in silence, as though everyone had forgotten their lines.

"Izzy, I could use some help," Elizabeth said when no one else offered. "Could you take the girls to tennis? Please."

"It's my first day of summer break," Izzy said. "Doesn't Dad want to take them?"

"I don't want to take them to tennis," William said.

No one spoke. Elizabeth leaned heavily against the wall, and for the first time Isabelle noticed that she was wearing two different scarves, one lavender and one green with a paisley pattern that looked like an infestation of orange bugs. Something was very wrong with every single person in the kitchen.

"Fine," Izzy said. "I'll take them."

And so she found herself in possession of her two nieces, walking across the golf course to the club. Both of the girls were quiet at first. The scene at the house had obviously shaken them. But as they walked, Lucy's quietness became noisy. She was summoning resentment; Isabelle could hear it in the angry swinging of her arms. She started clapping her hands in the direction of invisible insects. Caroline was more tentative. She had her father's nearsightedness and had been wearing thick glasses since she was a toddler. Isabelle felt for her, stuck in a family of people priming themselves for a fight. The rocks, the police, and all of Isabelle's charming lies must have been difficult for her to understand.

When they arrived at the courts, Lucy tore her racket out of its case and ran to her side of the court. Caroline was slower. She didn't have a racket; she had to borrow one from the pro shop. She kept dragging her feet. She tied her shoelaces with excruciating attention to detail. By the time she was out on court, a little crowd had assembled to witness the commercial adorableness of Lucy Adair, approximately the same size as her tennis racket, her blond hair in two stiff braids, bouncing a ball on her strings and humming to herself. Izzy sat down on a bench to watch. Lucy was launching forehands that a person her size had no right to launch. In another life, Izzy might have smiled at the sheer guts of that tiny girl to hit such shots, but in this life, at this country club, she felt nothing but the greedy eyes of the gathered crowd fastened to her niece.

"Check out that little firebrand out there," she heard Jack say from behind her. She didn't turn around to acknowledge him.

"Hi, Izzy," Abby Weld said to Izzy's back. She turned and attempted to smile. Abby was wearing a tennis dress. Her ponytail was tied with a white ribbon, all wrapped up and ready to be given away. Jack stood beside her, proud dad. The kind of dad who puts an Amherst bumper sticker on his Volvo the very second his daughter gets in.

"It's a treat to see you here, Isabelle," he was saying. "We haven't seen you at the courts in years!"

There was nothing to say in response. Seeing him and Abby together had always struck Isabelle as a sad joke. Sometimes the joke was on them, sometimes on Isabelle. She wished she could get away from Breacon and never see them again.

"That Lucy's a real firebrand," he repeated. "She looks just like your sister out there when she was a kid."

"Diana had the bowl cut, though," Izzy muttered, compelled against her will to a modicum of sociability.

"You Adairs were always talented."

Izzy turned back to her nieces on court. Caroline was playing obediently, as though counting every step, measuring the arc of her swing. She took the ball too late. It was heartbreaking, how careful she was with each of her movements, how reluctant she felt about forward motion. Lucy played differently. She was careless, unhindered, springing on the ball like a young bird of prey.

Behind her, Izzy felt more people gathering. A lady's clinic ended, and its members assembled by the fence, clucking among themselves over Lucy's general panache. Jack said something and they laughed harder, at which point Lucy, startled, looked up as if she'd noticed their presence for the very first time. Her brow furrowed. The cloud of this morning returned with a vengeance. For an extended moment, she glared at the offending gaggle of ladies, then turned and missed the next serve that Caroline launched over the net. Her brow furrowed even more deeply. She muttered something to herself while she walked to the other side, then lost the next three points.

"She's got a little temper, doesn't she?" Jack said. Lucy fumed at him before serving so hard and long, the ball clattered against the back fence. Jack chuckled and Isabelle felt sick.

By the time they switched sides, Lucy had lost two straight games. She moved forward with murderous intention. At the net post, she gave Izzy a single hateful glance and muttered under her breath, "Shitbagger can of a pile of sluts."

Izzy's mouth dropped. Lucy proceeded to her side of the court.

"Did she just say 'shitbagger'?" Abby Weld laughed.

Izzy stood and walked out to Lucy. She could feel Jack's eyes on her. Across the net, Caroline watched, shifting from one foot to the other. "Lucy," Isabelle whispered. "Lucy, what did you just say?"

Lucy glared at her strings.

"Lucy, what did you just say?"

"Nothing."

"I mean it, what did you say? I'm not mad, I just want to know what you said."

Lucy approached until she was close enough that Jack Weld wouldn't be able to hear her, then whispered with reverberating force: "I said, SHITBAGGER CAN OF A PILE OF SLUTS."

"Wow," Izzy said. Lucy looked up at her, jaw jutting. "Wow, Lucy, that's pretty expressive."

Lucy adjusted her strings, attempting to restrain herself and failing. "THEY'RE WATCHING US," she whispered violently, "LIKE WE'RE ANIMALS IN A SLUTTY ZOO. LIKE WE'RE SHIT PANDAS IN A SHIT-FUCKING ZOO."

It was loud enough to cause Caroline to come running over. "Lucy, shhh," she hissed. She was clutching her water bottle, splotchy-cheeked with distress. "Don't say that stuff, it's not nice. I could hear you all the way over there."

"No, Caroline, it's okay," Izzy said. "She's angry. It's okay."

"They're bad words," Caroline said, her splotches deepening.

"It's okay, Caro," Izzy said. "She's right. She shouldn't have to be watched if she doesn't want to be." She turned to Lucy. "Those shitbaggers don't get to watch you if you don't want them to."

Lucy's mouth opened a little. She stared at Izzy. She quieted so miraculously that Caroline breathed a sigh of relief. Her splotches cooled. "Shit pandas!" Caroline whispered.

"You know," Izzy said, "we don't have to stay here. We could just stop."

Lucy and Caroline appeared shocked by this news, as if giving up a tennis reservation were tantamount to running naked through the country club, cursing at the top of your lungs.

"These shit pandas will watch us for the rest of our lives unless we stop. You can't satisfy a shit panda: give him an hour and he'll ask for a lifetime."

"Shit panda!" Caroline giggled.

Izzy felt good. She felt like she was giving them a thing that was important. "Let's get out of this shit-fucking zoo and go somewhere else. Let's get away from this slut pile once and for all."

They left Lucy's racket behind. Elizabeth could pick it up in the lost and found. They were leaving the shit pandas behind.

Jack Weld could fuck himself. The ladies' clinic could look down their noses. What did she care? They were escaping out Clubhouse Road, Lucy was skipping at her side, Caroline was babbling something, and Izzy was thinking that maybe they could go downtown on the train. She could take them to lunch at that restaurant by William's office. They moved in a green shade, under the arms of the Osage orange trees that lined the street, dropping their fruits like small green brains. The world was still new; the flatness of summer hadn't settled. Lucy, skipping ahead, picking up oranges and flinging them off to the side, giddily turned and called back, "WORM BONER!"

"That's good!" Izzy called.

Lucy skipped forward, then spun and called back again, jumping up in the air for greater effect: "WORM BONER AND A PILE OF RUSTY SLUTS!"

Izzy laughed again, and Caroline joined her. Lucy, proud of herself, spun around once more, and as she spun she vaulted forward suddenly, flung down on the ground by her own propulsion. When she got up—reluctantly this time, some of her energy siphoned—there was a red caterpillar on her eyebrow. As Izzy watched, the caterpillar expanded, clinging close, and then there was a curtain of blood falling over Lucy's eye. For a moment, Lucy looked as though she would either smile or kill someone, but instead she started to cry. She lifted one hand to her face and brought it down, soaked in blood.

They would have to go back. Izzy had wounded a child who wasn't her own, and they would have to go back. She ran toward Lucy, picked her up and held her close, then headed back to the club with her niece's hands around her neck like little panda paws.

She found Jack Weld in the clubhouse bar. "She needs stitches," he said, taking Lucy out of Isabelle's arms. By the time someone got him a medical kit, Lucy's eyes had fluttered shut. He laid her down on a leather couch in the men's locker room, which was cleared for the occasion, and Abby took Caroline home. Sitting by Lucy's feet, Isabelle watched while Jack pulled his needle in and out of Lucy's eyebrow.

"She'll be fine," he said without looking up from his work.

"Sure."

"There might be a little scar, but that's it." He snipped his thread with a pair of miniature scissors, then stood to throw the needle away. Alone with Isabelle, he was less boyish and light. On his way back from the trash can, he glanced at her. "Are you okay?" he asked.

"Fine."

He set to work cleaning up the medical kit. She watched his hands crawling over his various tools.

"My dad says he can't smell anything."

He looked up quickly, then returned to his work. "Oh?"

"Yeah. He's been saying it all morning."

"That happens sometimes after a stroke. Damage to the olfactory bulb."

"Is it permanent?"

He zipped up the medical bag. "Yes, it is. I'm sorry, Izzy."

"He seems different."

"That's a big loss. Scent. It's connected to memory."

"Yes."

"Look, Isabelle," he said, reaching the limit of his sympathy, "here's a prescription for a painkiller Lucy can take. She'll need it for a couple of days. After that, it might itch a bit. That's fine. Try not to let her touch the stitches. You can make an appointment with her doctor to get them out in a week or so."

"Okay." She watched him preparing to leave. He would go home to Abby and his wife. They would make lunch, and they would sit together as a family. It was all so unfair that it broke Isabelle's unfeeling heart. "Jack?" she said. He turned around. She fumbled for her switch, trying to brighten, to soften her rock-hard face. "Jack, this carriage house thing is killing him. Do you think you could help? We just need one person to agree to a delay."

He glanced over his shoulder toward where his fortunate life was waiting for him to return. "I'm not sure. There's a rodent problem. It's unhealthy."

"A few more days won't hurt," she said, loathing the tone in her voice. "There've been mice in there for years. A few more days won't hurt." Having waded in, she let the water rise up around her head. "I can't leave him like this. After all these years and the kind of daughter I've been." She focused on her sneakers; it was impossible to look at him, having said this to his face.

He was quiet for a long time. "I'll see," he said, and that was all.

When he was gone, she lay down next to Lucy and pressed her face against Lucy's warm cheek. It smelled like medicine and grass. "I'm sorry, Lucy-bug," she whispered. "I'm so sorry I wasn't more careful."

Chapter 8

They didn't get out to canvass the neighborhood until late afternoon. First there were the bulldozers, then the police, then Lucy's accident, and afterward Elizabeth had to be called at the studio. It took several hours for the accusations to build, and by the time Adelia called them for canvassing, it was clear that neither Isabelle nor Elizabeth was in a diplomatic frame of mind. Adelia was intensely agitated; she had counted on more Adairs than only Diana to help win over the neighbors.

"Don't worry, Adelia," Diana said. They were waiting in the foyer, and Adelia's face was pinched with anxiety. Diana attempted to sound soothing. "We don't need them to come. We can cover the street on our own."

Adelia didn't answer right away. She looked past Diana, up the empty stairs, hoping against hope that Elizabeth might appear. Diana could understand the hesitation; over the past few years, she had lost her confidence in social situations. Around new acquaintances, the shift in her personality was fine. But for people who had known her when she was young, the difference was disappointing. She felt it and instinctively became apologetic for having lost touch with the personality they'd liked, embarrassed about presenting them with the new, less impressive incarnation of Diana Adair. This was why Adelia had hoped to accompany Diana on the neighborhood rounds, and because of it, she was nervous about the idea of Di meeting neighbors on her own.

"I didn't have the chance to make my cookies," Adelia murmured, still searching the stairs for the apparition of a more sociable sister.

"It's fine, Adelia. The cookies don't matter."

Adelia snapped into focus on Diana. Elizabeth was not going to appear, the cookies would never get baked, and Diana would have to suffice. Her mouth set in a grim line, Adelia accepted these setbacks bravely, and the two of them—doomed little cadre—headed down the driveway to launch the neighborhood initiative. Green spinners were parachuting down from the June trees, and Adelia assumed a military posture as she surveyed the cul-de-sac.

"You'll go right," she said. "The Welds, Suzanne Legg, and Anita Schmidt. Or Arthur. Obviously, they're the most important."

Diana felt her face freeze. "Could I go left?" she asked.

"I'd rather you went right. I'm afraid I've alienated Anita."

Diana's stomach tightened. This was all wrong. She couldn't see Arthur this way. Adelia had asked her to dress up for the occasion, but in the hubbub of Lucy's accident, she'd forgotten. Now, the idea of seeing him, wearing these jeans, pleading for the carriage house, was nearly unbearable.

Adelia watched her, lips tightening. "Oh, Diana, if it's going to cause you to freeze, I suppose it's best if you go left."

"Okay," Diana said. "I'll go left." She watched while Adelia marched toward Anita's house, then she turned and embarked on her route. Yusuf Uzmani hadn't gotten home from work. Diana left him a note on stationery she'd unearthed from a drawer in her middle-school desk. It was bordered with pink flowers and bluebirds, and using it made her feel like a child, but it was the best she'd been able to come up with. "Dear Mr. Uzmani," she wrote with a felt-tipped pen she'd used when drawing up plans to run for student council. "I stopped by to talk to you about my family's carriage house. I look forward to meeting you, and welcoming you to the neighborhood, very soon. Yours, Diana Adair."

Her next stop was Sheldon Ball's house, white-pillared and imposing on the corner. Sheldon, with whom she played tennis when she was a teenager, grinned when he opened the door. He looked as though he might hug her, then restrained himself and invited her into the living room. His movements were so jumpy that Diana worried he might upset one of the strange dripping vases that his mother had kept on the sideboards. He was wearing the same tiny tennis shorts that he'd always worn when they played league together, revealing legs that were as muscled as an acrobat's. He still walked on the balls of his feet. The only difference between Sheldon Ball now and Sheldon Ball then was that his bald spot was wider in diameter.

"Take a seat!" he told her. He remained standing, shifting from one foot to the other, beaming intensely.

Diana settled onto the plastic-lined couch. It crinkled as she moved. There was still that flock of pink plastic flamingos in the back of the room. Those birds, the product of Sheldon's mother's eccentric sense of humor, had grown eerie under his stewardship.

"Sorry about the couch," he said. "Mom used to keep it covered in plastic, and I haven't changed it since she passed." His face dropped, and he stopped shifting. Motion coiled in his muscles. After a minute he brightened again, and it was a relief to watch the coiled motion spring outward. "It's great to see you, Di. I remember playing with you like it was yesterday!"

For Diana it was a lifetime ago. She only vaguely remembered his style of play and could not for the life of her recollect how she felt when they walked home from the courts. She could remember Sheldon's mother saying at one point that she'd never seen Sheldon so happy as when Diana called for a match. Sheldon had been in his midthirties at the time. He'd been living at home since returning from college. Every day he walked to the club to play his acrobatic, heavy-handed tennis. He didn't seem to relate well to other adults; his laugh was the kind of laugh that caused everyone to fall silent around him.

"Do you remember men's league?" he asked. "With Bobby Flaherty and Ted Cheshire?"

Diana smiled automatically. She remembered, but the memories were so distant that they barely registered in the emotional centers of her brain. She was distracted by her diplomatic task, by the pink flamingos and the slick plastic crinkling beneath her.

"Hey, Sheldon?" she said. "I wanted to ask you about the carriage house."

He stiffened.

"I'm sure you know my dad just had a stroke. He'll be fine, I think, but he's struggling. He can't smell things. We think the carriage house might make a difference. If we could save it."

Sheldon wandered over to the flamingos. He stood in their midst, bald spot gleaming, a Floridian Saint Francis.

"I don't know," he said. He put his hands on his hips and leaned to the left. "I just don't know. I have to talk to Jack Weld. He's my partner in summer league. I know he's spent a lot of time on this."

"We're just asking for a little more time. We'll get it off her property and fix it up so there's no more rodent problem."

"Yes, but I need to talk to Jack."

"Couldn't you just do me this favor?"

"I don't know. I haven't heard from you in years. You never once called me to play when you were back on vacation."

I was thirteen, Diana wanted to say. *You were thirty-five.* "I'm sorry, Sheldon," she said.

"I wouldn't have expected that, you know? I trusted you."

He was standing there with his hands on his hips, surrounded by his mother's undiscarded things, burdened and resentful. "I'm sorry, Sheldon," Diana said, and she meant it. "The truth is that it's been hard to come back. I compare myself to the way I used to be."

"I would have understood," he said, looking down at one of the flamingos so that the circle of his bald spot pointed directly toward Diana. "I would have understood that."

His racket bag was propped in the corner by the front door. There was a coatrack with his sweaters and his coats; at its top, like a disoriented tropical bird, was a red knit hat with an enormous pom-pom. Diana felt tired. There was nothing else she could say, so she stood to go. "Maybe this time we could play," she said. "I'm home for a while. I'm not as good as I was, but I'd love to play sometime if you'd like."

He crossed his hands over his chest, unwilling to give in so soon.

"I have to go, Sheldon. I'm sorry."

Once Diana was outside, she tried not to turn around until she reached the Cheshire house. Mrs. Cheshire came to the door in a housedress. Her hair was molded into a stiff salon updo, as it always had been in Diana's youth, the same unnatural chestnut brown.

"Di, sweetie!" she said. "Come on in."

Diana shook her head. "No, I don't want to bother you. I just have a quick question." Mrs. Cheshire's heavily lipsticked smile froze at half-mast. A defensive smile, metallic and well fortified. Diana knew that Mrs. Cheshire took a moral stance against Adelia. She understood that, from the perspective of the neighbors, the friendship with William seemed inappropriate. Still, she couldn't help but think that these women's principles were self-serving, kept for the pleasure of keeping principles rather than out of concern for Margaux's well-being. And Diana felt for Adelia. Once, Adelia caught Diana in the kitchen and told her, "You know I'd never try to take the place of your mother." It was irritating but also sad. Of course Adelia would never take the place of a mother. That was terribly obvious. But Adelia was *there*. When she walked in the front door, you could feel the warmth of her arrival from wherever you happened to be in the house.

"Mrs. Cheshire," Diana said, "I know that things have been difficult between our families recently. But my dad thinks of your husband as one of his good friends."

"Yes, dear, of course," Mrs. Cheshire said. Her lipstick resumed its smile formation.

"And I know you were Mom's best friend on the street," Diana lied. Margaux never had a best friend on the street. When Diana was little, Margaux told stories about the farm where she grew up, and about the antiques shop she helped her mother run; a boy from the neighborhood had helped them lift the heavier furniture. He was a friend. Margaux was wistful about such friends of her youth, but she resisted William's attempts to guide her into relationships with the women of Little Lane. The more enthusiastic he became about a potential friend, the more Margaux resisted. She never felt comfortable with those women; dinner parties, his favorite events of the week, were always painful for her. Once, while grocery shopping, Diana and her mother hid behind a pillar of bananas when they noticed that Beebee Cheshire and Elaine Weld had entered the store. They stayed there for twenty minutes, until the women had finished their shopping, watching through yellow foliage as Beebee and Elaine loaded up their wagons and drove out of the parking lot. When they stood up, Margaux brushed off her skirt as though nothing had happened. "We should get Nilla wafers," she said. Diana felt as close to her mother then as she ever had in her life.

"Your mother was the most darling woman," Mrs. Cheshire was saying. Her lipstick pursed, approximating sympathy. "I feel just awful for her. It must be difficult, I'd imagine, to have Adelia in the house so much. I'm not sure I'd understand if I were in her place."

Mrs. Cheshire was close enough that Diana could smell a combination of hair spray and powder. She wanted to look away but warned herself to maintain eye contact. "It's hard to know," she said. "She doesn't seem to notice. Right now it's Dad who's really struggling, and Adelia helps him." Diana felt Mrs. Cheshire scrutinizing her, preparing to share notes with the neighborhood if she failed to produce some sign of daughterly distress. For the sake of self-preservation, Diana was tempted to gratify her, but in the end she cared about Adelia too much. She steeled herself to continue. "Dad hasn't been the same since the stroke," she said. "If we could save the carriage house for him for a few more weeks, I know it would help."

Mrs. Cheshire stiffened, her sympathies rebuffed. "I'll have to talk to my husband," she said. "He understands the politics of the neighborhood better than I do. I've always been a dunce about these things. But I hope we can help. Anything for your mother. She was a darling when we first moved in." The taut smile returned, and Beebee Cheshire and Diana faced each other at the threshold, neighborly and removed, until Diana waved and moved on with her route.

When she returned to the house, Adelia met her on the front stoop. "Did you get anyone?" she asked.

"Maybe the Cheshires. She said she'd talk to her husband."

"I knew you could get them! She'll want to do it for the sake of your mom." Adelia clapped her hands in front of her chest. She looked like a child preparing to pray. "So maybe the Cheshires," she breathed. "And not only them, Diana. Arthur Schmidt has come to our rescue. Can you believe it? He agreed to a stay on the demolition. He was apologetic about the police. He understood everything. He was *wonderful*."

Diana watched the last spinners falling slowly down through the evening air. "So if the Schmidts agree, and maybe the Cheshires, that's enough for a stay?"

"It's enough!" Adelia said, then caught herself. "Di, listen. In my excitement, I asked him to dinner."

"Who?"

"Arthur. He was so wonderful that I asked him to have dinner with us."

"What did he say?"

"He asked if all of you were home. I said you were, but that you would have to stay in, to take care of Lucy." Adelia paused, clearly waiting for a reaction; Diana's throat was tightening, but she tried to maintain an easy expression. "I only thought," Adelia continued, "after your reaction this morning, I shouldn't put you in a position you couldn't get out of."

"That's fine," Diana said. "That's what I'd prefer."

"I actually suggested he come over for dinner, so that you could come and go, but he wouldn't hear of it. He didn't want to inconvenience us, with Lucy upstairs and your father just back from the hospital. I told him we'd take him out to Traviata."

The tightness in her throat was replaced with dull understanding. After all this time, Arthur wanted to avoid her. He wanted to go out to dinner so he could avoid seeing her at the house.

"You don't mind, Di?" Adelia was asking. "You'll take care of Lucy? Otherwise Elizabeth could stay home, or Isabelle. It's completely up to you."

"No, that's perfect," Diana said. "That's perfect, Adelia. Let's leave things just as they are."

By the appointed time for dinner with Arthur, the atmosphere in the house on Little Lane had elevated to a frenzy. Diana realized they'd been isolated a long time, more deeply than she'd understood. They'd existed alone, deep in their sense of superiority. The prospect of one dinner out with Arthur Schmidt sent them into paroxysms of preparatory activity. In the kitchen, Adelia rehearsed a speech about how grateful their family would be for the chance to remove the carriage house. William came downstairs in a tie no one had seen before—dusty brown crepe with silver bullet-point dots—and Adelia sent Diana to find him a new one. Elizabeth had arrived an hour early from the house on Wimberlyn Street, children in tow, jangling with bangle bracelets and hoop earrings; now she was running down the stairs in search of a missing hair clip. Diana followed her with a red and blue alternative for William. In the living room, Isabelle, shimmering in a purple dress that made her look like an Italian movie star, looked up from the magazine she was reading and examined the tie. "No," she said. "He won't look like himself." Diana turned to go back upstairs and saw that Margaux had come down. She was standing on the landing, holding her purse in one hand.

"When are we going?" she asked, scanning the foyer.

Diana blinked back at her mother. Usually, there was a serenity to Margaux's vague wandering that was familiar and continuous with the person she had always been. This pointed distress was new and confusing.

"We're going to dinner with Arthur, Mom," Izzy said from behind Diana. Her voice was crisp and capable. "You don't have to come if it makes you nervous."

Margaux peered, unconvinced. "Ah," she said. "I see."

Louise materialized above her. "Where are you running off to, young lady?" she asked, and Margaux looked up, relieved.

"I think I'll stay, if they're all going anyway," she said, moving back up to her studio.

"She's not used to all these people in the house," Izzy said, and then Elizabeth was rushing out from the kitchen with a bottle of children's aspirin. "Take these up to Lucy?" she asked breathlessly, catching Diana by the arm. Diana started when Elizabeth touched her. "What's wrong with you?" Elizabeth asked. "You look like you've seen a ghost. If you're going upstairs for another tie, can you take this to Lucy?"

When Diana was halfway up the stairs, the doorbell rang. She stopped, unsure whether to move farther up or down. Behind her, Elizabeth ran to the door, bracelets jangling. Diana thought about running up the stairs to escape, but the idea of him seeing her in flight made her stay where she was, back turned, clutching the bottle of aspirin. The door opened. Elizabeth said his name. There was the clanging sound of a hug, and then Diana heard his voice. The same voice. She turned around. For a moment he looked up and half caught her eye where she was standing on the stairs.

"I'm taking these to Lucy," she said, too softly for anyone to hear. He nodded curtly up at her, then turned to smile at Isabelle, who had glided into the foyer. Diana felt the heat of a blush rising to her cheeks, so she turned and fled up the stairs to the bedroom where Lucy was resting. Her hand was trembling slightly when she reached out to brush Lucy's sweaty bangs away from the bandage on her face. Trying to calm herself, she leaned forward and kissed the girl's forehead; Lucy, still sleeping, moved closer to Diana's hip on the bed, her body curved like a parenthesis. Diana breathed. She could hear the family clustering in the foyer, preparing to leave.

"We're going, Diana!" Adelia finally called, and there was the sound of the front door closing, the car's engine starting in the driveway. The headlights sent a wash of pale light across the room, and then they were gone.

Hours later, when they returned, Diana joined them in the kitchen while they reviewed the success of the night. Her sisters had softened, polished to a rich glow by the chance to display themselves again. There was the glimmer of jewelry, Elizabeth laughing, another round of wine being poured. Isabelle lingered in the kitchen, leaning over her forearms on the island while Adelia retold a story that Arthur had delivered. Even William had collected himself. There was a look of satisfaction, if not optimism, about him tonight. His white hair, combed neatly from its side part, seemed less faded than it had since he came back from the hospital. From her side of the kitchen, Diana felt as though she were watching luminous fish swimming across an aquarium.

"I could have listened to his stories all night," Elizabeth said. "Really, I haven't laughed so much since I left L.A."

"He's gotten more handsome than he used to be," William said, sitting at the kitchen table. "I remember him having a slouch."

"He *is* more attractive, isn't he? And he's done so well for himself. I had no idea he owned the Eldridge; *everyone* goes to the Eldridge. I'm sure Mark's been there; I'll have to ask him next time." Elizabeth sipped her wine. "We tried to get him to come say hello to you, Diana," she added. "But he was so sweet about Lucy. He said he didn't want to disturb her."

Diana pulled out a stool so that she could sit.

"He's grown into his nose," William continued. "I remember his nose being bigger. But he's grown into it. I think if you met him on the street at this point, you'd think he was a good-looking person."

"He was so reasonable about the carriage house," Adelia said. "He agreed that it's gotten out of hand. He was sure he could buy us some time."

"That's wonderful," Diana said, her voice faltering.

"It's nice to see when a person grows into his looks. So often it works the other way," William said, a touch of accusation in his voice.

"Yes, William, that's fine," Adelia said. "But did you hear what we said about the carriage house?"

William's expression darkened. "It's too far gone. It will fall apart, even if we get it across the fence." He considered his terrible tie. "That house was perfect once. In another time."

"We can rebuild it," Diana said.

"We'd need an excellent architect," he muttered, getting up from his place at the table to pour his wine down the drain. "This wine tastes like ash. And the architects in this town are no good anymore." He resumed his place at the table.

"You could do it," Elizabeth suggested, sweeping over to the table to sit beside him.

"I'm too tired," he said.

"Diana could do it," Adelia said.

"Diana hasn't even graduated yet. She's taken six years, and she hasn't finished her degree."

An awkward silence settled into the kitchen.

"Well, it's a start that he's going to speak to Anita," Adelia said finally.

"He was nice to be around," Isabelle said out of the blue. "He has a nice way to him."

"I completely agree," Elizabeth said. "I *needed* that. I *needed* to relax for a while. I can't tell you how much I have needed to sit back and have a glass of wine and an actual *meal* with some people my age."

"You drank too much," William said.

"I had a glass and a half," Elizabeth corrected him. Wounded, she pushed her glass to the side. "Di, how's Lucy?"

"She's fine. She hasn't woken up since you left."

"Oh, *good,*" Elizabeth said. "You were darling to stay with her. I wish you could have come with us."

"Me, too, Lizzie."

"We talked about you, you know," Elizabeth continued, attempting to be generous.

"Arthur said you've changed since he saw you last," William said. "He said you were so different, he hardly recognized you at all."

The air in the kitchen felt like rising water. Diana looked at both her sisters: could they also feel the thickening air? Isabelle, unnoticed, poured herself a glass of wine. Elizabeth glanced at hers but didn't touch it. Adelia, looking through the kitchen window to the slanting shape of the carriage house as it rose out of the darkness, murmured, "I think he can help us persuade her."

"He seemed like he wanted nothing more than to get that building off his property," Elizabeth said. "Don't you remember? When he said it belonged to the Adairs and had nothing whatsoever to do with his family?"

And then all of them were talking about the issue of the carriage house, and Diana was left alone in her corner of the kitchen. So she was changed to the point that he couldn't recognize her. He had used those words. She couldn't blame him. She *had* changed, and why would she expect Arthur Schmidt to be generous about that? She had faded. It had never hit her quite as fully as it did just then, in the kitchen, while Isabelle and Elizabeth laughed, their earrings glimmering. How unfair for unhappiness to also make you look dull. As though it weren't enough to feel unhappy, you also had to fade.

"I could help with the house," she said, and as her words rang out through the kitchen, she had the strange sensation that even her voice had changed beyond recognition. "I really could," the voice persisted. "I could draw up a plan, and we could use that to rebuild it. I know that building as well as anyone."

They all stopped talking and turned toward her.

"I could do it quickly," she said.

"You've never finished a thing in your life," William said. He stood from his chair with measured dignity. "I have had a terrible day," he said. "And now I will go to sleep."

They waited for his footsteps to climb the stairs. "You'd do a great job of drawing a plan," Elizabeth said once he was out of earshot. She repossessed her wine.

"You would," Adelia agreed. "Just give him a couple of days." She patted Diana's hand in a way that was neither pitying nor gentle but could only be classified as fierce, then made her way up to the guest room. Elizabeth yawned and followed, and Isabelle waved good night. Diana was alone. Without them, all the various elements of the evening resolved into the stillness of an empty kitchen, and Diana Adair closed her eyes and tried to remember the sound of her old voice, the way she once looked, when Arthur loved her and listened to her and recognized her still.

On Monday morning, Diana woke to find Lucy staring at her. Her wide eyes were close enough that Di could almost feel the sweep of her eyelashes when she blinked; the yellow in Lucy's irises made her eyes the blue of a deep bruise. The stitches had puckered her eyebrow, the soft skin around it pulled taut.

"Hi, Luce," Diana whispered, reaching out to touch her warm cheek.

"Hi, Aunt Di. You wanna go outside and play?"

"Right now?" It was early enough that the light through the shades was watery.

"Right now."

Outside, Diana sat on a damp chaise longue while Lucy collected insects on the lawn. Diana liked to be awake this early, before the rest of the world had risen. Things were so new, emerging out of the nighttime cool. In Texas she would pour herself coffee and sit down to work at her desk at five A.M. before the creaking of the floorboards above her announced the awakening of the couple who lived upstairs. Then she could sharpen her pencils, roll a sheet of paper out over her desk, pull out her measuring tools, and draw. Unencumbered by the long accumulation of errors that occurred over the course of a day, Diana imagined buildings. She drew in the company of a bird that lived in her driveway. Its call punctuated the morning, a long, hoarse *craake.* The sound of a rusty gate swinging wide open, allowing a new day to enter and wash the house clean with its light.

At that time of day, Diana loved her apartment. It was nearly empty, pristine in its emptiness. In the living room, a blue couch and a table. In the bedroom, a mattress, her desk, and a bookshelf full of architecture texts. She liked it that way: simple and spare. She tried not to keep any food in the fridge. Nothing that could pile up. In her drawings, people could live cleanly and efficiently. Modern human beings, sharing each other's heat and cool air. She imagined idealized downtown blocks, carless and compact.

By seven o'clock, Diana would start to get hungry, so she'd pour herself a bowl of cereal. By the time she'd finished the second bowl, the equilibrium of the morning had shifted. The house creaked and sighed, adjusting itself to the livelier presence of her waking neighbors. Diana felt leaden. When she returned to her drawings, the lines were less straight than she had imagined, the designs less crisp. By noon, Texas light had armed every aspect of the day. The sun was direct and unstinting, unfiltered by trees. With each new motion, Diana felt as if she were resisting defeat. In class, she took notes dutifully but had no recollection of what she had learned. By the end of the day, she could no longer imagine the people who would live in her buildings. Her teachers felt she had talent but hadn't yet found her voice. Her adviser asked her to decide what kind of architect she'd like to become. He offered a list of suggestions: schools of thought she might join, theories she could espouse. He seemed to think it ought to be clear. What kinds of structures did she want to build? Diana couldn't tell him.

Once, in a past life, she would have been sure. When she was playing tennis, she knew who she was. She had a ranking to measure her value. People recognized her from tennis magazines and televised tournaments. She met with her coaches every day to ensure the progression of her talent. When tennis ended, she felt as if a door had closed behind her, stranding her somewhere she didn't recognize. There was no numerical system to quantify her life. Her coaches no longer checked in on her. She took for granted how surrounded she was when she was playing her sport. She was so alone out there on court, talking to herself about footwork and strategy, but she was at the center of a universe. After she quit, she was like a planet that had fallen out of its orbit.

At night the other students met for drinks or worked together in the library, but Diana ran. Through neighborhood streets at first, past chain restaurants and apartment complexes, then into Shoal Creek Park, along the dry creek bed littered with pale rocks, under the arms of live oak trees draped with Spanish moss. When she got to town lake, she turned around, heading again into the world of the living, past bike shops and pet salons, home to her apartment. She never ran in loops: just straight out and straight back. The accumulations of her day could be whittled down if she ran long enough. She could almost remember the old quickness and ease. The sure trajectories. Her presence within her body, directing its forward motion.

Now Lucy rattled back to the patio with a jar in her hands. The insect inside was iridescent, oil-slick, its wings tucked close to its body. "A Japanese beetle," Diana told her, and Lucy tilted the jar so the beetle scuttled forward against the slope, struggling to maintain its position. "Have you found any snails?" Diana asked. "With silvery trails and little forked tails?"

Lucy grinned. "No, but there are hundreds of whales!" She headed out into the green.

Drawing her knees up to her chest, Diana watched as Lucy threw herself down by the compost pile. Beyond was the Schmidts' house—its familiar squatness, the bright orange shutters, that broken screen door into the kitchen, from which Arthur suddenly stepped out. Diana froze. She considered pretending she hadn't seen him, but she'd already caught his eye. He smiled; a polite smile, nothing more. He was wearing glasses that made him look owlish; she'd never seen him in glasses before. For some reason, Diana shrugged, and his smile grew on one side. He seemed undecided as to whether to move forward to talk to her. She, too, stayed still, watching him. Something hovered between them. Then Lucy darted from the compost heap to the dogwood tree, and whatever had been holding them in stillness was broken. Diana followed Lucy's movement. When she turned back toward Arthur, he was gone.

"Di Di Di!" Lucy shouted. She was jumping up and down in her urgency.

Commanded to do so, Diana approached.

"A moth tent!" Lucy whispered, pointing up into the branches of the dogwood tree.

The tent was spun between three branches, pulling them closer, three wooden axes around which silk threads had been woven so densely that they were almost opaque. Inside, the ghostly forms of black eggs clustered close to the branch, swept by leafy shadows. They gathered there before they went out into the world. Diana blinked at them. She wondered if, as moths, they ever dreamed of their days in the green shade of the nest, or whether that part of their lives dropped away forever with flight. Lucy was chattering at her side, but something was welling in Diana's eyes, blurring the nest, and she couldn't look down. She could see how pathetic she must seem to a person like Arthur. How useless and sad, having come home at her age. Having wanted nothing more for years than to come home, to be as she was when she lived there. "Luce, I'm done now, okay?" she said. Lucy tried to cling to her arm, but Diana pulled herself roughly away. It was too much to be out there, in the space between their houses. In the place where they used to be young together, and from which he had offered to take her away.

Chapter 9

On Tuesday, Arthur called Adelia at work to let her know that Anita would open the carriage house for inspection. Anxious to cement this surprising alliance, Adelia invited him over to a dinner party with some of the neighbors on Friday; they settled on Monday, since he had a meeting in New York that would keep him there for the weekend. Adelia's satisfaction over this small victory floated her through the workweek. On Monday morning, she took another personal day and woke before dawn in order to plan.

It was still dark when she made her way down to the kitchen and brewed a pot of coffee. The house above her was full of sleeping people. Since William's stroke, the girls had gravitated closer, so that after Diana announced she wasn't returning to Texas, Elizabeth started spending more and more time on Little Lane until she and her daughters arrived with sleepover bags. The house on Little Lane became, overnight, a place where lost adults retreated to find the threads of the life they were supposed to lead. Now, behind closed doors, the various wounded parts of this once-great family slept. William in his bedroom, the girls in theirs, Margaux in her studio high above them all. And downstairs, restless Adelia, hatching her schemes.

It had been a rainy night, and there was a damp weight to the light as it rose. These earliest hours were always the worst for Adelia. They made it possible to wonder whether she had been wrong to work so hard for the carriage house. Whether she had been wrong to move into this house, or even, for that matter, to move back to Breacon. Like the spokes of an asterisk, each of these doubts fed back to the carriage house. If only it could be saved, then. But William seemed agitated about the idea of a removal. It didn't excite him as it once had. Moreover, he didn't want to draw the plan himself. He didn't want to hire another architect. And he didn't want Diana to draw it. In the early-morning dampness, Adelia faced the idea that perhaps the carriage house was a fight she was pursuing merely to keep pursuing a fight.

She took a sip of her coffee. It smelled like coffee. This was a smell that William would never again comprehend. Since last Sunday, Adelia had started to smell things she hadn't smelled in the past, aware that William couldn't. She smelled the staleness of upholstery in her car. She smelled tar in her office parking lot, noodles eaten days ago in the office break room, the faint scent of metal left on her hand after turning a doorknob. These aspects of the world were lost to William for good.

In Dr. Ravitsky's office, Adelia asked if there had been any other damage besides the wreckage in William's olfactory bulb. Had any other parts been changed by that moment when his brain struggled for breath? "Not that the CAT scan reveals," Dr. Ravitsky said. "But it's worth staying alert to these things. Keep an eye out. Let us know if anything shifts. And be aware that the emotional effects of sensory deprivation can be significant. It's hard to lose any channel of connection with the world." Adelia asked about getting back to work. "It's up to you," Dr. Ravitsky answered, addressing William. "It should be safe to go back at this point if you're able to avoid too much stress. But again, I'd ask you to stay alert to any differences in your perception."

Adelia watched William carefully on the car ride home. He seemed removed. He stared out the window, and his reflection floated on the glass. Physically, he was still her William. There was the handsome line of his jaw, the youthful fullness of his hair. But something had changed. The thought of his girls gave him none of the old pleasure. Last night, before bed, he and Adelia had shared a mug of tea at the kitchen island, and he'd said, "Elizabeth was never a very good actress, was she?" "Don't say that," Adelia said. "And now she's too old," he muttered, more to himself than to Adelia. "She was the most outgoing girl, but now she's gotten old."

In the car, she tried to start a productive conversation. "Will you go back to the office tomorrow?" she asked, and he shrugged. "They'll manage without me for now," he said. "For how long?" she asked him, and he glared at his reflection. "For now," he repeated. "It's my grandfather's firm. What can they do? They won't notice, anyway. I haven't been on a project in years. The secretaries can manage without me." He sat with his hands crossed over his chest, irritated that she couldn't understand the bleak reality of his professional life.

Now, sitting at the kitchen table while everyone above her slept, Adelia blinked back loneliness. If she didn't spur herself to action, she would be lost, sitting there, surrounded by gloom, excessively aware of the smell of her coffee. Getting up from the table, she found a piece of paper in what used to be Margaux's desk. She sharpened a pencil at the ancient crank sharpener. There was the smell of wood shavings and lead as she set to work on a plan.

A dinner party for Arthur to celebrate the truce. He had shown real character in standing up to Anita. Yes, the word was *character*: the willingness to engage in contentious situations for the sake of preserving your values. She would make her special chicken. Arthur was a restaurant person, so she had to make something good. This she wrote on her list: "Special Chicken Ingredients." She underlined it twice. She might have been intimidated by the idea of making dinner for someone so involved with gourmet cooking, but Arthur had seemed eager to come. She frowned and underlined "Special Chicken Ingredients" once more. There was, of course, the question of why Arthur cared enough to help them. The thing with Diana had ended badly, and now poor Di was changed beyond recollection. Still, Isabelle was ever the charming companion when she chose to be, and Adelia could tell that Arthur enjoyed her company. At Traviata, Isabelle sat beside him, radiant in the secret way that she hid from Adelia. Several times during dinner, Adelia noticed Arthur watching Isabelle, as if remembering something.

Or perhaps it was just that he was lonely in his grandmother's house. Adelia wished she had a better grasp on what it was, exactly, that was drawing him to the aid of the Adairs. Perplexed, she returned to her list. She licked the tip of her pencil and tasted the metal on her tongue. In total, there would be nine people, since the Cheshires had declined her invitation. On a sticky note, glommed on to the foil-enfolded lasagna that Beebee had left on the Adairs' front stoop. There was something morbid about the impulse to leave a casserole out on a stoop. Every time Adelia discovered one, she thought of abandoned foundlings. And the note had been a terrible blow. They could not count on the Cheshires to vote for a delay. The Welds would be there. Surely, at a dinner party, sharing a meal on the back patio where William had thrown so many successful parties, Jack Weld would remember the contours of the friendship that used to exist between the Welds and the Adairs. There would be candles. In a soft light, they would put aside their conflict and agree on a solution. There would be four Adairs. Five if Margaux decided to join them, which she would not. Plus three Welds, a Schmidt, and one Adelia Lively. Ten chicken breasts. Shallots. White wine, cream, butter, capers. She would ask Elizabeth to cut flowers for the table. Elizabeth was always excessively extravagant, but this was an important dinner. Adelia wanted it to be an elegant affair, because William had always loved elegance. He shone in those scenes. Since coming back to Breacon, Adelia had spent countless evenings on the patio watching him, vivid in a green or yellow sweater, holding a glass of wine and entertaining the entire table.

For several years after Margaux's diagnosis, William continued to throw dinner parties. Margaux attended, presiding at her place without engaging much in conversations. Sometimes you could catch her gazing out across her garden, evidently thinking of something worlds away from the party clamoring around her. Adelia always wondered how Margaux could tear her eyes away from William. How could she remove herself while he asked her to remain? At some point she stopped coming down for the parties. "She's not feeling well today," William explained to his guests, as though Alzheimer's were a temporary affliction. Guilty Adelia was sometimes offered Margaux's empty seat. Eventually, the guests stopped coming. Perhaps they were mortified by the idea of laughing on the patio while Margaux suffered above them. Perhaps they felt that Adelia and William had gotten too close. Maybe the excessively attractive teenage girl who sometimes wandered out and drew their husbands' eyes caused the neighborhood women to want to stay away from the house.

Adelia wasn't blind to this phenomenon. She could see that Izzy was too attractive. There was something wrong with her prettiness as it had combined with solitude. She was never surrounded by friends. She occasionally developed relationships with older men—coaches, teachers, even Jack Weld for a while—that struck Adelia as inappropriate and actually rather stomach-turning, although she never found the nerve to confront Izzy about it. Izzy had never tried to fit in, and Adelia had the sense that if she were to instruct Izzy on the merits of normal relationships, a glint of unbearable scorn would appear in Izzy's eye, so she avoided the issue completely. She watched while Isabelle distanced herself. After her brief and successful tennis career, she seemed to repel the other girls her age, but that never appeared to sadden her. In fact, she embraced her isolation. There was a brief period when she seemed inordinately close to the art instructor at school, who must have been nearly thirty at the time. Once Adelia caught him dropping her off in the driveway. And then she never saw him again, and Adelia almost regretted that, since Isabelle's constant aloneness resumed. She applied herself minimally to her schoolwork, choosing to read for hours in the isolation of her bedroom. As a result, when she came downstairs to a dinner party, her looks seemed as if they had been sharpened to a dangerous point by the hours she spent alone. It was no wonder the wives inched closer to their husbands in a house that Isabelle moved through.

But there was also Margaux upstairs, and undomestic Adelia, and William entertaining while his guests edged farther away. For whichever of these reasons, the dinner parties tapered off. After that, it was just William and Adelia sharing a glass of wine on the patio, eating take-out from Traviata, talking about their days at work like an old married couple who never shared a marriage bed.

For Adelia, it was mostly enough to spend those evenings

with him, listening to anecdotes about tasteless client requests, pretending that he was the man she had chosen to marry. Since moving in, she had considered the prospect of sneaking from the guest room into his bed, though it was painful to think of sleeping with him for the first time in this state. After so many years of dreaming that he could be hers, to finally climb into his bed when he was disappointed and lost would be a sadness Adelia wasn't sure she was ready to know. So she remained in the guest room, plotting the removal of the carriage house to its rightful position.

Behind her, the front door creaked open. Louise, laden with a folded umbrella, a tote bag full of magazines, and a Frappuccino from Starbucks, entered the house.

"They're sleeping," Adelia whispered, pointing upward, surprised by the vehemence of her desire that the girls be allowed to rest undisturbed.

"Ah!" Louise said, lifting her eyebrows. Her whisper was shatteringly loud. "The little angels." There was something in her tone that Adelia didn't like. A note of conspiracy, perhaps, as though the two of them were in league against the Adairs. Adelia lifted her finger to her lips more severely this time. "Shh." Louise nodded, that amused look clinging to her face, then repaired with a notebook and an *Us Weekly* magazine to the chair in the TV room, and Adelia was left alone again to await the unfolding of the day.

Surprisingly, the girls were helpful in planning the party. Before leaving for her job at Bed Bath & Beyond, Isabelle offered to pick up bread and cheese at the specialty shop. Adelia thanked her, gave her a twenty-dollar bill, and refrained from telling her that the Welds were coming in order to avoid an unpleasant reaction. Elizabeth was delighted at the idea of a dinner party and offered to bring votive candles for the patio. Only Diana remained reluctant. If she were honest with herself, Adelia couldn't entirely blame her. What happened between Diana and Arthur had clearly meant more than Adelia had known. Adelia understood this increasingly, watching Diana in her faded form, quailing whenever Arthur's name came up. Still, she wished Diana might summon some courage. Some energy, at least. Instead, she offered to babysit Elizabeth's kids. Adelia assured her that they could entertain themselves upstairs. She insisted that Diana be present at the party. It was time for someone to force her to engage. To remind her that when she smiled, it used to light up rooms; she could smile that way again if she tried. Diana took it bravely, which was a pleasant surprise, then excused herself to walk the contractor around the carriage house.

That afternoon, as Adelia returned from the ACME in Brynwood, Isabelle arrived with a bag of cheeses and a long baguette. Adelia set to work laying the chicken breasts beneath waxed paper and pounding them with the mallet she'd picked up from her house on Mather Street. When the chicken breasts were thin enough, she returned them to the refrigerator and went out to the yard to check on Diana. The contractor was gone, and Di was alone, considering the house. "The wood is worse than we thought," she said. "There's going to be a lot of damage when they move it. He says it's doable, but we have to be prepared for a major renovation."

"We are," Adelia said, but Diana kept looking off into the space surrounding the carriage house. By the time they got back to the kitchen, Elizabeth was slicing bread at the island. She was wearing a red bolero jacket over her flounced brown skirt. Adelia bit her tongue: for some reason Elizabeth was confident about her style sense, and there was no reason to undermine her convictions now. Diana ran upstairs to change, and Adelia joined Elizabeth to start work on the salad. When the dressing had been mixed, Isabelle came in from the back patio wearing a white sundress, her hair braided. She seemed almost like a little girl in that sundress, with that braid, and Adelia felt a pang of sympathy for her. She wasn't heartless, though she sometimes chose to be cruel. Her father's situation would have affected her. She had chosen that dress for his sake. Even if her youthfulness was feigned, she had feigned it for him. Adelia gestured toward a cutting board and Isabelle joined her, taking a knife from the drawer. It was a happy moment, standing side by side with Isabelle, slicing shallots while Elizabeth chattered. The three of them, working together in the kitchen to create a dinner for William Adair.

But then Diana came downstairs wearing a pink dress from high school that no longer fit her properly. She kept tugging at its side, slouching to conceal the fact that it was too tight in the chest. Adelia tried to remain focused on the chicken. She opened a bottle of wine and poured a cup of it over the casserole dish. Diana fidgeted at the end of the counter, unsure how to occupy herself. Adelia poured more wine. Frustration scratched at the back of her throat.

"I have a terrible headache," Diana finally said, as though to excuse her unhelpfulness.

"I'm sure it will go away," Adelia said, grinding pepper. It was an ancient grinder, crusted over with residue; to grind properly took great force and determination. "Right?" she asked. Diana looked back helplessly. She tucked a strand of hair behind her ear, and it immediately fell. "You might," Adelia attempted, measuring a quarter cup of capers, "doll yourself up a bit, for fun, don't you think?" Isabelle ceased chopping; Adelia felt a downward slant in her expression. The moment of union with Izzy was already lost. It had come so quickly, and now it was gone.

"I don't look good in makeup," Diana said. "Really, this is the best I can do."

"I could lend you a skirt," Elizabeth suggested. "And some lipstick."

"I don't look good in lipstick. I'm telling you."

"You're fine," said Isabelle, chopping again. Her expression was flat.

"Yes, you're fine," Adelia repeated, slicing the garlic thin. "It was only a suggestion." She shoved the chicken into the oven. "All of us are absolutely fine," she said, and slammed the oven door shut.

Chapter 10

On Friday, when Adelia asked Louise to stay overtime for the dinner party on Monday, she was happy to agree. This had to do in part with a desire to research her novel, in part with the fact that overtime was sacrifice, and Louise had been searching for penance since Sunday. On the previous Friday, the first day of Brad's Philadelphia business trip, her resolve to withhold herself had remained flinty. Friday was a positive day for Louise. While Margaux was upstairs painting, Louise wrote an entire chapter about Adelia throwing rocks at Anita Schmidt's construction team, taking care to note the ghastly nightgown Adelia was wearing. She was proud of herself. She imagined giving interviews during which she called her novel a "psychological thriller of miniature proportions." She was not sure what this meant, but it had the rhythm of a comment that would go over well in interviews. Buoyed by accomplishment, she attended a spinning class after work, showered, and applied a pore-cleansing face mask before settling in for an evening at home. It was ten-thirty by the time Bradley called, and even though she was two thirds of the way into a bottle of wine and halfway through a terrible movie about teenage ballerinas, she refused to meet him on the premise that she was busy writing a novel. "You're writing a novel?" he asked, and laughed. After hanging up on him, Louise poured herself another glass of wine and made a mental note to include a character named Bradley Barlow, whose main attribute would be a constant gravitation toward failure despite his obsession with achieving success.

On Saturday morning, an atmospheric shift occurred in Louise. She reread her chapter about Adelia throwing rocks and realized that it was completely unbelievable. No one who had not lived with the Adairs would believe that a non-mentally-ill woman in her fifties, with a successful legal career, would actually find herself in the situation of throwing rocks out an upstairs window in order to prevent the demise of a carriage house. Furthermore, Louise began to see that from her first chapter on, she had described the Adairs as though they were the busty heroes of a romance novel and not the characters of any respectable story. The novel was not a psychological thriller of miniature proportions. There were no miniatures, only great fat mistakes.

This epiphany depressed Louise so severely that she called her only friend in Breacon and invited her over for a glass of afternoon wine. This friend was a slightly unhinged Welsh nanny named Arlene. After two bottles of wine, Louise and Arlene rewatched the ballerina movie. This time they perceived, with galvanizing unanimity, that ballerinos were far more attractive than either of them had previously imagined. This inspired them to open another bottle of wine, which in turn inspired them to go out to the local bar in search of good-looking dancers. Dressed in short skirts and Louise's most precarious high heels, they teetered down the hill outside of Louise's apartment to McGillicuddy's.

As it turned out, McGillicuddy's was not a ballerino hot spot. Still, after three lemon-drop shots and a drink that tasted like caramel, Arlene had straddled a man too old to be trolling McGillicuddy's for nannies. Abandoned, Louise ordered another caramel drink and contemplated either a) seducing the bartender or b) calling Brad. In the morning she awoke with the awareness of Bradley's arm on her back. She groaned. With great bursts of hangover erupting in her temples, she managed to extricate herself from his weight in order to root around for her clothes.

"Are you leaving to work on your novel?" he asked while she searched for her tank top, and by the tone of his question, he might as well have asked if she were leaving to fly to the moon.

"Yes, as a matter of fact, I am," she said.

"Will you put me in the acknowledgments?" he asked, watching her from the royal ease of his naked recline.

All Sunday afternoon, no matter how she tried to distract herself, she couldn't stop wincing at the thought of his arm on her back. It was all her fault. She had made herself available to him. She felt like a receptacle. Twice in the course of the afternoon, she had to sit down and put her head between her knees in order to avoid getting sick. By the time it was dark, she had eaten an entire frozen pizza and watched the ballerina movie again. This time she cried when the bulimic ballerina told her pushy mother that she was sick. "I'm *sick*, Mom," Louise said in unison with the ballerina. "This is your *dream*," the mom said. "No, Mom, this is *your* dream," said Louise and the bulimic ballerina. Together they ate a pint of ice cream and fell asleep while the Latina dancer performed *Swan Lake*.

On Monday morning, Louise woke before it was light. She went on a run in her neighborhood, and halfway through, it started to rain. Louise stopped running, closed her eyes, and said out loud for all of the stormy heavens to hear, "You have one more chance, Louise. *Please don't screw this up.*" On her way to the train, she dropped the ballerina movie off at the video store, bought herself a Starbucks, and threw out the notebook with the chapter on Adelia pitching rocks. Whatever she wrote would be more careful this time. These were not bulimic ballerinas she was writing about; they were real people, with real personalities to contend with.

When she arrived at the Adairs', Adelia was sitting at the kitchen table, so small in her nightgown that Louise was tempted to go sit beside her and hold her hand. But it was her task to notice carefully, not to intervene, so she went off to the TV room with her magazines to wait. After Isabelle left, Louise spent the morning watching Margaux paint. For an hour or so she snooped around in Izzy's bedroom, and at noon she went down to the kitchen to make a turkey sandwich for Margaux, which was when Adelia cornered her and asked if she'd mind staying through dinner.

"We're planning a party," Adelia said, using the same tone with which a politician might say, "We're planning to occupy a developing nation in order to get our hands on its oil." "Do you think Margaux would like to come?"

"Parties confuse her," Louise said. "I'll ask, but I think it's best if we respectfully decline."

"That's fine. Whatever you think is best." Adelia blinked. Louise waited. "And also," Adelia continued, "do you think you might stay late tonight? I could pay you overtime. We could use some extra help. This party means a great deal."

And so Louise was granted a reprieve from going home and checking her machine for a message from Brad, and at the same time she received a penance for her sins. Upstairs, on the floor of the house reserved for forgetting, she asked Margaux about attending the party.

"Why do they want me to come?" Margaux asked. "They'll be just fine without me."

"Yes, but they'd like you to be there," Louise assured her.

"I don't see why," Margaux said, shaking her head. Louise felt a flush of pity for her own mother back in Melbourne, whom she had often made to feel as if she were encroaching in undesirable ways.

"Because you're a lovely person," Louise said. "And they love you."

"Oh, I don't know," Margaux said, standing up and brushing the wrinkles out of her linen pants. "I don't know why you'd say that." She took a wet paintbrush and placed it in the graveyard for unwashed brushes, then muttered something about going out to the garden. In her wake, Louise remained in the treasure trove, trembling in her nosy excitement. She counted to twenty, giving Margaux time to retrace her steps, before pulling out the latest journal.

November 1988

It's been months since I've written. I haven't been up to recording my thoughts. I sometimes feel our brains protect us by forgetting. My meeting with Dr. Worthington was terrible. I keep hoping the memory will fade, but the worst things stay vivid as the best grow dim. "Who is the president?" he asked me. And "What year is it?" I remember those things. It's not the basic facts I forget. Then his tone shifts. "This is the age when your mother got sick. It must be difficult to think about, isn't it?" I didn't answer him. The thought of my mother made me want to lay my head on Dr. Worthington's desk and never open my eyes, just to dream of her forever. "Do you sometimes feel depressed, Mrs. Adair? Do you have feelings of despair?" I could barely bring myself to answer him. I sat there shivering. It has always been the saddest thing to me, how fully people fail to understand each other's minds.

But here is something I'd like to remember, from the time just after our marriage. We took the train from the city to have dinner with William's parents. His father took me out to the carriage house. I tried to focus, but he was carrying a glass of bourbon, and its ice cubes were clinking. "It's the finest example of shingle architecture in North America," he said. "William's always loved it, ever since he was a boy." I tried to act as though I loved it, too, but to me it seemed lonely. A carriage house. A house never lived in. Full of the ghosts of old cars, elaborate machines, and horses that waited through long nights, their dark shapes fading into the darkness. Nothing more than a passing through on the way to somewhere else.

William's father could see that I was pretending. "William used to play here with Adelia," he said, eyeing me. "Did you ever meet Adelia? She was William's first love. We were all quite close with her." Her name rang in my ears. Adelia. When he said it, I finally knew who William was hoping I'd become.

In the first year of our marriage, I'd walk into a room where William was sitting and I'd have to try to remember: who is the person I'm supposed to be? It always confused me. I felt myself getting it wrong, although William was too determined to give up. But that afternoon, with William's father leering over the rim of his glass, I knew that Adelia was the woman I was meant to be. It made me terribly sad, but I hoped I'd meet her one day. Adelia, the woman I was not. The woman I am not still.

On the train ride home I asked William about her, and he looked as though I'd slapped him across the face. "Who told you about Adelia?" "Your father," I told him. "Adelia Lively was a girl I played tennis with when I was a kid," he said, but he didn't talk to me for the rest of the ride. When we went to sleep that night, I lay so far to the side of the bed that it was a struggle not to fall. It felt good, working all night to keep myself from slipping off the edge. I never fell. In the morning I was exhausted but proud of myself. William never knew. He ate his breakfast quietly, then left to go to work.

That year I was pregnant with Elizabeth. She is the child of William and a woman who was not.

Chapter 11

After they got the chicken in the oven, Isabelle went out to the front stoop. The vision of Adelia pounding chicken breasts, jaw clenched, telling Diana how to doll herself up, had annoyed her. She needed a breather before dinner started. She sat with her toes pressed against the cool flagstone of the front walk until she felt the door open and close behind her.

"Hi, Izzy-belle," William said, sitting beside her.

He hadn't called her that in years. Izzy leaned toward him slightly and let the sound of that forgotten nickname hover. A breeze lifted around them. The linden trees were blooming, dropping swathes of pollen so that the air was hazy with gold, and the smell of honeysuckle wafted up to the front stoop from the fence along the Schmidt property, where Margaux had planted vines before her diagnosis.

"What are you thinking, Izzy-belle?"

Izzy shrugged. She could feel her father's desire to unravel the things he'd said in his hospital room. She, too, had things for which she would like to apologize. They waited at this cusp.

"You haven't disappointed me," he said finally. "I was wrong. You haven't disappointed me."

"It's okay, Dad," she said. "I wish I'd turned out differently, too."

"I don't," he said. His voice trailed off into the hazy air. They sat together quietly while the evening dropped its mantle over their expectant shoulders.

"That honeysuckle smells nice, doesn't it?" Izzy asked.

"I can't smell it."

"Oh, Dad. I'm sorry."

He didn't say anything, only squinted out into the distance. "I wish to hell we could skip this dinner party," he said.

"Are you not feeling well?"

"Oh, I'm feeling fine. I'm fine."

"It seems like things are working out with the carriage house. That's good, isn't it?"

"I don't know. The whole thing is a mess. I'll die soon, and then what will it matter whether that carriage house is standing?"

"Don't say that, Dad."

"I think maybe I've been holding on too long."

Isabelle was quiet. In the evening breeze, the lindens' branches creaked. Behind the house, the yellowwood would be sighing in response. Since she was a little girl, she had fallen asleep to that sound. She was about to close her eyes to listen when she noticed that the Welds—all three of them, a little phalanx—were walking across their lawn. Elaine was holding a salad bowl. Jack was gesturing in a way that made it seem as though he was telling them a familiar joke.

"What are they doing?" Isabelle asked her father.

"Adelia invited them. I don't know why."

Isabelle watched them advance. Abby was laughing at her

father, favoring him the way daughters always do. Her hair was pulled back in a tortoiseshell barrette.

"He'd burn down my house to humble me," William said, rising to greet them. "But what does it matter anymore?" Isabelle stood beside him. Her shoulders felt bare in the sundress she'd chosen to wear. The familiar shame began to creep up from her stomach. To combat this, she straightened her posture and imagined she was participating in a military ceremony conducted by an absurd little army, rather than standing with her ailing father while their victorious neighbors approached. With a little effort, she could substitute a degree of detachment for the confusion of feeling that was even now taking hold. What smug ambassadors the Welds made, marching over the lawn. And what a motley delegacy she and her father must have seemed, standing on the stoop to welcome the conquering heroes of the Little Lane Wars. White flags should have been waving, pins on lapels glinting, and everyone ought to have worn their white gloves. Set apart from all this, she tried to smile coolly, but she could feel Jack watching and the smile got stuck.

What a stupid child she had been, to have allowed this to happen. Preposterously daring, encouraged by warlike Adelia toward kamikaze types of behavior, full of dumb belief in her own intrepid potential. The first time she asked Jack into the empty house, it was on a clever little dare with herself, like swimming down to the pool drain from which you suspect a shark might emerge. After tennis, she invited him in for lemonade. Sitting with him in the living room, rather than playing tennis at the club, was invigoratingly scary. Izzy thrilled with fear that she felt must be profound because she so little understood its actual source. Her mother was upstairs, but she'd never come down. Izzy and Jack were alone. This seemed to present a challenge to them both, but Izzy was learning to throw herself before all sorts of interesting challenges. Given the circumstances, she felt she was performing beautifully. Jack told jokes. Izzy laughed carelessly, as though nothing were unusual. The second time he came over, when she brought him his lemonade, she stood very close to him and held out his glass. She felt this was an elegant and daring addition to the scene as it stood. *Thank you,* he said, looking up at her. She realized she was much too close, but she was determined to hold her ground. She stayed where she was, acting as well as she could. He didn't reach for his lemonade, only watched her where she stood. His face had gotten nervous. Something buzzed silently, and Izzy stood frozen before him.

After a long time, he laughed. An unpleasant laugh that made her feel like a silly little girl, as if she had lost a silent bet they had made. Later, when Adelia came home, Izzy told her that she hated Dr. Weld. Adelia put down her groceries and considered Isabelle, and Izzy thought she could see a shift in Adelia's face. Adelia understood. Only she looked triumphant, as if Izzy had beaten him. She stood with her hands on the countertop, considered the situation for a moment, and then a little competitive light flared up in her eyes. Something played on the corners of her mouth. "He's just fond of you," she said, and arranged another court. They played again the next week, and Jack asked to come back to the house. The week after that, Izzy quit.

But it was she who had invited him first. That was the thing that now caused her shame, standing beside her father in her childish sundress. When she quit, Izzy thought she'd escaped just in time. Everything remained as it was, only she had a little more knowledge. It gave her an edge on the rest of the neighborhood. On neighbors like Abby, suburban and sheltered, sealed off from the actual world. Only now, with Abby standing in front of her, emerging out of childhood at the right time, glowing with the hope of it all, Isabelle wanted to go upstairs and cry. So Abby was the last one standing after all. Isabelle was a wasted attempt, dressed in a girlish costume, and her father was getting old. It was Jack and Abby who had risen above them in the end.

"The garden looks lovely, William," Mrs. Weld said, holding her salad bowl to one side.

"Just beautiful," Jack agreed. He pointed toward the larger linden. "That's quite a tree! I'm surprised it hasn't gotten blight. Lindens don't seem to survive around here."

Isabelle thought she might gag on his cheer, but she noticed that Arthur was walking up from his grandmother's house. She felt a rush of gratitude for his solitary form, moving up the slope of the street. Leaving the Welds behind, she ran out to meet him, her feet bare on the warm grass.

He watched her coming toward him, surprised at her hurry. "Hi, Izzy," he said. He laughed gently. She almost could have taken his hand.

"I'm so glad you're here," she said. All around him the pollen was falling. "Do you smell the honeysuckle?" she asked. "Mom planted it."

"I know," he said. "I remember. Every time I smell it, I think of her. How is she?"

"Sort of the same. I don't really notice a difference."

Arthur didn't rush to console her, but there was comfort in his presence. Isabelle walked close enough to feel the barest outline of his arm against her arm. When they reached the stoop, she stopped him. "Do you want to go upstairs and see her?"

He looked startled by the question. "Who?"

"Mom."

"Oh, of course," he said. "I'd love to."

Quietly, so that no one could catch them, they slipped up the stairs. Isabelle knocked lightly on her mother's closed door. "Mom?" she called.

The door opened a crack. "She's sleeping," Louise whispered.

"I brought an old friend of Diana's to see her. We thought she might remember him."

"Should I wake her?" Louise seemed disinclined to move from her post. She seemed disinclined, in fact, to move anywhere at all.

"No," Arthur said from behind Isabelle. "No, it's fine. We'll come back later."

Isabelle stared at Louise. Louise stared back. *Why are you in there, then?* Isabelle wanted to say. *Shouldn't you leave her alone if she's sleeping?* "Is she coming down to the party?" Isabelle asked, as though there were any question of Margaux coming down to entertain.

"She's not up to it today."

"When will she eat?" The question was pointless: Margaux had always eaten privately.

"I'll bring her a plate," Louise said. She considered Isabelle through the crack in the door. "I can wake her up right now if you'd like."

"Really, it's fine," Arthur said. Louise remained motionless.

Izzy shrugged. "Another time, then," she said.

At the top of the second flight of stairs, she stopped. "Stay here with me for a minute?" she asked Arthur.

He sat. Izzy joined him, sitting close. So close he could have put his arm around her and drawn her toward him. They remained in silence for a while. Finally, he spoke. "Should we go down?"

"Just a minute more. I'll have to smile so much once we're there."

He waited, leaning back on his elbows. He seemed like the kind of person who could sit and wait with you forever.

"Do you think it'll work?" Izzy asked him. "Moving the carriage house?"

"I'm not sure," he said. "It's pretty damaged."

"Diana says she could draw up a plan. In case it falls apart in the move."

"She said that?" He looked at her sharply.

"Yeah," Izzy said, noticing the change that crossed his face when she brought up Diana. She felt a pang of jealousy that her sister could command the interest of someone like Arthur after all these years, because of something that had happened between them when they were Isabelle's age. "I'm not sure why," she continued, feeling the way he watched her with heightened interest while she talked about Diana, "but she suddenly cares about the carriage house. You should see her whenever the conversation comes up. She hasn't cared so much about anything in years." Izzy edged toward a question she'd never asked. "What happened with you and Diana? I was only nine. I asked my father once, and he said you two were just close friends. But it was more than that, wasn't it?"

"It was a long time ago."

"I can't imagine her dating anyone now," Izzy said. Arthur didn't respond. She wanted to keep him there, solidly alone with her. He was twisting a carpet fiber between his forefinger and his thumb. "She's lost something," Izzy said. "I blame Adelia. There's something about Adelia that makes you want to give up. When I used to play tennis, she coached me between games. She'd get down in front of me with those beady eyes and say, 'You've got to be *aggressive*.'" Isabelle noticed that Arthur was smiling slightly.

It was a gratifying thing; he seemed like a person who wasn't overly polite about smiling. "'You've got to be *aggressive,*'" she said again, bulging out her eyes, hoping she'd make him laugh. "That was her only coaching advice. She wanted it so badly, you were afraid for her. It made me crazy for a while. Then I got it. You just have to stop. You can't keep trying for people like Adelia or they'll tear you apart."

"You're probably right," he said, but he was a little distant, working at loose threads in the carpet.

She kept talking, hoping to reel him in. "Di never learned that. She's loyal to a fault. She would have done anything to make them proud. She probably would have kept playing tennis forever if she hadn't gotten hurt. She might still be playing satellites, struggling in the rankings, beating herself up."

He turned toward her finally. "And you think she should have stopped?" he asked. "Before she had to? When she had the choice to do it for herself?"

His face was long and pale. He had collected himself behind that face, and now he sat beside her, complete in his way. She thought about turning on her charm switch, but something about sitting alone with him, while the light from outside shifted down to darkness, made that impossible to do. "I'm glad you're here," she said.

"Me, too, Izzy-belle," he said. "After all these years, it's good to see you again."

Chapter 12

Despite Adelia's lack of talent for entertaining, despite her unfounded confidence about the pounded-chicken dish, Elizabeth had managed to make the patio look elegant. It was as beautiful as it used to be when Margaux spent all day preparing for a party, coming home with armloads of flowers and polishing silver for hours. She used to hum to herself while she set the table, and then she'd fall into anxious silence as soon as the guests arrived. As a child, it was painful for Elizabeth to watch her sitting off to the side, hoping she'd be forgotten. Adelia had none of Margaux's artistry, but at least she could be counted on to try, and what Adelia lacked in taste, Elizabeth could furnish. She had cut a bunch of Margaux's peonies and placed them at the center of the table, heavy-headed and white, like a bunch of brides. She'd set votive candles everywhere, even on the outstretched palms of Margaux's gnomes, peeking out of shady coverts. In the candles' flickering light you could see moss on the rocks around the pond. The bullfrogs were croaking, and out on the lawn, fireflies lit and then extinguished their lamps.

Elizabeth felt young again, sitting out there on the patio. Arthur had brought a bottle of good white wine, and when she poured glasses, the candlelight filtered through the pale liquid in faint webs. She was sitting beside Arthur, and he was actually interested in her acting career. Not since coming back from L.A. had Elizabeth talked to an engaging young person like Arthur, who cared about things like her audition with Woody Allen, when he told her that her face was too striking to play the part of a prostitute. Arthur laughed when she told it, that old familiar story. She was just out of college. Diana was winning matches, Izzy was cute, and Margaux was functioning. And Woody Allen gave Elizabeth his number and said he would write a part for her that was less compromised. He actually said, "The part of a woman who has never heard of a thing called compromise, for a face like your face." She hadn't told that story in years. It was refreshing to remember, to lean forward the way Woody Allen did when he talked, dipping into her Woody Allen voice.

Telling the story again, she felt her face coming alive as it once had. When she was younger—and it was only a few years ago, really—she was so sure of herself. When she walked down the street in L.A., people turned to look at her. Of *course* Woody Allen came up to her after a jazz show and invited her to audition. Of *course* famous directors who saw her at the restaurant returned and asked to be seated in her section. She never questioned herself. But people in the suburbs didn't understand her style. They didn't understand the subtleties of her talent. She nearly died when she moved back with the girls, especially after finding out that Mark was seeing his ex. After everything they went through! They built a *family* together. Elizabeth despaired in the little rental house William found for her, driving the girls to school in the morning and coming home to take long naps on the floral sofa, knowing that Mark was probably having breakfast with a producer and afterward coming home to *their house,* usurped by that woman. Mark was probably screwing her on the bed that was once their marriage bed, for which Elizabeth had found an adorable farmhouse quilt without ever suspecting that it would be put to that particular use. To think of them on that quilt! Even worse, maybe they were planning a dinner party for the friends who once were Mark and Elizabeth's but now belonged solely to Mark and his ex, as though Elizabeth had never existed, and perhaps they were going to eat in the dining room with the farmhouse table that she'd found in Sonoma on a wine-tasting trip. It felt like death, lying facedown on the rented floral sofa, remembering the wood grain of the table that used to be hers. Facing an eternity of floral upholstery, knowing that her life once kept to a bolder print.

But she was stirring again on the patio, surrounded by her flowers, gesturing to Arthur with a glass of wine in her hand. It didn't matter that it was Adelia opposite Daddy. At least Adelia was functional. At least she cared about bringing the family together around a dinner table. The house felt more vibrant than it ever did when Margaux presided at its center. With all the candles lit, the patio reminded Elizabeth of the first house she rented in L.A. with three of her best friends from college. They organized dinner parties in the backyard under strings of Christmas lights that they slung from the lowest branches of the jacaranda trees. While they laughed and drank cheap wine, she could feel herself lifting out of her chair to float over the guests. It was as though only she could hear a chiming above them all and was swimming up through the air to put her ear to its source.

She got that talent from Daddy. He had always presided over a party. Now he was different, but there was still something exciting about his posture at the head of the table. To help him remember how he had risen for dinner parties once, Elizabeth became especially animated. She demonstrated the poise that he and she had always shared. This was why she was the daughter of whom he was proud, because she still glimmered with promise. The others could feel it around her. Dumb, simpering Elaine Weld was nothing compared to Elizabeth. Jack was impressed with her, and she gave him a large proportion of her attention in the hopes that he would change his mind about the carriage house. When she looked at her own hands around her wineglass—her fingernails painted red to match her new jacket—they were vivid against the darkness of the night. She had not lost the power to light herself so that people would see. Abby asked about the girls, so Elizabeth called them down to sing a song, and they were adorable in their nightgowns, sleep-stricken and luminous. Lucy's pink gown, with its vertical pleats, was out of a dream. It was the one that Mark had brought her back from New York when he shot the Verizon commercial that would pay her college tuition; they'd saved together for the lives of their children. At the back of Lucy's head, her hair had tangled into a nest where she'd gone to sleep on her ponytail, but she was blissfully unaware of that; it might have been a chignon for all the grace with which she carried it. A perfect child, hovering at a perfect age. She sang Cosette's song from *Les Misérables* while Caroline accompanied her on violin, and Lucy was brilliant singing that song, her little face melting as though she knew what it was to be orphaned in Paris. Even Daddy smiled while she performed, and after the final notes—she sang them kneeling on the flagstone, gesturing up toward the stars—Jack sprang to his feet and shouted, "Bravo," and Adelia clapped so hard it must have hurt her palms. Even though Isabelle was watching Jack with the thinly veiled hostility that made people nervous when she entered a room, she looked lovely in that white dress, her dark braid melting into the garden behind her.

Elizabeth didn't feel jealous of Isabelle's looks. She and her sister were equally attractive. They came from a striking family. That was what Elizabeth used to feel sure of. She had taken that confidence with her when she moved to L.A. after college, when she had the carriage of a beautiful person. The carriage of someone who would certainly succeed. She'd lost it at some point, but she could feel the old sureness again. Jack Weld understood its importance. She could see him glancing over at Isabelle when he reached for the bottle of wine. They were so beautiful, the Adair girls, that you wanted to watch them, to touch them as they passed by your life. Arthur was here because of that, too. He and Isabelle had been laughing together all night, leaning in to each other, because the world gravitated toward a person who had made herself bright.

Only there was Diana, sitting so quietly it hurt to look at her. She seemed uncomfortable in her dress, and all night she had been lifting her hand to her temple, as if checking to be sure it was there. She had said nothing other than "I'm fine, a little tired, but fine." She radiated the desire to be somewhere else, off on her own, where she would not have to talk or laugh or engage. It made Elizabeth furious; one had obligations to one's family! Everyone at the table politely avoided looking at Diana. Only Arthur occasionally watched her, turning his eyes away from Isabelle, lingering on Diana's face when she was looking in another direction. Elizabeth wanted to shake her. *Straighten your shoulders!* she wanted to tell her. *Give him a smile, at least!* Because Arthur was obviously trying to see if anything remained of the Diana he once knew, and if Diana didn't attempt to carry herself with some remnant of poise, he would conclude that she had irrevocably altered. But

Diana *could* be beautiful. She, too, was related to Isabelle with her violet eyes. She only had to struggle a little more fiercely with whatever was bothering her, and she could be herself again. They had all struggled, but in the end they were an impressive family. They would be all right. They could still light up the evening if they wanted to.

When the audience had ceased to applaud, Elizabeth kissed the girls on their warm, fragrant heads and sent them up to bed. She explained to Jack that Lucy had taken acting classes when they were in L.A., and that he should hear her sing Grizabella's song from *Cats,* and Elaine asked whether Elizabeth herself was auditioning again. Attuned to their interest, Elizabeth lifted up, expanding vastly under the sky, capturing all of their eyes, and this was closer to the life that she was meant to live than on any evening she had spent since coming back to Breacon after the divorce.

She felt so confident that when she went in to get the dessert, she shut herself in the laundry room and called Mark. She leaned against the cold rim of the dryer while the phone rang, sipping her wine, thrilling with her newfound strength, and even though he didn't pick up the phone, she left a message saying, "M, it's me, I just wanted to say the girls have been so sweet tonight, and I was thinking of you, and I want to just forget about our fight last week." She hung up the phone and was alone again with her wineglass and her red-painted fingernails, and then she animated herself to pick up the dessert plates and walk out to the patio with the fruit tart as though playing the role of a charming hostess, as though she were Elizabeth Taylor or Grace Kelly, and her tart was beautiful, each strawberry and nectarine lacquered with sugar glaze. It was a tart to be proud of, even in the company of someone used to the Eldridge, even after that terrible chicken.

She smiled while she served the tart, holding herself tall, aware of the guests' attention and plating perfectly proportioned slices.

When she went in to pick up the dessert forks—she had always loved their silver filigree, their complicated tines—Adelia came with her, and she, too, was triumphant. She said, "Isabelle's lovely tonight, isn't she," and "You look just gorgeous in that color red," and Elizabeth *loved* Adelia, even if she was a challenging person to love, no matter what the neighbors might think about her moving in while Margaux was upstairs. She wasn't *sleeping* with William, after all. She was just *closer* so that she could try *harder,* and the efforts she made swelled Elizabeth's heart. Adelia murmured, "Do you think Arthur might be interested in Isabelle?" and "I think I might ask Izzy to talk to Jack Weld, to see if there's anything more he can do." Elizabeth grasped that Adelia was never going to give up on the carriage house, and this reassured her. It made her hopeful about the state of the universe, about the arc of their family plot, and while she listened, Elizabeth allowed her head to incline to one side, aware that the light was striking the graceful line of her jaw. "We'll get it back, Adelia," she told her, stoic yet tender. Adelia nodded. "I'll just have Isabelle talk to him; she used to be so persuasive." Elizabeth remembered when they had been the kind of family whom people ask to take pictures of at the beach. When they were older, the local paper ran articles about them. *Golden Girls,* one headline read when both she and Diana won the regional championships in their age groups. There was a picture of her and Diana sitting on the living room sofa, with Isabelle standing beside them in braids. *The Adair girls look like Uma Thurman's younger sisters, but don't let that fool you out on the court*. They were famous in Breacon. They played on varsity when Diana was in middle school. Boys had to ask Elizabeth to go to prom at least a month in advance or they knew she'd be taken. One fall she starred in the high school play, and her tennis team won states the following morning. Back then she'd been so sure of herself that getting a divorce would have seemed like an utterly impossible thing. Having lived through impossibility, she held the dessert forks close, feeling their cool points against her chest.

"Could you take these out?" she asked Adelia. She went back to the laundry room full of magnified sensation and called him again. Again, he didn't pick up, so this time she said, "M, I will love you for the rest of my life because you are the father of our girls," and when she hung up, she felt pleased. It was a beautiful thing to say. She was a woman who was full of noble ideas, and perhaps she had forgotten that sometimes, but she remembered it now. She remembered who she had always been, and when he saw that, he would leave the usurper again and invite Elizabeth back and they would be whole in a city that did not make her feel so horribly out of place.

When she went out to the patio, Isabelle was whispering with Arthur, and then Jack tapped on his glass with his dessert fork to get their attention, and when he had drawn them in, he said, "First of all, I want to thank you all for hosting such a wonderful party. And second, I just wanted to let you know, because I'm sure it's in the back of your minds, that I haven't forgotten about the carriage house. The neighborhood is dead set against it, and there are the rats to deal with, of course. But who knows, there may be things I can do. I'd like to be able to help, if I can."

"If we could only have a few more days," Diana said. This was a shock, since she'd been virtually mute throughout the course of the party.

"I don't know what a few more days will do," Daddy said. Elizabeth noticed that he hadn't brushed his hair as he usually did.

She wished she could fly to him and smooth his hair, of which he had always been so proud.

"Just to move it," Di said. "A few more days to move it out of Mrs. Schmidt's yard . . ."

"It will fall apart," Daddy said.

"There's extensive termite damage," Jack agreed. "Di, I appreciate your determination, but I'm with your father here. I just don't think it'll hold."

"I'm working on a plan," she said, her voice as stiff as the collar of her dress.

"She says she's working on a plan," Daddy said to Adelia across the table. "How long do you think we'll have to wait?" He smiled, as though expecting Adelia to laugh, but Adelia only looked down at her tart. Everyone at the table was quiet, and Elizabeth felt as if she could pierce her own heart with the tines of her dessert fork, and even Adelia could think of nothing to say, so that everything at the table but the flame of the candle was motionless, until Arthur spoke up.

"I'd like to see it, Diana," he said. Diana nodded to herself, refusing to acknowledge him. He was watching the side of her face, his head tilted slightly, and Elizabeth wanted to force her sister to look up and show some gratitude for the interest he had taken. But Diana murmured something unintelligible, and William remained stubbornly silent, and Elizabeth wondered whether this depressing moment would last until everyone decided to leave. Then Arthur rekindled his conversation with Isabelle, and Adelia said something funny to Elaine, and there was life again on the patio. Isabelle went on pulsing with her prettiness, and upstairs Caroline was sleeping with that nearsighted furrow between her eyebrows, and Elizabeth revived enough to engage Jack Weld about his practice. Things were fine except for Diana sitting with that hand against her temple, looking exhausted. It might have gone on for hours, everyone was having so much fun, except that Arthur glanced at his watch and said he hadn't realized how late it was. Then the Welds were gathering their things, and Daddy was sitting there looking off into the night, so Elizabeth rushed to see them all off. She was a good hostess. She packed them slices of tart to take home. She thanked them. Elaine Weld complimented the candles, and Elizabeth walked with them out to the front stoop, where Arthur kissed her lightly on the cheek and a wave of honeysuckle swept over her so that she felt lyrical and generous. When they had gone, she went back into the kitchen, past Adelia consulting with Isabelle at the kitchen table, and shut herself in the cool angles of the laundry room. She wanted to leave him one last message, to let him know how lovely the evening had been, but this time he picked up and said, "What, Elizabeth, what do you want?"

Even that didn't bother her, because she had remembered herself. She had remembered the grace she had taken with her out to L.A.

"I'm just calling to tell you I've had a wonderful evening," she said.

"I'm glad," he said. Nothing more.

"Yes," she said. "And I'm calling to say I remember how I used to be. It's strange, I can remember it perfectly now. I just feel sorry that I forgot. But I remember now, perfectly."

"Yes," he said. "Okay."

And then she heard someone in the background, and the possibility that the ex was there, in the house that used to be her house, occurred to Elizabeth, and the laundry room was drained of air. She reached for her glass of wine, felt the thin cylinder of its neck between her thumb and forefinger.

"I remember how we used to be," she faltered.

"I have to go. I can't have this conversation now."

"You picked up," she said.

"You called three times. I was worried about the girls."

"They're beautiful," she said, summoning her dignity, lifting her face against defeat.

There was a silence on the other line. "I can't talk to you right now," he said, and there was the click, and then silence ringing, and she couldn't feel any of her large sensations anymore. And this time when she walked back out to the patio, she saw William with his disheveled hair, and she saw that Diana had gone off somewhere, and Isabelle was walking over to Arthur's house with a bottle of wine, and the candles had burned down to nothing so the gnomes stretched out their empty palms, and at the center of the table the peonies bent their heavy heads so low it seemed their bending necks would break.

Chapter 13

After the dinner party, as she climbed the stairs to her room, all she could hear was his voice. "I'd like to see it, Diana." Her name in his voice. He said it just when the silence had gotten cruel, but he waited until that point. It was clear that he hadn't forgiven her fully. When he was most vulnerable—abandoned by his mother, facing an uncertain future—she had let him go. Years later, why would he want to intervene on her behalf? He hadn't looked at her all night. From the beginning of the party, he was occupied with Isabelle, laughing at her jokes, letting her whisper in his ear. Diana had a headache all night. She thought the party would go on forever, those candles burning down to the last drip, Isabelle flirting, Elizabeth demanding more than her fair share of attention, Jack Weld flashing his lupine smile. And Arthur, sitting so close, withholding himself. But then, for the second time, he intervened on her behalf. At the moment when she thought she couldn't sit at that table any longer, he looked at his watch and ended the party. As if he knew. As if he'd noticed her headache, felt it, and refused to let the party go on.

Her notebook was resting on her desk. Its black cover was closed. Inside, the pages were empty. Over the past few days of promising to work on a plan, its pages had become more and more empty. The more time passed, the denser her notebook started to look, as though if she tried to lift it, it would be heavy with sketches of nothing. Tonight she picked it up and put it under her arm. When she went down to the kitchen, Isabelle and Adelia were talking at the table; they didn't look up from their conversation to acknowledge her. Elizabeth was absent, and the door to the laundry room was shut. Diana went over to her mother's old desk to pick up one of the pencils that jutted out of the flour jar; it smelled like fresh wood shavings, as though Margaux had just sharpened it in the crank sharpener that crouched like a metal frog on the corner of her desk. Margaux had always liked her pencils perfectly sharp. She used to draw maps of the garden, labeling each new shrub with its Latin name. As a little girl, Di liked to be close to her mother when she was engaged in projects like that one. Just to hang around her, allowing her elbow to brush almost imperceptibly against Margaux's. Seeing how long she could keep it there before Margaux moved her elbow away.

Since the diagnosis, Di had spent less time with her mother. Maybe she'd grown tired of the long silences; maybe she was afraid of the similarities she might notice. Now she lifted Margaux's pencil up to her nose. It smelled like the inside of a new house. Holding it in her right fist, she walked through the garden to the carriage house and took a seat on the bottom step. She waited for her eyes to adjust to the darkness. Without opening her notebook, she looked around. The ceiling was tall. Two stories and nothing but the narrow loft between the floor and the roof. It stretched up and up, arching over its termite-infested beams. She closed her eyes and felt what it meant to exist in a room of that shape. She felt the top of her head rising up toward the roof. She breathed, her rib cage a structure of arched wood beams, clasped around space that was empty except for herself. She opened her eyes again. Something was moving outside. From the frame of the door, Diana saw that Isabelle was striding across the lawn with a bottle of wine. She stopped at the Schmidts' kitchen and knocked at the screen door. Arthur came out, and while they talked, he leaned against the frame of the door. Then they were moving toward her and the carriage house. Diana ducked back inside. She held her breath as the sound of their voices approached, then stopped in front of the door.

"Let's stay out here," Arthur said. Diana could hear them settling down on the grass in front of the door.

"Have some," Isabelle said. The wash of a bottle passed through the night.

"Thanks. I'm glad you came over. I've been alone in that house every night since I came back."

"How long have you been here?"

"Almost a month. I go up to New York sometimes, but mostly, I can work from the house."

"How long are you planning to stay?"

"I'm not sure."

"You're loyal."

"You would be, too."

"I'm not sure," Izzy said. "I was watching Dad at the table tonight, wondering how much would I do for him to help him now that he needs me. I'm really not sure."

"If it came down to the wire, you'd be there for him."

"I don't know. I'm not sure I have that kind of loyalty. Di's the only loyal one, and look what it's done to her."

Inside the carriage house, Diana winced. She tried to think of the ceiling's loft to comfort herself. She tried to imagine flying up into its rafters.

"What has it done to her?"

"You saw her tonight."

There was a long pause. Diana listened for what he would say next. "I guess there are kinds of loyalty that aren't advisable," he said.

"You can say that again," Isabelle said, and then there was another silence. "Adelia wants me to talk to Jack Weld about the carriage house. She says he's 'fond' of me. She thinks I could persuade him to block the demolition."

There was a silence, but Diana could hear Isabelle getting angry. That Diana could hear the sound of Isabelle getting angry must have been a sign that there was sisterly closeness between them, despite the fact that there was so little understanding. Why did it make Isabelle so upset, the idea of talking to Jack Weld? Why did she flicker on and off so wildly? Diana could hear nothing but the sound of Isabelle pulling every inch of anger from the widest corners of the sky into her dense, unknowable center.

"Why does she think he's so 'fond' of you?" Arthur asked.

"I don't know," Izzy said. Diana could hear wine sloshing forward as Izzy tilted the bottle to drink. "We used to play tennis together," she said. "Jack and I. One day I came home and told Adelia I hated him. She said, 'He's fond of you,' but there was this awful little smile on her face. She was proud of me for drawing him in. It made him seem foolish. That's what that smile meant. When she scheduled another match for us at the club, I went, but this time I felt powerful. Like I was on a special-ops mission with a stolen identity. Like I could be any kind of person at the drop of a hat. Does that make sense? I thought I could be anyone." Izzy broke off as if considering the veracity of her testimony so far.

"It's what good parents tell you, isn't it?" she continued. "That you can be anyone you want to be? Or maybe that's wrong. Any*thing* you want to be, not any*one*." Izzy paused. When she started again her voice was more flat. The thoughtfulness had passed, replaced by something else. "Anyway, I believed it. Anyone I wanted to be. I was no one; I could be anyone. It was our shared conspiracy. Our little joke. The kind of joke that you know, even while you're telling it, is actually sad. No one's going to laugh, but you can't go back. You've already gone too far. I felt it as it was happening. For a second I was powerful, but it slipped out of my hands. At some point, you can see it in everyone's eyes when they look at you. They can tell you took it a little too far. They know you crossed over." Isabelle paused to take another drink of wine. "Sometimes," she continued, "if you try on a certain kind of person for size, you end up getting stuck inside her. For years I've been stuck, and all I want to do is get out of this neighborhood so maybe I can be myself someplace where no one knows me. Someplace where people don't think their cul-de-sac is the world. With stakes that high, as though the neighborhood association is the UN, and war is imminent, and sacrifices are necessary. I just want to go someplace where I can look back at all this and laugh and know that none of it mattered. But now Adelia wants me to talk to Jack to plead for the life of my father, and to tell you the truth I'm half tempted to do it, even though the whole thing makes me sick."

After a long time Arthur spoke. "I'm not sure . . ." he started, then stopped. "I'm sorry, Izzy."

"Could you wait here?" Isabelle said. "While I go get another bottle from the basement?"

"Do you think you should? We've had a lot. And you're not really supposed to be drinking, are you?"

"No, I'm not."

There was another silence so long and complete that Diana worried they would hear her breathing. Finally, Isabelle broke it.

"Can you smell the honeysuckle?"

"Yeah," he said, his voice soft and even in the night.

"Dad can't smell it anymore."

"That's terrible."

"I imagine him losing pieces of himself, one by one, until he's completely gone. And then there will be nothing left. Only Mom, fading away, and Adelia. But he's the only parent I've really had."

"I know."

"You've never even had a parent. You're here for your grandmother, and I won't lift a finger to help my own father."

"I admire you, too. Your independence. You know what's important to you. You'll choose your loyalties."

He was speaking directly to Diana. The rebuke was so pointed that Diana wondered if he knew she was there, if he was speaking those words to her so she'd know why he hadn't forgiven the way she followed her family's advice.

"What's important to me," Isabelle repeated. She laughed a jagged laugh. "Like not caring about this fucking carriage house. Like wishing it would burn to the ground and we could all find better things to worry about."

Arthur was quiet.

"Will you stay out here with me for a while?" Izzy asked. "I'll get another bottle of wine. I feel so strange."

"Izzy, we should go back in," he said. "Or I'll stay out here, if you really want, but I don't think you should get more wine."

"What I'd like is to have another couple of drinks, then help my father get his historical carriage house, then leave this absurd little suburb forever. I'd like to drink another glass or ten of wine, then close my eyes and open them in a world where miraculously, the carriage house would fly to our backyard, where we'd all be ourselves again so that I could leave us behind." She laughed harshly, and then there was a tense silence. Finally, the sound of Isabelle standing. "I'm going home," she said. "Thanks for talking."

"You're sure you don't want to stay?" he asked. "I'm happy to. Were you finished with what you wanted to say?"

"Sure," she said. "Sure, I'm all finished." There was the sound of her movement through the grass, and the feeling of his presence, alone with her in the dark. Diana stayed quiet, holding her breath, until he, too, stood and walked away, and she was free to breathe. When she had exhaled fully, and her breath had settled into the beams, Diana opened her notebook and drew the shape of the roof. She drew its long straight spine, the wooden ribs that curved away from it, tapering into the walls. And when she had drawn that skeleton—capped by the iron weather vane that spun its ghoulish wings in the wind—she drew the outlines of walls, rimming negative space. To get the shape of the windows right, she ran her finger along their sills, leaving pale stripes in the dust. They were tall and narrow, strict in their corners, and she took comfort in running her finger along them until she felt the shape of a rectangle open in her chest, through which there was the possibility of escape. Then she rushed to her notebook to draw them: six windows, narrowly rectangular. Her hand pressed so firmly that a thin wake of lead dust trailed her pencil as it moved. This she picked up with the tip of her finger, ever so gently, to keep it from smudging. When the drawing was done, she held it before her and felt cleaner than she had in a very long time.

It wasn't as if she'd forgotten that Arthur hadn't forgiven her. She still remembered that William had lost his ability to smell. She knew it was in June that Margaux announced she was sick, when Isabelle stuck her fork in all those lanterns, when Elizabeth was pregnant and they were all beginning to fade. Those recollections were sad, but she was starting to sort things more clearly. Tomorrow she'd bring back the measuring tools. She could draw up a blueprint in William's basement studio. She'd like to talk to Isabelle and tell her something that would calm her down. She could find out what happened with Jack Weld, ask her about growing up alone in the house with the absence of a mother and Adelia up the street. She'd like to talk to Elizabeth about the divorce. And she could remind herself that even if Arthur hadn't forgiven her, he didn't want to see her suffer. He cared enough that he wouldn't allow her to get hurt. She could go on like this, living in this way. She could keep a straight line, clearing the floor of her mind so that corners could form in the shape of a house.

Chapter 14

He had been thinking, before Isabelle strode back over the lawn with an empty bottle of wine in her hand, that his family had embarrassed him tonight. In the past, William had always imagined his family was the envy of every other household on Little Lane. He had always suspected Jack Weld of jealousy, because his daughter was passive and his wife was a drip. But tonight, for the life of him, he could not see what evidence had caused him to hold such convictions.

Before dinner, he watched them fluttering around in their various preparations, like so many frantic insects trapped in the house, and he felt sorry for them. He felt for Adelia, who had draped herself in small hard jewels in an attempt to seem more womanly. Because Elizabeth had flown to Adelia's aid in preparing for the party, he felt intense fondness for Elizabeth, with her unkempt hair and her inexplicable jacket. He even pitied Diana and promised himself he'd be kinder the next time the topic of the carriage house came up. And when he saw Isabelle coming down the stairs in her white dress, looking like the little girl of whom he had been so proud, he felt a pang of regret for having accused her of disappointing him.

But at dinner, with the Welds gathered at his table, he saw his family through their eyes, and he was embarrassed. He saw, from the slight lift in Elaine Weld's eyebrows when Adelia served the chicken, that Adelia was not his wife. As she served the guests, uncomfortable with her jeweled wrists in oven mitts, he could see that Adelia was not the woman he'd married, and she had no right to assume such a familiar place in his house. Her chicken tasted like pounded rubber soaked in brine. She was not a wifely woman. Perhaps he had known this when he married Margaux. Perhaps it wasn't only wounded pride but the knowledge that, despite her perfect topspin, Adelia Lively was the kind of woman who creates inexpensive dinner menus while dreaming of vengeance, a woman with none of Margaux's softness, without even the decent curves of a woman such as Elaine. Understanding this made it difficult for him to look at Adelia. He tried to avoid her gaze. He could tell that no one liked her chicken.

And his daughters. He saw them as Elaine must have seen them. Elizabeth kept running in and out of the kitchen as though her ridiculous jacket were on fire. Diana slouched the entire evening with nothing to say for herself. And Isabelle, who had looked so pretty when she first walked down the stairs in that white dress, spent the entire dinner flirting with Arthur as though she were a prostitute. Three times he caught Weld watching her while she whispered in Arthur's ear, her cheeks glowing in a way that made William feel ashamed for her sake. Three times he imagined her as Weld did, and it nauseated him. When he compared Izzy to Abby, who ate her chicken politely and listened while Elizabeth blathered on, he wanted to grab her by the braid and drag her upstairs so she could learn how to act like a decent child again. He could see Jack Weld thinking: *My daughter would never behave that way, whispering at the table, disrespecting her elders, smiling as loosely as a hussy.* He could see the flush of triumph that spread itself over Weld's face, and it dawned on him that Abby Weld, whom William had never credited with much, had grown up gracefully. She had learned to be less plain. And what had happened to Isabelle? Had she always been so flimsy in her character? Perhaps he had fooled himself. Perhaps the promise he saw in her had never existed after all.

The only member of his family of whom he had been truly proud was Lucy, singing that song from *Les Misérables*. It revived his belief that there was something special about the Adairs, some quality that other people lacked. But then Elizabeth sent her upstairs, and it was as though the lights went out on the patio and everything was drained of the color it had acquired while she was spinning around in her pink nightgown under the starry sky. William was forced to remind himself that, after all, his own children had been like that when they were young, and look how they ended up. At which point he caught sight of Diana watching Isabelle and Arthur as though they were falling slowly into a black hole from which they would never emerge.

As he was recollecting this, alone at the table in the wake of the party, Isabelle walked across the yard with an empty bottle of wine in her hand. William did not want to think where she had been, or how she had disposed of that bottle's contents in the space of twenty minutes or less. When she sat at the table, he noticed that her feet were bare and there were little flecks of grass around her ankles, as if she had been turning cartwheels after the grass had been mowed. It was such a childish thing that he wanted to take her in his arms and demand that she remember who she was, because for the life of him, he couldn't remember.

"Hi, Daddy," she said. Her voice was so hard that he understood the grass on her feet had deceived him. They sat in silence for a while, and William occupied himself with counting Margaux's irises. He was at twenty-seven when Isabelle reached for the bottle of wine left on the table. He was at forty-four when she finished her glass.

"How do you feel?" she asked. He told her he was fine. When she poured herself another glass, she caused him to lose his count. Determined, he started over at forty-one, but again his counting fell apart because he couldn't believe how quickly she polished off the second glass. She was eighteen years old. She was a little girl. Why she had chosen to act this way was beyond him. She was no longer pretty in that white dress, which was skimpy around her shoulders.

"Daddy," she said. It irked him that she had taken to calling him that now, after all these years. "I'm going to go over and talk to Jack Weld about the carriage house."

He didn't say anything. He tried to find the black shape of the bullfrog that was making so much noise.

"Daddy, do you want me to go over and talk to Jack Weld about the carriage house?"

"Isabelle, I don't care. I do not care about the carriage house. I do not care about Jack Weld. It doesn't make the slightest difference to me whether you talk to him or not."

She finished the bottle of wine. The speed with which she drank it disgusted him as he counted Margaux's irises, looking away from her, hoping she'd leave him alone.

When she was gone, William was startled to realize that tears were coming out of his eyes. This surprised him. He hadn't cried in a long time, and he had felt none of the warning signs that usually preceded the welling of tears. There was nothing. No building up, no intensity of sensation. Only a spontaneous effusion of water, a vestigial fatherly response that had no basis in actual emotion. He sat there, leaking tears, until he realized that Margaux had come from behind the house and was bending down in the bed of ferns that she'd planted along the edge of the property. He watched her through his leaky eyes for a while. She was wearing a pale lavender dress with fluttery sleeves and a sash around the waist, as though she had stepped out of that old photo of her as a bridesmaid at her sister's wedding. Each of her motions among the ferns—she was cutting and placing them in a square glass vase—was deliberate and fluid at once. Because her dark hair was spread over her back and her shoulders, whole parts of her faded into the night. In the way that he knew how, he had loved her, and she had chosen to disappear. He had never been disloyal; it was she who had left him behind. He wasn't absolutely guiltless, of course. She had told him she didn't want children, yes. She was firm about that. Perhaps she knew somehow that she wouldn't last. But he had imagined a family! A family of beautiful girls. He imagined Lizzie and Di, and then he imagined Isabelle. He hadn't known how sharply Margaux would decline.

When she finished cutting ferns, she turned and noticed him sitting at the table. She lifted one hand to wave. He lifted his. He wondered if she could see his meaningless tears. She hesitated, holding her glass of ferns, tilting her head to one side as if trying to place him precisely, as if attempting to put a name to his face.

Margaux, he thought. *Wife, if only you were here.*

But already she had disappeared through the laundry room door, and she was no more gone than she had been when she was standing there.

Later Adelia stuck her head through the sliding door and asked if he would come inside.

"No," he said, looking out at the garden.

Her head stayed there, insistent and stuck. "William, what's wrong?" she asked.

"I'd like to be alone," he told her. He had never told her that before, he had always wanted her presence close by.

"No," she said. "No, you can't be. I need you here with me."

"Go inside, Adelia."

"No," she said again. "Not unless you come with me."

Her head refused to withdraw, and so he stood, and he observed that the unbidden tears had stopped welling. When he followed her inside, there was something reassuring about the brisk way she took the stairs, as though she were reminding each one of its place. He followed her. It was nice to follow someone after all. She turned down the bed and pointed him toward the pajamas she had laid out on his chair.

"Get in bed," she said. No, she was not a wifely woman, and yet she was right here, as important as she had always been.

"Stay with me," he said.

She hesitated, focusing on his pajamas.

"I need you here with me."

She folded her arms across her thin chest. She was not a wifely woman, but she was his Adelia. He had lived with the benefit of her closeness since he was a boy. Now he could feel her tumult. The close, palpable snarl of her confusion that could almost be mistaken for anger. Without speaking, without looking at him, she kept her arms folded. She was pressing her lips together very hard, blinking as she used to do when someone had insulted her but she refused to let them see her cry. He almost pitied her, but he couldn't let her go. He remained still before the bed. He would not lie himself down until she decided to stay.

"I need you here with me," he said again.

"I've been here with you from the start," she said. William moved to sit with her, but she pointed once again toward the laid-out pajamas, and William, grateful to be given a plan, did as she directed him.

Chapter 15

The windows of the Welds' house were brightly lit. They looked like amber lozenges, soft around the edges, melting into the night. Seeing them made Izzy remember her throat; she was thirsty. "Windows are the souls of a house," William used to tell her, before the architecture lessons had ceased. The Welds' house was bright with rectangular souls that she wanted to drink. She stopped by the mailbox, alone in the gaping night, watching the house. The air smelled of cigar smoke and summer; he must have walked down this driveway, smoking a cigar, under the swarming black leaves. His lingering presence caused Isabelle to pull up short, caught in the netherland between two imposing houses. She wondered why a person should feel so left out of the world in which she was meant to exist. Before her, the long screened porch was empty. Behind it, the lights in the kitchen were on. All three of the Welds were moving around one another like woven strands. Jack was vivid. Around his family, in the privacy of his illuminated kitchen, he ascended into ecstasies. She watched him laughing at something that Abigail said. He reached over and gave her a high five. What a ridiculous motion, the high five. Two needy hands, stranded together. But the Welds laughed. They moved around one another and smiled. After a while, Abby kissed them both and then went upstairs. Jack and Elaine were alone in the kitchen. The dance broke up. Jack stood at the sink, washing dishes. Elaine moved over to the door, looking out. Isabelle would have been worried that Elaine could see her—it seemed she was staring directly at Isabelle—but she knew that from inside the house she was only a part of the darkness. Elaine couldn't see her, standing by the mailbox, all angle and stiff white dress, feeling like an angel of vengeance with her bare feet against the angry gravel of the driveway. Jack leaned away from the sink to say something to Elaine, and she responded with a single word, facing the yard. Then she turned and left the kitchen. Upstairs, a light went on. Abby moved over to the window and lowered the blinds. *So be it,* Isabelle thought. *Let the blinds drop on Abigail Weld. Let her sleep a deep and oblivious slumber.*

Jack finished with the dishes. He dried his hands on the dish towel and moved through the glass door to the screened-in porch. He sat in one of the wicker chairs and lit a cigar, cupping the match with his hand. When he sat up, sucking in with his cheeks, Isabelle watched the cigar's tip crumple to a rim of red ash. His body had blended into the darkness, but she could see the circular shine of his eyes moving, scanning the night. She wished she'd picked up a handle of something out of William's liquor cabinet. She could have used its glass weight in her hands. She thought of turning around and going back home, but the idea was repulsive to her, and when she took a step forward, the gravel under the soles of her feet was pleasantly painful. She felt sharpened by the sensation as she walked, pressing her feet against the stones. When she worried he'd hear the sound of her steps on the gravel, she switched over to the lawn.

He didn't see her until she was close to the porch. If she hadn't been wearing the white dress, he wouldn't have seen her at all. She could have walked right up to the porch and draped herself across the screen like a huge luna moth, camouflaged by darkness, invisible to human eyes. But he saw her dress moving and stood up. He walked over to the screen.

"Isabelle?"

"Hey."

He glanced behind him into the house. The kitchen was empty. "What are you doing?"

"I wanted to ask you something."

"You shouldn't sneak around like this. If you want to come in, come in. I'll get you a glass of lemonade. We can sit in the living room with Mrs. Weld."

"That sounds like a ball."

He sucked on his cigar, watching her.

Isabelle attempted to make her voice gentler. "You wanna come outside with me?" she asked. "We could sit in those chairs." She gestured toward the two iron lawn chairs, stripped of their cushions, that had lounged unused at the side of the Welds' house for years.

The rim of his cigar flared and crumpled, unfolding petals of ash. "This is ridiculous," he said.

Isabelle couldn't be sure, exactly. Her brain felt hot. There was the helping of her father, the spiting of Adelia, the desire to feel something painful again. She looked up at him. She knew that, in theory, she was beautiful, her white dress shining against the darkness of her hair. She commanded her looks to reach out and wrap around him where he stood on the porch. She could see him softening. The breeze moved the hem of her dress around her legs.

"Go home, Isabelle," he said, but this time his voice was quieter.

"Am I different now? Than when I was a kid with all the promise in the world?"

"You're still a kid. You're Abby's age."

"She's done better than I have, hasn't she?"

"I never compared the two of you."

No, he hadn't, had he. She'd already had enough. Bile was rising in her throat, and she had to concentrate to keep it down. "I'll go," she said. Her eyes narrowed. She could feel them sharp as stones. "But can you do something about the carriage house? It seems like you owe me a favor."

He turned and stubbed out his cigar. When he came back around, something had changed in his face. "I said I'd see what I could do. I'll do my best. I don't know what you've imagined, but I don't owe you any favors."

"What's your best, Jack? What's your very best?"

He studied her, head tilted to one side. "You know what my best is, Isabelle? Nothing. I don't owe you anything, and I won't do anything for you now that you're threatening me. My best is nothing. Whatever importance your father has invested in the carriage house means nothing to the outside world. That building is no more than a rat-infested dump, and to be honest, I'll be delighted when it goes. I've looked forward to it for a long time. I'm going to sit here and smoke a cigar, watching, when that thing finally falls."

Isabelle breathed in, taking her time. "When you win this war, Jack," she said at last, "you're still going to be just another middle-aged man, married to a woman you can't remember loving, wishing you'd become the person you used to hope you'd become."

"Sure, Isabelle," he said.

"You're still going to drive to work in the morning, and you'll stroll around the hospital and tell yourself that you're somehow important. But when you come home at night, you'll miss this fight with my dad because it gave you some intensity, at least."

"Well said, Isabelle. You have a way with words, don't you."

"And then without a feud to keep you distracted, you'll look around and get that your wife is boring, your daughter is average, and you're nothing more than a little boy pretending he's grown up into a man."

He waited until she was finished. "And you'll be nothing more than a girl who threw her life away to make the point that she could."

Her breath caught. "I won't let you," she said, although she had no idea what she meant.

"Go home, Isabelle. Go home and get some sleep." She didn't move, so he shrugged, turned his back on her, and went into the house. The light in the kitchen switched off. A new darkness descended around her. She waited for a while longer, until the house started settling into the night, then opened the screen door and sat in the wicker chair he had been sitting in. She toyed with the matches he'd left beside the ashtray. She ran one finger through his discarded ash, then put the finger to her lips; it tasted acrid. On the other side of the porch were a hopper of tennis balls and two rackets leaning against a card table. She examined these and all the easy familial comfortableness that they stood for. She settled into Jack's chair. Then she got up and tested the kitchen door. It gave with only the slightest creak, so she walked in and tried the cabinet beside the sink for liquor. She was right; people's liquor cabinets exhale a special allure that makes them easy to find. She took a handle of bourbon out to the porch and settled into the wicker chair. There was something extremely pleasant about drinking directly underneath the room where Abigail Weld was sleeping peacefully. Izzy looked out over the lawn. It was too late for fireflies, but the bullfrogs were croaking. Over in the Adair yard, in the silt of the pond, the frogs' pale gullets were extending and collapsing. In the carriage house, the rats had been hiding all day, and now they were venturing out of their holes. There were whole nests of rat babies over there, and rat mothers scurrying around, scavenging for food. There were mice, too, with translucent ears and trembling noses. And termites burrowing into the honeycomb rafters. All of them would be lost when the carriage house went down. Isabelle took another swipe of cigar ash and tasted it again, and she thought if they were going to be lost, it might as well be now. You could fight for something only so long; at some point you just have to stop. You have to pack up your bags and get out. She imagined whole trails of exile mice wearing little straw hats and pioneer bonnets, pushing their children ahead while behind them, their city burned to the ground. And this was very sad, so sad it was practically unbearable, and Isabelle felt she couldn't put it off any longer. If they were going to be banished, she wanted them to just fucking get out. Why wait around in a sinking ship? Why wait for Jack Weld to come in with his wrecking ball ready? Better to do the thing herself. She didn't want him to watch it go down. She took a final swallow of bourbon and put the matches in her pocket. On her way out, she stole the ball hopper and one of the tennis rackets, then trooped back down the driveway. The soles of her feet didn't hurt anymore. By the time she'd crossed the Schmidts' lawn, she had formed a coherent plan, and she stopped in front of the carriage house with a sense of immediate purpose.

She took a ball out of the hopper and held it in the palm of her left hand. At one point in her life, she'd loved the feel of a tennis ball in the cup of her palm. Now she held the ball and tried to remember the old comfort, but that was gone, so she whispered, "Fuck it," and lit it on fire. It was hard to light at first, but then the flame caught so quickly she was afraid it would burn her, so she took the racket in her right hand and launched the flaming ball out toward the carriage house. It arced through the dark like a comet. Isabelle's eyes widened in appreciation of its beauty. It was the most beautiful thing she'd seen in a long time. She lit another ball and lobbed it, a little higher this time. It was like a Viking funeral ceremony. She was shooting flaming arrows, and the carriage house was like a big canoe in the lake of the night. She struck another match. She was giddy with the scent of unnatural smoke. She was seeing them off. She was seeing all of them off, and when they were gone, she would turn back and move away from the shore. In the thickening haze of smoke, it looked as though the carriage house were moving away from her, a big slow canoe receding into a mist. "Here is for the mice," she said to herself. "And here is for the rats, and the termites, and the old falling rafters. Here is for my sisters, and here is for my mom." Each time she lobbed another ball. "And here is for myself," she said, just to keep talking. She kept on lobbing until she burned a hole in the strings, then dropped the smoking racket on the grass and headed back to the driveway. She found the keys that William always left in the ignition of the Jeep, and she thought she would be sick, but then she rolled down the windows. The breeze rushing past her settled her head, and she told herself she needed to go on a drive, away and away and away and away, a drive so endless there would be no need to imagine it ever coming to an end.

Chapter 16

When the first ball of fire broke the windowpane and bounced four times across the floor, Diana watched it as if it were an exotic bird. It was intensely bright, the orb of bluish heat at its center dripping with gold. The second one bounced outside the open door, then rolled into the entryway, where it kept to itself, a lonely little blaze. Watching it, she smiled. It was the strangest, most beautiful thing she had seen in a long time. Only when the third ball hit the window frame and bounced back out, landing in a pile of shrubbery and erupting into flame, did Diana become more practical. She thought of running into the Schmidts' house for water, then stopped. Judging from the speed at which the shrubbery was going up in flames, she wouldn't have time for that. She remembered that you were supposed to throw blankets over fire. She'd have to climb up the old stairs to the loft, assuming those blankets were still up there. She should probably run for help. It was an ancient building, condemned by the district. But it was also her father's carriage house, the carriage house she shared with Arthur, and she was running up the stairs before she had time to hesitate. She nearly broke an ankle when one of the old planks gave out beneath her feet, but she had hold of the loft's floor by then, and she found firm enough footing on the next stair to scramble up. The blankets were heaped there, so inviting that she almost wanted to lie down in them, wrapped in their old scent, allowing the smoke to billow up around her in plumes.

By the time she had an armful of blankets, at least a dozen more balls of fire had been launched into or around the carriage house, and flame from the first one was licking the wall in a ribbon of bright tongues. There was one at the base of the stairs, too, but the crown of fire around it was small enough that Diana started her backward descent. Only when she reached back with her foot and felt nothing but air—the bottom half of the stairs had collapsed entirely—did she understand that she would have to jump into the fire. She hung there for a minute, barefoot, strangely calm, perversely imagining that perhaps she should wait, but the wood was burning her fingers, and she knew she would let go soon except that suddenly someone reached up and took hold. She released her fingers and fell into him. He helped her outside. For a moment she thought of holding on to him, grasping this unexpected closeness while she could, but the carriage house was burning. Three jags of flame lined the door as if it were a hoop of fire in a circus trick. Inside, the floor shimmered with gold.

"Did you call 911?" she asked.

"No," he said, "I thought someone might be in there, so I came."

"I'll do it," she said, and ran inside, and when she came out again, he was still standing there, holding the blankets. She took them, went back through the flaming hoop, and threw them down, as best as she could, over the shimmering floor. Smoke billowed up around her and she retreated, coughing. Arthur took hold of her elbow. "Don't go back in, Diana, it's only a house."

She pulled free of him and ran back out to the road, as though that would hurry the fire trucks, and when she did, she saw that the Jeep was gone, which was curious enough to give her a chill. When she crossed back through the yard, she passed a tennis racket with a black hole at the center of its strings and a half-full hopper. Only then did she realize that the orbs of fire had been burning tennis balls.

She joined Arthur again. "We have to go look for her," she said.

"Who?"

"Isabelle. She took the Jeep."

He looked down at the tennis racket in her hands. "She was drunk?"

"Yes."

"I should have stayed with her."

"Just come with me," she said. He followed her back to the house. Inside, she ran up to William's room and saw, in the darkness, Adelia lying beside him. She was wearing her white flannel nightgown; he was dressed in striped pajamas that made him look like a child. They looked like children curled together, Adelia's head against his shoulder and her arm across his chest, his hand holding the elbow as if to lock it in place. Diana knew she should feel betrayed on her mother's behalf, but there was something so tender about her father's hand holding that elbow, and outside, the carriage house was burning. Diana knelt at Adelia's side and put one hand on her shoulder.

"Adelia," Diana whispered. Adelia peered at Diana through the darkness. "The carriage house is on fire. The fire department is coming. I'm going out to look for Isabelle." Adelia blinked, still comprehending. "I'll call you later. It's going to be okay."

The air outside smelled like smoke and June trees. The bullfrogs had gone quiet; everything was oddly hushed except for the static crackling of the fire. The dark sky behind the house had been pushed aside by an uneasy halo of peach-colored light. Arthur and Diana didn't speak as they climbed into the car and turned down Little Lane, passing the screaming sirens on their way onto Clubhouse Road.

"Will they save it?" he asked when the screaming had faded behind them.

"No. They'll stop the fire, but they won't save it."

"I'm sorry," he said. She looked at him for the first time. He was wearing the same plaid shirt, over the same gray T-shirt, that he had been wearing at dinner. His hair smelled like smoke. She remembered, now that she was seeing him, the particular line of his profile.

They drove down Clubhouse Road, under the Osage orange trees, out Buckley Street past St. Matthew's church, to Breacon Avenue. They passed the tennis courts on their right, lined by chestnut trees. Diana watched them slide away. "Why did you go back into the house that morning you saw me in the garden with Lucy?"

She could feel him glance at her, then look away. "It's been hard for me to see you," he said. He was quiet for a while, and she kept her eyes on the road so that he would continue. "For me, what happened between us was real," he said at last. "For a long time, it was hard to forget. Even now seeing you is difficult."

"I'm sorry, Arthur," she said. Through the open windows, the wind brushed by her. Everything was passing so quickly. Now, in the eerie light of this evening, that morning in the garden seemed impossibly distant. Even the way she'd missed him all those years seemed like an ancient artifact, something that could be talked about without too much embarrassment. "It's hard for me, too," she heard herself saying. "I've changed so much since we were together." It would have pained her to admit this before, but she was long past that point.

"We all have," he said. For a while they drove in silence, the car full of wind and the sound of leaves passing outside, until Arthur turned to her again.

"Where would she have gone?"

"I don't know."

"Where are you going?"

"To school, I guess." By instinct, she was following their old route to high school. Through Breacon, over the bridge, west toward the city. Already she could feel the dangerous curves of Kennedy Drive in her hands. She had steered that road for years, driving with Izzy to school. In the winter, icicles as long as yardsticks dripped down the sheer rock face along the western side of the road, and in the spring, trickles of water poured through the moss that grew in its crevasses. There were three different memorials at treacherous points of its route. It curved in ways that were difficult to manage. Beside her, Arthur looked out the window. The night rushed in, lifting the scent of smoke in his hair.

"How did you know I was in there?" she asked him.

"When I was talking with Isabelle, I had a feeling you were inside. I saw the fire and I wanted to be sure." They passed the Fishers' horse farm on the left. Diana could see the shadowy outline of three horses close to the fence; when the car passed, the shine of their eyes shifted to follow it. They crossed the bridge that spanned a deep valley of treetops. The wire ropes at the side of the bridge were intact; there was no tangle of metal where a car had taken flight. Arthur turned in from his window. "I should have stayed out there with her. She was telling me something important, but I missed it, I think."

"It's not your fault. I'm her sister, and I barely know her."

Trees passed. The cool night was untorn, and Diana began to feel that she had anticipated excessive danger. When they came to the turnoff onto Kennedy Drive, the air outside smelled of dripping water. She steered Adelia's car around steep curves, her nerves suspended by immediate focus. The road was as it had always been, back when they were children going to school, and it was only at the last sharp jag of the road, under a ledge of stacked rock, that they saw the semicircle of blinking lights, so bright that the wreck they enclosed was invisible from the outside. Diana parked the car.

"It might be my sister," she said to the officer who tried to block her way. He stepped aside and Diana pushed through. There, at the center, the Jeep was on its side, wedged into a tree. Behind it, the world had lost its resolution, nothing but a blur of rock and tree and electric pulsing light. The turned car looked like a statue, a piece of public art that had been there as long as the tree that had bitten so deeply into its side. One of the upturned wheels was spinning; the others were still. Diana felt Arthur beside her.

"Where's the driver?" she asked in the general direction of the lights.

"They took her to the hospital," someone told her. "They just left. Is she a relative?"

"My sister. Is she okay?" She tried to focus on the officer and noticed that he was clutching his hat.

"She was alive when they took her. Unconscious, but alive. They drove her to Breckenridge."

Diana looked at Arthur. "You don't have to come with me."

"I want to." His face was crossed with alternating shadows of red and blue.

He drove this time, away from the throbbing lights, along the rock face of Kennedy Drive. Diana's head was spinning, so she put the window down, and there again was the smell of water and moss, laced with rubber and gasoline. She closed her eyes and imagined she was young again, and that Isabelle was even younger. They were driving to school with Elizabeth, protected by the surety of their childhood. When they pulled into the hospital parking lot, her head cleared. The urgency of the luminous red letters, EMERGENCY, focused her, and the mathematical grid of the parking lot. The useful architecture of a place devoted to injury. She could hear the jangling of keys in Arthur's pocket as he walked alongside her. The receptionist, at her broad, clean desk, directed them to Isabelle. They had placed her in the children's wing; she was in surgery, listed as critical; they could wait in the visitors' room. They took the elevator together. In the waiting room, they sat in small plastic seats, red and yellow and blue, surrounded by LEGOs, stuffed animals, and battered coloring books. When she turned toward Arthur, the familiarity of his profile opened a hairline crack in her rib cage; her breath caught at the sharp sensation. "I'm going to call the house," she told him, and left him in his little chair. When she came back, a nurse was standing with him.

"You're her sister?" the nurse asked. Di nodded. "She's unconscious. Her spleen ruptured in the accident. Dr. Bellamy performed a splenectomy; it went fine. He's closing the incision now. She suffered head trauma as well, and her collarbone is broken. But there was no damage to the spine. She's lucky for that."

"Will she be okay?" Diana asked.

"She's in critical condition, but she'll stabilize after the surgery. We'll run a CAT scan when her alcohol level is down. But there's no paralysis. No damage to the spine. No other internal bleeding. She's lucky."

"When can we see her?" Arthur asked.

"Not until she's stabilized. You can wait here. Dr. Bellamy will speak to you."

They sat together, shoulders close. There was a basket of *Highlights* magazines in the center of the room and a crate of inflatable basketballs. "I'm exhausted," she said. Her weariness at the dinner party had been nothing more than practice for this. This, finally, was what she'd been waiting for.

"Here," he said. He put a child's pillow on his shoulder.

"You're sure?" she asked, and as soon as she felt the ridge of his shoulder against the shallows of her temple, she closed her eyes and slept.

When she woke, Adelia was sitting beside her, holding her hand. William was standing by the window with his hands clasped behind his back. He was wearing the same green sweater from dinner. In the hospital light, it looked faded and bare.

"She's stable," Adelia said, blinking through her glasses. "The doctor said the surgery went fine."

Diana breathed. "What happened to the carriage house?"

"It doesn't matter," said Adelia. She was gripping Diana's hand so hard that Diana could feel each one of the bones in her fingers. "It's fine. It doesn't matter at all."

"Did Arthur leave?"

"He left after we found out that the operation went well. He stayed until then."

"How's Dad?" At his name, William turned from the window, and Diana saw that his face was streaked with tear tracks.

"He's going to be fine," Adelia said. "Everything's going to be just fine."

· Book 2 ·

I must go uncertain of my fate; but I shall return hither, or follow your party, as soon as possible. A word, a look, will be enough to decide whether I enter your father's house this evening, or never.

—Jane Austen, *Persuasion*

Chapter 17

She had hoped the move down to the shore would be a way of starting fresh in a better climate. When Adelia announced one morning in early July that a temporary move might help, Elizabeth couldn't have agreed more readily. There would be water, and sand, and a new set of neighbors. It seemed like it would ensure an upward turn of events. And yet the low point of the entire Summer of Tragic Accidents came on the day they left for the shore. At that point in the thirsty summer, when the kids were sticky with heat and cross at her for not having a house with a pool, Elizabeth was tired down to the center of her bones.

This summer was meant to be her summer of recovery from divorce. After a year of numb survival, she would come alive again. By fall, she was supposed to have found a wealthy but liberal Breacon businessman who supported the arts. He would be a distinguished person with a youthful physique and lines around the eyes, maybe some white at the temples. Proud of Lucy's precociousness, excited about taking Caroline to science fairs. In bed, before they fell asleep, he would kiss Elizabeth on the forehead and thank her for being his wife. With a man such as this, the old inklings of inspiration might stir in her. She might start considering roles. Once again she could find herself acting as she used to be able to act, throwing off her life and stepping into another one as if the passage were as easy as breathing. As though the return could never be in doubt.

But the summer of recovery had spiraled in a matter of weeks into the summer of Daddy's stroke, then into the summer of Diana flunking architecture school, and finally, into the summer of Isabelle's recovery from absolute psychotic break/splenectomy. Through all of these recoveries, Elizabeth was expected to be the stable one, the favorite daughter with nothing to complain of because she wasn't teetering on the brink of collapse. It was exhausting and it was unfair.

While Isabelle was in the hospital, Elizabeth wasn't as galled as she later became by the fact that no one brought up the carriage house, which looked like the charred carcass of a prehistoric mammoth. She allowed Isabelle two weeks of grace to heal from her surgery, during which she delivered the books that Izzy requested without once mentioning the fact that they were all disturbingly immature. Isabelle gravitated toward children's books: the mice warriors who lived in that monastery, *The Wind in the Willows,* or *James and the Giant Peach*. Elizabeth never questioned her demands for simple sentences. She campaigned only once to have Isabelle moved to the adult section of the hospital. After that failed, she continued to chauffeur Lucy and Caroline to see their train wreck of an aunt in the children's wing. When Diana brought Isabelle the ridiculous marker set, Elizabeth didn't protest about signing her enormous cast, although she resented the fact that a person who had gotten herself into a drunk-driving accident should be having her arm cast decorated in purple Magic Marker.

As long as Isabelle was wearing those hospital gowns that made her look more gaunt than usual, Elizabeth was willing to allow her an extended childhood. She looked so fragile in the bed, reading her mouse books, that Elizabeth pitied her despite the fact that she *burned down* the one and only structure that held out hope for the disappointed Adairs. Not to mention that she totaled the Jeep, which was like killing a beloved family pet. That Jeep had been with them since Elizabeth and Diana were in high school. Elizabeth was once invincible in that hunter-green Cherokee. She used to drive it to parties where she was the envy of every girl in school, wearing her French-rolled jeans and her side pony and perfume from the Body Shop. While Isabelle was in the hospital, Elizabeth was able to shunt these feelings off to the side for the sake of Izzy's recovery. She almost never complained about the strain of balancing trips to the hospital with work in the studio and care of her kids, as well as spending time with Daddy, who was at that point taking long naps in the afternoons with the sheets pulled up to his chin as if he, too, were a child.

After a certain point, all of these sacrifices started to wear. And even though she started to orient her yoga classes around the issue of forgiveness—doing backbends and heart openers, reading mantras about letting go, and asking everyone who was lying in savasana at the end of class to offer forgiveness to one person against whom they were harboring a grudge—she herself usually spent the majority of savasana sitting on her cushion in front of the class, eyes closed, thinking about exactly what she would say to Isabelle when she got out of the hospital to let her know how very deeply she had fucked things up.

When Izzy did come home, Adelia threw her a party. It was Elizabeth, of course, who picked her up. When they walked in the front door, there was a banner hanging in the foyer that read

WELCOME HOME ISABELLE, and somehow someone had induced Margaux to wear a party hat and stay put in the living room without getting up every two minutes to ask, "When are we leaving?" as though everyone in the family were late for a crucial appointment they had all managed to forget. There was Margaux in her party hat, smiling, and there was a massive sheet cake, and Lucy was blowing on that screaming party horn so furiously that Elizabeth thought she would lose her mind if someone who was not a lunatic didn't intervene to set the world on its feet.

Adelia must have seen that she was upset, because she took Elizabeth into the laundry room and said, "Is there something on your mind?" "Yes," Elizabeth said, "there *is* something on my mind, as a matter of fact, which is that she is not a little girl! She is almost eighteen, and she *burned down the carriage house*, and no one has mentioned that, but it did happen, and I have not forgiven her." Adelia, whom Elizabeth had expected to be on her side because no one had been more resolute than Adelia about the issue of the carriage house, simply said, "She's been through a lot." As though that solved things. As though Elizabeth hadn't recently been through a lot herself, and as though it did not pain her to be asked to constantly act like an adult so that her sisters could act like children. So that Mark could live in L.A. pretending he was not a father. Dating a girl-child, a person who was not a mother, with whom he drank good wine and had good sex and did not feel any of the oppressions involved in responsible living. As though it weren't difficult for Elizabeth to be grown up while all around her everyone enjoyed protracted childhoods and somehow only she—who should have been in L.A., going to auditions, because it was not yet too late for her to succeed—was supposed to be beyond that stage. *Do you mean she's been through a lot as in she's recently become an arsonist and a drunk driver and a totally destructive wreck?* was what Elizabeth wanted to say. Instead, she went back out to the party, where Lucy promptly blew that goddamned horn so it hit Elizabeth in the side of the face, and Daddy was sitting at the kitchen table like a captain settled into his cabin while his ship inevitably sinks. And Diana was off somewhere drawing in her journal, and Margaux was holding her untouched plate of sheet cake as though she had no idea what to do with it but didn't mind holding on for a bit. As though she had no clue about the mishaps that had happened, which she probably didn't, because she had opted out so thoroughly that she wasn't even aware she had two grandchildren, let alone a pair of other daughters whom *she* should have been mothering so that her oldest daughter could enjoy what remained of her youth.

Looking at her mother holding her cake, waiting for someone to sweep in and carry it off, Elizabeth was reminded again of the early days of her childhood, when she was in the chubby phase before she blossomed, and Margaux used to say, "You're the strong one, Elizabeth. You have toughness. I can't imagine how you came from me." Elizabeth always hated that, because it implied that Diana was the talented, sensitive child and Elizabeth was nothing more than a kid with some fight. Remembering that long-lost refrain, Elizabeth comprehended that she had fulfilled the prophecy. She had become the one who was holding things together while everyone around her fell apart. This made her even angrier, because it is a sacrifice to be so tough. Being the tough one often involves giving up on being gentle or prettily kind. It doesn't make you popular. It doesn't get you parts as a lead, and it doesn't keep you a husband. Sitting toughly in the kitchen, while the celebrators gathered around Izzy with her cast, Elizabeth thought that this must be what veterans felt like. Having given up on their right to be gentle and then getting avoided at family parties. People never praise you for your toughness. They feign innocence and tell you to be forgiving. They say, "She's been through a lot." No one pats you on the back or throws you parties. They avoid the fact that it's crucial, when the world is collapsing, to have someone around who promises she won't go down in flames.

As a result of her feelings during the party, Elizabeth tightened. The next day in her early-morning class, she made an announcement during downward-facing dog. "We've spent two weeks on forgiveness," she said, sitting on her cushion. "But today we are warriors. Today we are focusing on our strength." All class they did nothing but warrior ones and warrior twos and sun salutations, and class went well because the truth was that every housewife in that studio had been dying all year for permission to turn their lives into a serious fight.

The lowest point came later, on the day they left for the beach. After Elizabeth had allowed herself to start dreaming about wearing a bikini and sitting on warm sand. She and Adelia packed everyone up, buckled everyone in, and remained generally responsible for getting the whole demented show on the road. In the Acura, Isabelle was sitting in the back with Lucy and Caroline, and Adelia was up front with Elizabeth. Diana was driving William, Margaux, and Louise in the rental car. They had finally put some distance between themselves and Little Lane when Lucy announced that she wanted to read her book in the car. Elizabeth told her it would make her sick, and Lucy said, clearly for the benefit of Isabelle, "FUCK SICK," and Isabelle started laughing, and after a month and two days of being a warrior, Elizabeth spun around and said, "GROW UP, ISABELLE, YOU'RE NOT A LITTLE GIRL!"

A shadow passed over Isabelle's face, and everyone in the car got quiet. Adelia's expression hardened. The silence became thick. Elizabeth tried to start two conversations—one about fossils, for the benefit of Caroline, and one about tennis, for the benefit of Lucy—but both girls were somber and mute. Adelia glared out the window, unrelenting. Elizabeth switched on the radio. In the attempt to find something mature, she selected the classical music station, although she associated classical music with costume drama and found it slightly excessive. The song that filled the uneasy car was unsettling, some kind of piano piece that made you imagine a violently lonely and possibly deformed man playing his instrument alone in a dark room at the back of a large house. Still, she held on to the strains of the music as though they were the only solid things in the car, more concrete than the unknowable shifts in her family's moods. As she listened, a sensation of panic began to rise within her. It was the same thing repeated over and over. Low and simple first, then higher and more complicated, then so elaborate that she felt the lonely pianist must have three hands. Over and over, different voices repeating the same urgent refrain, and none of them getting closer to solving the problem. Elizabeth's heart beat in her throat. She kept the car steady as they progressed along the six-lane highway, moving away from the suburbs, passing and getting passed, but inside the car the music wrapped around itself in endless cycles, and Elizabeth felt as though every one of them in the car were drowning, unable to find the final iteration of the problem they started with. "A fugue in six voices," the radio announcer explained after the piece had ended. Elizabeth was steering the car off the highway, following the directions she'd printed out on Little Lane. Then the music was replaced by commercials, the lonely pianist lost to the world, and Elizabeth switched the radio off. Silence resumed, vague and tumultuous even as the streets settled into quaint numbered blocks of lawn divided by hydrangea shrubs. Unbroken, it expanded into intensified uneasiness: a fugue in five silences, Elizabeth thought, and wished for the comfort of sound.

When they pulled into the driveway of the rental cottage, Isabelle very softly asked, "I should try to grow up?"

It was neither a statement nor a question. No one could answer her. Then she stepped out of the car and walked into the cottage, which incidentally was adorable, and should have made everyone happy, and which Elizabeth had spent a long time finding online. Instead of admiring it, however, everyone bent to the task of clearing out the car. After Lucy and Caroline went inside and Elizabeth's arms were full of bright plastic beach bags and pillows and a box of children's books, Adelia cornered her behind the car and said in the most terrifying tone Elizabeth had ever heard, "*Who do you think you are?*"

Elizabeth stared. She was at a loss, because she had done *nothing* but try to be strong. She had been Adelia's only ally in this, and now Adelia had turned on her and was hissing, "*She can be whatever age she wants to be. Just leave her alone.*"

And then Adelia went off to look for Isabelle, leaving Elizabeth to clean out the car.

So that was the low point. Scooping beach toys out of the car, completely alone, while Adelia sympathized with Isabelle for reasons that Elizabeth couldn't understand. Her children were hauntingly quiet all afternoon. They were soul-stricken in the inexplicable way that affects only children, for reasons that adults have long since forgotten how to feel, so that when she went into their room to ask how they liked it, they murmured obedient necessities, trying to reassure her, and went back to playing a secret game. Elizabeth felt useless, standing in the doorway, wondering when, in the process of this harrowing summer, her daughters had gotten so close. And then she went back outside, through the front porch with its rocking chairs, to the yard with its white picket fence where she had imagined she would spend the last weeks of the summer feeling less abandoned and angry.

Then Diana pulled up in the rental car, and while the others unpacked, Margaux got out and joined Elizabeth in the yard to survey her temporary garden. They stood there in the crabgrass, she and her mother, for a long time. Elizabeth refused to say a word. If her mother wasn't going to talk, she wasn't going to, either, but then two minutes later Elizabeth said, "I forgive you, Mom." Margaux didn't say a fucking thing. So Elizabeth revised her opinion and said, "I don't forgive you, Mom. I absolutely *do not* for*give* you."

Margaux's eyes were fixed on the hedge of hydrangeas across the street, in the yard of their new neighbors. "No, you shouldn't."

Elizabeth stared at her, because that was the first real *response* she had gotten from Margaux since she was about twenty-six years old and had just had Caroline. Twenty-six years old! It was too young—she wanted to scream this across the water to the younger version of herself—but she had been such a motherless girl, and she was so excited to be loved by Mark, and she was hoping to be a proper adult. Now her mother was with her, and Elizabeth had so many questions, she didn't know how to begin. Already Margaux's face had been wiped blank. As though no motherly words had come out of her mouth, she started moving around the perimeter of the fence, and then she wandered around to the backyard, behind the screened-in porch, to inspect the flower bed there. Elizabeth trailed behind like a little girl, wishing she would deliver more lines.

"Mom," she said when the silence was too much, "Mom, I feel so angry."

Margaux bent down at the edge of the bed and pulled out a weed by the roots.

"Mom, I feel so *old*. It's too soon to feel like this."

She was talking to herself, because Margaux was entirely devoted to the task of pulling weeds. But since she was already having a solo conversation, she kept at it, realizing that there was something soothing about having a conversation with your mother, even if she'd tuned you out.

"I can't remember what it was like to be young." She considered her mother's back, her dark hair pulled into a bun, and felt a frantic reaction of hollowed-out love. "Even when I was young, I felt old. You called me the tough one, remember?" Margaux didn't turn around. She pulled another handful of weeds, shaking the soil out of their roots. "Mom, do you remember telling me that I was the tough one?" she asked again, and Margaux leaned back on her heels and looked up at Elizabeth. Her eyes widened, as if for a moment she recognized that this was her daughter whom she had lost on the way.

Elizabeth drew a quick breath, startled by the presence of her mother's gaze, then blurted out, "You used to say that I was the tough one. As though that was my *thing*. But was I more than that?"

"I wanted that," Margaux said, wiping a strand of hair away from her temple with the back of her wrist. "For you. You were so little, and I worried you'd feel lonely. I hoped you'd be tough."

Elizabeth stared. She was literally brimming with questions, and she wanted to embrace her mother, and for some reason she wanted to remind her that she didn't show up for the high school production of *Don Quixote* in which Elizabeth played Dulcinea. Which was ridiculous, because Margaux didn't show up for *any* plays and probably had no idea that Elizabeth was an actress. That was fine. Elizabeth had to remind herself that was fine, because toughness was a thing Margaux *wanted* for her, not some terrible part of her core. So Elizabeth said, "What was I like, Mom? Do you remember? Do you remember me?" All at once the idea of someone remembering what she had been like before all this, what the original version of her had been like, was very important to her. It was *crucial* to her, and if her mother could just remember, Elizabeth felt as though she could start all over again. All these things were spilling out of Elizabeth even as she saw that Margaux had checked out and was focused on weeding the garden. She looked up once more, but this time she seemed annoyed, as if Elizabeth were intruding and she had no *idea* what this chattery person was talking about. The motherly interlude had passed as quickly as that.

Elizabeth stood up and let her weed. She took a deep breath. She closed her eyes and heard her mother say it again: *I wanted that for you*. The sweetness of it washed over her, and suddenly she smelled the ocean, the enormous soft sweep of it, and when she opened her eyes, she realized that she could see it through the gap between two houses, a shading of pale sand into blue that became deeper as it moved closer to the sky.

Chapter 18

William sat on the front porch and rocked, slowly. He did not like rocking chairs. They made him feel like an infant or an elderly man. And yet there were no other types of chairs on the porch. Margaux was kneeling in the front yard, coaxing a rose up a stake using brown twine. They had been living at the beach only a week and already she had made something out of the garden. Last week she mentioned roses, so William brought her eighteen cuttings from the garden emporium. They were so leafless and stark that William couldn't imagine them coming back to life. For a week after planting the branches, Margaux kept them covered in mason jars. A garden of glass jars lining the fence, alien and lunatic, but when she removed them, the cuttings had sprouted leaf buds, hard and bright as enamel.

At this point in William's life, Margaux's devotion to the garden was interesting to watch. When they were young, it had only wounded his pride. When he brought her back to the house on Little Lane, he was overflowing with pride. He was giving her the house of his childhood, the largest one on the hill. A house that had inspired his ambition, a house that made him think of pilgrims and the open sea. It was his father's house. He wanted Margaux to enjoy it. He wanted her to cherish its every brave angle.

He could tell from the start that she did not identify with the house. She wandered through it as though visiting a museum with strict rules about touching the exhibits. She was never a good housekeeper; she accumulated trinkets and cared for them assiduously, but she never cleaned the furniture, so that under her tenure, dust began to pile on all the old artifacts of Adair life until William finally hired a cleaning woman. Once the cleaning woman took over dusting the trinkets, Margaux focused her attentions outside. This hurt him. Almost from the moment his father died, William had looked forward to making the house his own. His and Margaux's family home. But she gravitated outdoors. From the start, she was moving away.

She planted peonies in the beds under the kitchen windows. Then she dug a bed around the outside crescent of the patio and filled it with irises and foxgloves. The summer she was pregnant with Elizabeth, she dug out the pond. He worried every day that she would damage the baby, but no matter how many injunctions he delivered, she returned each morning with her shovel to dig. By the time Elizabeth was born, Margaux had filled it with water, with lilies and goldfish and the copper fountain in the shape of a bullfrog.

Once she moved out to the garden, she never moved back in. Not to eat toast in the breakfast nook, not to feel the cool marble of the dining room floor under her bare feet, not to sit by the fire under the arched ceiling of the living room, not even to care for the potted ferns that he carried into the kitchen. When she was pregnant with Isabelle, she looked up from her book and asked if they could move to another house. William dismissed the comment as one of those whims that women come up with when they're carrying a child. How could she want to leave this house, his childhood home? After that, she was distant for a while, but he figured she'd work through whatever had gotten caught in her mind.

Now, as he watched her from his rocking chair, William understood that Margaux never did. She never crossed back over that distance that opened when she asked if they could move. He dismissed her and she never returned. In the days after Izzy's accident, Margaux had taken to wandering downstairs with her purse tucked under her arm to ask, with a worried look on her face, when they were going. "Are we leaving?" she'd ask whomever was closest. As though after almost twenty years, she'd picked up that conversation right where they'd left off, her question about moving unanswered. Who would have known that such a question could linger so long?

At first, William blamed the renovation for her lack of affection. If he'd brought his young bride back to the original—before the lightning fire, when it was built out of shingles rather than new stucco, when it was so big and shadowy that, as a boy, William imagined ghosts in the unused bedrooms—she would have fallen in love with its history. But not even the hush of the original carriage house had awakened her desire to stay. William had always taken the carriage house's magic for granted. From the moment he first walked through its old wooden doors, he understood its power. So did Adelia. But that ancient gravity was lost on Margaux. William brought her out there several times to show her the intricacies of its architecture. Once, after Diana was born, he hired a sitter, packed a cold supper and a bottle of white wine, and laid out a picnic blanket on the floor. At the hour when late-afternoon light filtered in through the owl's nest so that dust motes tumbled in illuminated rays, he blindfolded Margaux and led her out to the carriage house. The picnic was all laid out. But when he removed the blindfold, she looked startled and lost. His heart broke. He couldn't avoid the regret in her face. He tried to forget it while he poured the glasses of wine. He tried not to think about it while he unwrapped the ham sandwiches, while he laid out paper napkins and porcelain plates.

She ate only a bite of her sandwich. "This place makes me so sad," she said. "It's never been lived in. It's lovely, of course, but it's been vacant from the start."

And then Anita Schmidt discovered that the carriage house was on her land, and that was that. No, and then Isabelle Adair burned the carriage house down to the ground, and truly, that was finally that.

Adelia came out of the house with a glass of lemonade. Behind her, the screen door banged twice against its frame. She handed the glass to William and folded her arms. "I'm going, William," she said. It was Sunday; she'd have to go back to work in the morning. He looked up at her and saw that she'd followed his gaze out to Margaux, kneeling in front of her roses. "You'll be okay until Friday?" Adelia asked, still looking at Margaux.

"Of course." There was another silence that William knew he should fill, yet he had no idea what to say.

"She's already made the garden beautiful," Adelia said.

"She has a way with plants."

Adelia pursed her lips. She had been angry for some time, ever since she'd broached the subject of sending Margaux to a home. The word "home," used in that sense, made William shudder. Homes were for stray animals and psychotics. Houses, angular and brave: those were the structures for humans to live in. To be sent to a home was something Margaux had asked for several times after her diagnosis, but William wouldn't hear of it. His wife belonged in his house. She was so young. There were tests to be done, confirmations to be had. And even if the diagnosis was final,

William could care for his wife in her illness. When she got lost after one of her walks, he hired Louise. That was his decision. At some point Margaux stopped asking to go. Only after Izzy's accident, when Margaux's confusion deepened and she started perambulating the house with her purse, did Adelia bring the topic up.

It happened a month or so after she'd moved from the guest room into his bed on the night of Izzy's accident. They never actually slept together, but they both harbored an unspoken grudge about the fact that the change came on such a horrible night. William—and Adelia, too, he was sure—wished he could take it back. Save such a thing for a less fallen evening or never let it happen at all. And yet neither of them could summon the words to ask for belated reprieve. At night, he could feel her watching him from her side of the bed. He turned away from her. During the day, she hovered more closely, expecting something. He held her hand sometimes, drawing it close to him. A hand that had been with him his whole life. There was nothing he could say. When she asked if it was time to think about putting Margaux in a home, he snapped at her. "She's my *wife,*" he said, and Adelia walked away. Two days later she returned and suggested that maybe they should all go somewhere for a while, just to get away. He was more receptive to the idea than he could have expected. The girls were happy to be closer to water, and for whatever reason Margaux had been preparing all summer for such a trip, so when they told her the car was waiting, she didn't even ask where they were heading. When they got to the beach, William was surprised by how comfortable he found it. He could barely remember why he had always resisted his wife's desire to leave. Adelia—Breacon Adelia, born and raised—hovered around, displaced, and while he didn't want to hurt her, he knew she had no place in this house.

Now Adelia stood on the front porch, a small metal suitcase in her hands, waiting for William to ask her to stay. William rocked. How can you ask a woman such as Adelia to stay in a house such as this, with its rocking chairs and its wall-to-wall carpets, with Margaux coaxing her plants?

"I'm taking Diana with me," Adelia said. "I'll drive her to the airport tomorrow."

William winced. "She's coming back next week?" he asked, trying not to think too hard about Diana's belated efforts.

"Yes. I'll bring her with me on Friday. She gets back from Austin on Wednesday, but she set up a meeting with Wayne Contractors to go over the plans."

"I wish you wouldn't let her go."

"Well." Adelia said, snapping her face shut.

They remained together on the porch in silence, until Adelia drew an audible breath. She was disappointed in him, he knew. But he was too tired to say an elaborate goodbye. He rocked back and forth.

"Well," she said again. "I've given a grocery list to Louise." And then she moved off, her heels clicking down the front walk. At the gate she waved to Margaux, who stopped her work and lifted a gloved hand. Adelia looked back at William, one strand of her neat hair lifted up by the wind.

"Goodbye, Adelia," he mouthed, but she couldn't decipher the movement of his lips, so a look of terrible confusion crossed her face. She turned and ducked into the car, and Diana hurried out of the house with her bag and the excited flush that had come over her since she started sketching again.

"Bye, Dad," she said, kissing him on the cheek. "Wish me luck on Tuesday." She ran out to Margaux and knelt beside her. Margaux looked up; William hoped she was present enough to say goodbye to her middle child. The moment was too brief to know.

Diana hugged her mother and followed Adelia out to the car, and then doors closed behind them and the car slid away, leaving William alone with his absent wife, his two remaining daughters, and the children of Elizabeth's recent divorce.

Margaux moved between rose plants. Her determination to draw a garden out of this soil touched him. Here, in this bare place, where trees were stunted by salt. Where houses were permitted a single story of height. Where sand swept across the street and settled into the crabgrass, where the women wore bathing suits covered by shorts when they shopped at the grocery store, flip-flops slapping their heels. He was touched by Margaux's drive to lay down roots in front of this house when a Greyhound bus stopped four times a day across the street and angular Russian girls who worked as maids at the Sea Shell Motel embarked and disembarked, their faces pimply and blank above their polyester uniforms. When all along the street, neighbors hung American flags across their balconies and large-bellied men mowed scraggly lawns, sockless in their Docksiders.

William rocked, and considered his wife. Her determination was touching, yes. But still, William knew that the Adairs could not rebuild in this place, where the streets were arranged in a scientific grid and the houses laid flat as the sand. Where renters came and went and there was no recollection of grandparents who stayed, no remembrance of family here before anything else was built or torn down. The Adairs could continue, of course. They could continue here as comfortably as possible, but there would be no going back to the kind of family they were when they lived in the house his grandfather built. In the end, perhaps that was for the best. Perhaps his children could feel happy here, where there could be no going back to what they were in the past.

Chapter 19

Rock Harbor was boring, but at least there was water, and now Louise had the novel to keep her occupied. She watched everything that occurred in the rental house with an eagle eye. She imagined her tiny bedroom was a writer's den, and adopted a writerly schedule. She woke up at six and took a run on the empty beach, avoiding landed jellyfish the size of frying pans. From seven to nine she wrote, eating peaches until her stomach hurt. At nine she brought Margaux her breakfast, which Margaux preferred to eat alone. At the Rock Harbor house, Margaux had dropped some of her recent anxieties about getting ready to leave, falling back into the routines of her customary solitude. This was helpful, because it allowed Louise to return to her writer's den after the breakfast delivery. At this point in the morning, she took care to leave the door open a crack for maximal spying efficiency. Next she applied a Crest Whitestrip and settled in to wait.

The first rush of motion passed through when Elizabeth herded the girls downstairs to be fed before camp. There had been three camps so far: two weeks of tennis camp, and now a camp for aspiring marine biologists. The pre-camp rush was sometimes interesting—there was the morning when Lucy renamed her cereal options Honey Slut Cheerios and Golden Damns—but it wasn't the children Louise was interested in. She watched Elizabeth carefully. Since the move to the shore, she seemed to have gotten things together a bit. There was less to-do about minor events. She'd joined an experimental theater group at the Rock Harbor Community Center, and she carried a pocket-sized notebook everywhere, which she filled with ideas for performance art. She sat down more; in Breacon she'd seemed allergic to chairs. Now there was less rushing past, bracelets clattering, scarves flying. The experimental theater group practiced three nights a week. During the day, Elizabeth spent hours hunting for props at local garage sales. A heap of ancient housewares—including an old rusted refrigerator—began to accumulate in the garage.

It was a strenuously recreational universe they lived in, Elizabeth and her daughters. There was an ever renewing supply of camps, acting projects, and minutely scheduled trips to the beach. They were active, at least. They had none of the others' inertia. Once they had gotten themselves out of the house, a hole opened in the mornings. William ate breakfast in the kitchen only if Adelia were there, and her presence had waned. She came down the first two weekends that the Adairs stayed in Rock Harbor, but she never materialized the next weekend and came for an afternoon the following Saturday. Louise took careful note of this visitation schedule. The first weekend Adelia was there, she made a big show of staying in the downstairs bedroom, but Louise caught her sneaking upstairs, guilty in her nightgown. So she was sleeping with the old dog after all. This gave Louise hope for the plot of her novel, but sadly, the next weekend Adelia failed to arrive, and the weekend after that she came only long enough to let Diana visit with her family and then to cart her back to Breacon to continue "work" on the nonexistent carriage house.

Adelia's absence was strange because she had been such a constant presence in the house on Little Lane. Why risk neighborhood scorn in Breacon, then refrain from visiting the rental house? When Adelia did show up, she was strangely tentative. On Little Lane she ordered everyone around as though directing a ten-million-dollar movie every time she cooked a rubbery chicken. She was so bossy that Louise had privately taken to calling her "Adelia Big-deal-ia." In Rock Harbor, however, Adelia hung around the outskirts of conversations, watching William, blinking, looking lost. This new development presented a massive hurdle for the novel. How could Louise explain the undramatic dribbling off? Her tagline started to falter: lifelong friend moves in while demented mother is still living upstairs, then lifelong friend moves out, sadly, but without much dramatic ado.

Louise found herself wishing that William would buck up a bit. He obviously loved Adelia. Once Louise witnessed him reach across the table after breakfast to hold her hand without speaking, just looking across at her and holding on as if he could sit there forever. If he wanted her so badly, why couldn't he get her to stay? Instead, he settled into his Rock Harbor routine, showing as much spine as a jellyfish. In the mornings, when Adelia wasn't present, he took his breakfast up to sit with Isabelle; in the afternoons, he prepared himself lunch on the screened-in porch. For hours, he watched Margaux garden. He took to going out and attempting to help, kneeling beside her on a green foam pad he purchased at the garden emporium so that his knees wouldn't get dirty. At first Margaux packed up her things and moved inside as soon as he hitched up his khakis and knelt on his pad. He learned to keep a little distance, placing himself at some remove from Margaux's current project. He figured out that it was better not to insist too much on his own usefulness to her garden. Soon Margaux let him kneel beside her, even occasionally instructing him in the art of trimming herbs or staking tomatoes. Afterward, William proudly hung up his pad in the garage and removed himself to the screened-in porch to gloat over his progress as a gardener.

After a week of camping in the bedroom, reading children's books and eating melted peanut butter sandwiches that William carried up to her, Isabelle came downstairs. She'd lost weight and somehow looked younger since her accident. The first thing she asked for when she came downstairs was a new tennis racket, and as soon as the cast came off, she and William spent their mornings at the public courts. This became the peak moment of activity in the Adair family schedule, which faded into stillness toward the end of the afternoon. During the Adair family dinner, which Louise attended through a crack in her door, Elizabeth spouted the narrative of her illustrious day. The eminent architect pulled out weeds and his Hollywood-actress daughter performed at the community center, while his teenager read children's books and toyed with her food. William didn't seem unduly perturbed. He wasn't leaping around for joy, that was for sure, but he wasn't beating his fists on the walls. For the sake of her book, Louise wanted to remind him that these were not lofty occupations. She could not write a novel about a mildly content puller of weeds.

Louise worried about this for several days, until she came to the conclusion that all ambitions—no matter how grand—are incomprehensible to people who don't have them. You have to be caught up in the dream of something to believe in its importance. As soon as you take one step out of your dream, you suddenly know that it was only an excuse to avoid the fact that you're just another sad old tosser living out your boring life before you die.

It takes guts to face life without any ambitions, facing reality each and every ambitionless day. Knowing all this, Louise began to feel that she should give up on the goal of writing a book, until she decided that her book would be about a family whose ambitions had dried out, and therefore it would still be a real contribution.

If she didn't let the Adair family dinner get her down, Louise could stay in, microwave herself a bowl of rice with melted cheese and ketchup, and read Margaux's diaries all night. She'd pillaged the entire stack from Margaux's desk when the family moved down to the shore, and she kept them in a plastic crate under her bed. She perused them religiously. After reading about Dr. Worthington's original suggestion that Margaux might merely be depressed, Louise started to wonder whether Margaux had suspected her illness before she was diagnosed. Maybe she'd been waiting to inherit her mother's disease and had found it in herself before it could be medically confirmed. Her decline had been monumentally slow, even for an early-onset patient. She failed several comprehension tests, but in the beginning Dr. Worthington wasn't convinced her condition was Alzheimer's. It would have been impossible to know for sure. Unless you bored a hole in her skull and captured her brain on X-ray film, you couldn't know which parts of Margaux's tissue had faded to white.

Later, the voids in her memory became increasingly obvious. In her diaries, she took to occasionally asserting that Isabelle hadn't been born yet. Before Louise was hired, Margaux got seriously lost twice while taking a walk. Once they found her stuck in the middle of Kennedy Drive, cars screeching around her. And after Izzy's accident, with the anxious packing of bags and waiting by the door, Margaux acted more and more like a traditional patient lost in the middle stage of Alzheimer's disease. Still, there was an odd degree of watchfulness involved in the forgetting of the early diaries. Louise suspected that the seeds of the disease had lurked for some time in her mind before they took root. Pre-Alzheimer's Alzheimer's. Who knew how many of us had it? This idea also depressed Louise, so that between Margaux's anticipation of decline and William's blank acceptance of his family's fallen position, Louise sometimes had the urge to go out for a drink.

There was a tiny local bar called the Grubby Tub where Louise gravitated in these instances, to sit in a dark corner with one of Margaux's journals and a Guinness, trying to revive herself. Sometimes an Aussie tennis pro with a peeling nose and a yellow Jeep Wrangler arrived, each night with a different girl who always looked about seventeen. When he sat down, he winked at Louise, recognizing a fellow citizen, and once or twice he bought her a drink, but Louise was absorbed in the journals and didn't have time to run around in search of diasporic Aussies to shag. The second weekend that Adelia did not stay at the beach, however, the novel hit a wall and Louise fell into a new depth of malaise. That night at the Tub, she felt compelled to replace her Guinness with whiskey, at which point the tennis pro showed up on his own.

It was a tired old drunken story. Somehow Louise found herself back at his apartment, drinking crap red wine, smoking weed, reading him passages out of Margaux's journals, drinking more wine, waiting patiently while he pawed around. At some point a glass of wine was spilled. There was excessive laughter of the kind that hurts your distorted face after it dies down. Then there was more weed, more pawing, more wine, until Louise finally fell asleep in his asymmetrical arms.

In the morning, she woke up and took stock of the situation. She hadn't brushed her teeth, and her mouth tasted like an old sponge. She sat up: explosions in her cerebellum. On the floor there were two wineglasses, one broken, an empty bottle, and

Margaux's journal, ruined by a wine stain the size of a tennis ball. Louise groaned. She struggled to swallow, then picked up the journal and inspected it more closely. Oddly, the wine stain on its pages made her want to cry, and if she weren't so dehydrated she might have. She felt literally homesick, as if her distance from home had translated directly into cottonmouth and the throbbing in her temples. Oddly, she had the distinct feeling that she had betrayed her own mother by having read Margaux's journals to a stranger and then allowing him to douse them with wine. The bottom right corner of the page was unreadable:

November 1993

Today I asked William to send me to a home for the final time. I would like to remember that. I asked him over and over again, as if I didn't remember asking him only yesterday. Today I finally stopped. It was for their good that I wanted to go. I am aware that it is hurtful every day to be reminded that your mother can't remember the logic of your bond. It would be better for them to be with Adelia; she has a memory as loyal as an elephant's. But I can't insist anymore. He hasn't wrapped his head around the reality. He feels that nothing dramatic has changed. I want to explain to him that it's because there was never an enormous change. It was in me from the start. I've adjusted to it well. They say people with a strong sense of identity make the worst Alzheimer's patients. It's lucky, then, I suppose, that I was always a little apart from myself. It's only a surprise that William didn't notice from the start; I was not a woman with whom he should have had children. It was my fault, too; I thought maybe I'd become more real. Tod
went to the kitchen and there was a cake that said "Happy Twelfth Birthd
that Isabelle was born twelve years ago. It was a startling recollec
strange, but I sometimes think that Izzy hasn't been bor
Margaux hasn't yet been born. When are we born in

rather not stay here and fill her with doubt. I c
me stay. If it were not for him I could just disap
whether or not to remember me, but in any case they'd

Louise's chest ached. Forever, the bottom quadrant of Margaux in November 1993 was lost because Louise had taken it upon herself to shag a tennis pro. Because yet again Louise had forgotten the importance of her task. Because Louise was drunk and stupid and never could keep hold of any motivation, and this was why even a person as pathetic as Bradley didn't want to marry her. Because she was careless. She couldn't hold on to ambitions. Even her ambition to let go of ambitions got ruined. She was the kind of person who could discover a secret journal of forgotten things and decide to write a novel about it, then get drunk and spill wine on its pages, ruining the one thing she'd discovered and wanted to keep.

Chapter 20

For Elizabeth's experimental performance, William selected a pair of white khaki pants and a royal blue polo shirt. The belt he chose was embroidered with yellow whales. He had never thought of himself as a beach man, and he felt no different even after over a month in Rock Harbor. He did not like to sit on the sand. He did not like the endless leisure or how often people commented on the precise stage of their relaxation. He did not like how the only tennis courts in town were a set of eight old concrete courts, cracked by the sun and surrounded by a ten-foot wire fence as though they were basketball courts in an underprivileged neighborhood. At the beach, William was a man living in exile. He was born on Little Lane. He was a boy on Little Lane, he grew up on Little Lane, and he raised his children on Little Lane. When they packed him up in the rental car and shipped him off to the beach, there had been no other option but to leave his history there, on Little Lane, with the ruins of the carriage house.

Regardless, life continued. He was still a good-looking man. Outwardly, there was no visible sign that part of him was missing. There was no reason for him to give up entirely just because an important element of himself had been amputated and left behind. His resolve in this regard had been fortified by the recent improvements in his family's appearance. Since taking up with her performance art group, Elizabeth had started wearing simpler clothes. The flailing scarves had made him nervous, as if she were Amelia Earhart getting ready for a misguided flight. Now she wore sporty tank tops and jeans, and she had developed a healthy tan. Comforted by the thought of Elizabeth's improvements, William pulled a pair of yellow sport socks onto his feet, then slipped them into his Docksiders. He would not go to Elizabeth's performance sockless, though so many of the men in Rock Harbor had dispensed with socks for the summer. Even if it was an experimental art performance, William would not sink so low.

He examined himself again in the mirror. He was ready to go. No one could say that he had attended his daughter's performance in anything less than a dignified outfit. He carried himself down the stairs as an optimistic man carries himself, then joined his family in the Acura with a cheerful salute. He was pleased that they were going together, despite the fact that, in general, he did not like experimental things. His attitude toward them was this: experiment when no one is watching. Once your experiment was proved, he was ready to admire it. And yet there was a definite glow to Elizabeth, and less of those scarves, and William was determined to applaud the development. When he climbed into the car, which Diana was driving, he noted that the rest of his family had also improved since coming to the beach. This alone was enough to make William resolve to continue at the cottage. Their looks, earlier this summer on Little Lane, had caused him to question everything from his genes to the state of his country. Because his children had always represented life in America to

William, and they had always been hopeful-looking and fresh. In their mature years, it began to look as if they didn't care about anything at all. Having taken their looks for granted, they had allowed them to fade away. Isabelle, for instance, might have emerged from her hospital bed deformed, because she simply hadn't cared. Thankfully, she did not, except that she was missing a spleen and part of her collarbone was now a shard of titanium.

William glanced at her in the rearview mirror. She was gazing out the window. Something about her had settled since the accident. She bristled less. She wore sundresses and spent whole days at the beach, reading her books. Nearly every morning, she asked him to play tennis with her, and this was certainly a positive development. He started playing against her in his Docksiders, but recently, she had gotten good enough that he asked Diana to pick up his tennis shoes on her next trip back to Breacon.

For that matter, something had changed about Diana also. In the recent past, looking at Diana had given him a stomachache. Arthur Schmidt was right when he said she had changed beyond recognition from the girl who was student body president. She was still different—quieter and less athletic—but she had improved. He wished she would stay more often, without running back to Breacon to dredge up the carriage house, lugging tote bags of architecture textbooks. She indulged in excessive studiousness, and Little Lane was a depressingly hopeless cause for her to take on, but at least she had found her determination. She looked less perpetually limp. In recent weeks she had even developed a tan. He would have liked to have asked Arthur whether she was still changed beyond all recognition; for his part, William couldn't tell.

When they pulled into the parking lot of the Lee W. Greenfield Rock Harbor Arts Center, Adelia and Margaux were waiting on the sidewalk. Adelia was wearing sunglasses. Margaux had on a large straw hat that suited her well, particularly at the beach. A straw hat and a fluttery dress. When William first met her, she was sitting in the back row in art history class, spreading out a lunch for herself that was old-fashioned in its intricate presentation. She was a woman from another time in history. A more delicate time, or so he had imagined. He was twenty-one years old; what had he known about anything? She was, at any rate, exactly opposite Adelia, which at that point was enough to satisfy William. Adelia's refusal had stung him; in the aftermath, it was pleasant to impress a woman such as Margaux, with her nervous fingers and artistic eye for impractical details.

After all these years, it was strange to see her standing beside Adelia. Adelia watched the Acura pull up as though it were an incoming volley, as though she were ready to take it early, facing it down. Margaux gazed off into the wind. They were like two birds from entirely incompatible ecosystems, nestled on one branch. It was for his sake that they had both flown here. William knew this, and although he did not like the beach, he was not ungrateful for the unlikely migration they had made on his account.

When they walked into the arts center lobby, William appreciated that no one who saw them would think they were an unattractive flock. One might go so far as to say that they were handsome in their way. It wasn't the same surge of pride he'd felt when the girls were younger, when he took them out in a gleaming troupe and knew that everyone who saw them would be dazzled. But still. In the arching, spare lobby of the arts center, surrounded by glass and circulating strangers, they were a striking little tribe. William knew, of course, that it was considered vain to care so much about looks. In his case, it wasn't mere vanity. He believed that looks were representative of deeper qualities. He trusted—and he was not sure how others could bear to live without such belief—that a person's deepest self must be represented in his outward appearance. If not, then the world was a deceitful place. The fact that his family was attractive again settled him as he had not felt settled in weeks.

He chose a seat with Margaux on his left and Isabelle on his right. It appeared, from the program on his chair, that Elizabeth would perform second, in an experimental piece entitled "The Divorce." The first piece was entitled "A Diary of My Life in Sensation." The third and final piece was called "Birth." William did not look forward to either the first or the third. He did not like when people forced their diaries upon you, and he did not like the vaginal aggressiveness that defined much of the theater to which his daughter had exposed him. He allowed himself a moment to wish that his daughter had joined a Shakespearean troupe rather than an experimental gang. He had once seen her play Goneril in a production of *King Lear* and had been deeply moved by her regal carriage. He liked to imagine each of his three daughters in Shakespearean roles. Diana once could have played Portia, doling out mercy and punishment in the Venetian court. Isabelle could have been any beautiful heroine she desired to play. They tried to deny it, but they had presence, all of them.

And yet this piece—"The Divorce"—meant something to Elizabeth, and it was part of the improvement that he had seen in all his daughters since coming to the beach, so he settled into his yellow plastic chair and focused his eyes on the empty center, which soon would be occupied by the Diarist of Sensations. She arrived in a lab coat. Her face was unremarkable, and her body was shaped like an egg. "Please reach under your seat," she said, and William grudgingly did as he was told. There he found a glass jar, which he pulled out and held in his lap. "Please smell the contents of your jar, then pass it to the left." William opened his jar and smelled: nothing. From its viscous cherry-colored wash, he could see that it was cough syrup, and yet even this knowledge did not produce the illusion of scent. The next jar that Isabelle passed him was full of lotion. Again, nothing. The next contained a pile of grass cuttings. The smell of grass once reminded him—while walking across the golf course—of tennis and possibility. And now nothing: a nothing he would have to live with.

When the smelling exercise was over, the diarist placed empty watercooler bottles, their necks sawed off and their outer plastic smeared with Vaseline, over each audience member's head. Sealed inside his helmet, William could hear his own breathing. He looked around. Isabelle's face was blurred, but he could tell that she was smiling at him, so he smiled back. On his left, Margaux's face was distant, disappearing slowly while he watched. He reached out for her hand and found it on her lap. She let him take it. Her head was a watercooler bottle. They were both strange beings, headless and blurred. He squeezed her hand. It was like seeing her through tears, like seeing her when she had faded further than she already had. He wanted to hold her close. When the Diarist arrived to remove his helmet, Margaux's sudden clarity took his breath away. And then she released his hand, and the group was subjected to more sensory abrasions that William was able to withstand because he understood that if he waited long enough, Elizabeth would arrive, and the world would resolve itself into the intensity of focusing on one of his girls.

"The performance will conclude with a slow dance," the Diarist announced, wheeling out a coatrack laden with gray wool jackets. "Please dance with someone you do not know." William considered staying in his seat. He did not like when artists demanded that he participate in their performances. But Margaux was standing and walking over to the jackets, and when she put one on, she looked just like a young girl wearing her beau's coat on a cool night. Suddenly, William found that he, too, was standing, and then he was asking her if she would dance with him. The lights went out and an old waltz played. Above them, a disco ball cast flecks of light on the walls and the floor and the ceiling, and William pulled Margaux close to him so that her head was against his chest. He could almost imagine the way her hair used to smell when they were both young and flecked with a different kind of light. He held her against his chest, and after he danced with her for a while, a light mood struck him and he stepped back and twirled her away from him, the way they danced when they were young. She twirled twice in the rotating lights before her hand slipped out of his and she stopped twirling and looked at him from across a widening space.

The music dropped off and the lights switched on, and in the normal glare of the Lee W. Greenfield Rock Harbor Arts Center, William realized that Adelia was watching him, and had probably been watching the whole time he danced with Margaux and tried to remember the scent of her hair. He moved over to say something to her, but she became livid with energetic motion and a great bustling return to her seat. William, too, returned to his chair. He sat there in the harsh light, caught between performances, ignored by Adelia, and grew irritated again that he hadn't been able to smell the cuttings of grass. It wasn't long before Elizabeth came out, wheeling a refrigerator on a dolly behind her. William focused on his daughter, wearing an old-fashioned dress and bright red lipstick, her hair coiled in a bun. She faced the pea-green refrigerator in silence. Neither one of them moved.

The refrigerator became hateful as the silence deepened. It was too rectangular. His daughter was so detailed. Each feature of her face asserted itself, important, beside the bluntness of its right angles. The refrigerator glared; Elizabeth did nothing. William's toes tensed in his shoes. Time stretched out, expanding, compressing him so that the tension spread up his legs and into his diaphragm. If no one did anything, William was going to have to stand. He would have to go outside for air. He glanced around. No one else seemed as infuriated as he was. He wanted to batter that refrigerator into the ground. How dare it hunker there, unmoved, in the presence of his child. He was going to have to stand, but just as he started to, she moved. She hit it with her palm. William breathed. Again she hit it with her hand, then took off her high-heeled shoe and hurled it at the pea-green monster. The shoe bounced off, clattering on the floor. Elizabeth left the stage and returned with a crowbar. William loved the crowbar's sleekly evil shape. Elizabeth lifted it high above her head and let it fall on the refrigerator's crown. She did it again and again. William breathed in and out. This was motion. This was something *happening*. This was his daughter fighting, beautifully.

She was tearing into the refrigerator. One of the metal hinges on its door sprang off and flew across the stage. The door swung open like a broken wing and revealed the bare skeleton of its inner shelves. Elizabeth took to its side. She left great visible dents in its metal frame. The crowbar was coated in pea-green paint. To his right, Isabelle was laughing, and William was so relieved that he could have braved the flying crowbar to hug his daughter, whose hair had come out of its bun. She continued to fight. The refrigerator had taken new shape, as though crouching closer to the ground, cowering in fright. There was a great crack and sigh, and then it was falling backward, out of the dolly, onto the ground with a crash that caused a brief sharp pain in William's skull and scared three audience members out of their seats. Elizabeth considered the ruins before her. Then she sighed and dropped her crowbar, but something important had been accomplished. When she faced the audience and said, "The end," William leaped to his feet to applaud.

He was the only one who stood. The rest of the audience stared at him, but he didn't care. He applauded with more vigor. Elizabeth smiled directly at him, and it was the two of them alone. This was his daughter, who had fought for her place. This was his daughter, who was elegant and strong. In front of him, Elizabeth and the battered refrigerator. Behind his eyes, on the floor of his brain, the smoking carriage house, black against the unnaturally illuminated sky, and in front of it Isabelle in her white dress. And then there was Diana, half smiling in the way she did when he picked her up at the airport and she slung her racket bag into the back of the car. They were there, just beyond his reach. Daughters he couldn't quite grasp. He locked his eyes on Elizabeth, triumphant before him. He tried to focus completely while she was there on the stage. For a long time, she looked back at him, and then she looked away. Her eyes flickered over the rest of the crowd, and after she had received her applause, she bent, collected her crowbar, and set to work on clearing the stage.

For a long time he refused to sit. Not even his family stood with him. He was alone. Long after no one was clapping anymore, when Elizabeth had wheeled off the dolly and two strong women in dark clothes had come out to push the refrigerator off the stage, William clapped, until the inner space was empty again and the room was blank, and he knew it was time to sit but he didn't want the feeling to fade into the shell of a memory, like those useless cuttings of grass. Even after he sat, the recollection of having been so stirred remained with him, so he was able to tolerate the sight of a dozen unattractive women chanting in a circle around an overweight person crowned with thorns, who reached into her underpants and took out a chicken egg, then held it up to the audience as though she had done something more impressive than reverse a million years of evolution. Thus should not develop the human female, thought William, refusing to applaud when the troupe finally took their oviparous bows. He felt the presence of his family on both sides of him, women all of them. They were better than that. So much better than an unwieldy person brandishing an egg. Adelia, who had no children of her own, who had loved him fiercely as a snagged tooth. Margaux, whose face had become blurred. And somewhere between the two of them, his three girls. His girls who had somehow slipped away from him but whom he would watch for, every day, as long as he lived, hoping to glimpse them even briefly as they winged their way past.

Chapter 21

As soon as Diana finished the plans, she went back to Breacon to start work. She had her certification from UT, awarded after her defense of a new thesis: "Reconstruction of a Nineteenth-Century Carriage House." Her adviser, surprised by the new direction, congratulated her on having found her voice. On the plane ride back from Austin, Diana sketched memories of the woodwork in the owl's nest. She completed the blueprints in William's basement office; when she was done, she took the train downtown to print them at his firm. Back at the rental house in Rock Harbor, she stayed up late in her seafoam-toned bedroom, finalizing details.

As soon as she signaled to Adelia that she was ready to begin, Adelia drove her back to Breacon, promising to secure the building permits through contacts at work. When they arrived at Little Lane, Adelia dropped her off in the driveway. "You're not staying?" Diana asked. "I'll stay at my house for a while," Adelia told her. "You don't need me here." Then Adelia handed her a checkbook and gave her a kiss on the cheek that was so hard, Diana was certain it would leave a bruise.

While waiting for the permits to come through, she sorted through the building materials she'd salvaged from the fire, before the neighborhood association swept in to clean up the rubble. She kicked the bricks off the tarp she'd spread over them, then lifted it up like a large blue beach towel. Sixteen glass doorknobs from the cabinets along the sidewall. Seven cedar beams that had fallen during the fire and suffered minimal damage; the rest of the wood was useless, but these could be incorporated into the rebuilt structure. She knelt to smell them; first there was an ashy scent, but then she caught the ancient tabernacle smell. There was a stack of the cement slabs that had covered the floor, and the iron light fixture that used to hang from the ceiling. She passed her hands over their cool surfaces, then covered them again with the tarp. She was on her way inside to call the contractor when she saw Arthur emerging from the front door of his house, carrying a bag of trash.

She smiled as soon as she saw him. Her first instinct was to catch him before he disappeared back into the house, so she waved and shouted. He turned and smiled, the same half smile, and this time she crossed the lawn to his driveway.

"Hey there," he said when she reached him, and she wondered whether she should be smiling less drastically. They walked out to the plastic bins on the curb. When he'd thrown out the bag, he shoved his hands into his pockets. "How's Isabelle?"

"She's okay," Diana said. "She got her cast off a couple of weeks ago."

"That's good to hear." He hovered before her, hands in his pockets, so close she could have touched him.

"It's amazing how well she's recovered. She's a little different, I think, but I'm not sure it's bad. She seems less prickly. A little more childish somehow, but I guess that's not the worst that could happen. She's postponing college for a year, to volunteer at Breckenridge." Diana wasn't sure why she was going on like this; there was the possibility that he had asked the question only to be polite. But she worried that if she stopped talking, he'd go back into the house, so she continued to babble. "My dad's already talking about her reapplying to Princeton. Normally Izzy would hate that, but now she seems fine with it. She lights up when he mentions it. Which is so strange for Isabelle. Same thing with tennis. She didn't play for years, but now they go to the courts every morning." With this she abruptly ran out of things to say. Arthur was squinting at her in the brightness of the August sunlight. A space widened between them. Diana realized how much the Adairs had imposed on him this summer, without offering anything in return. "I'm sorry," she said. "You don't need to know all this, do you."

"It's fine. I asked."

"You've got enough to worry about. How's your grandmother?"

"Better. She finished round three of her chemo. The doctors say it went as well as possible."

"How's she taking it?"

"She's been pretty mean," he said, smiling. "She's a little mean already, but she's been a real medal winner this month. I think she's starting to feel better. This morning she thanked me, which was a minor miracle."

"You're good to be here with her," Diana said. "Loyal." The memory of his conversation with Isabelle on the night of the fire caused her to pull up short as soon as she said it. It seemed as though he was considering whether to say something, but she felt him decide against it.

"Will you stay now that she's getting better?" she asked.

"I'm not sure. It's been hard to be here alone. I miss the city.

The new restaurant opens in a month or so, and work is piling up."

She had to remember that he had a life in New York. The kind of life a promising young person is supposed to possess. It was possible that he had a girlfriend whom he was hoping to return to. A girlfriend who would be modern and independent, who didn't live with her parents, struggling to rebuild a nineteenth-century house that her sister had burned to the ground. That was the kind of girlfriend who made sense for Arthur. They'd become such different people, she and Arthur, and yet she was reluctant to let him go. She wanted to keep the small place she'd regained in his life. "You could come visit us at the beach, if you want. It's a real family circus. You'd think it was funny."

"It's hard to imagine the Adairs anywhere other than Little Lane. How is everyone?"

"Oddly enough, they seem fine. Maybe better than they were. My dad hated it at first—he's always been suspicious of vacation—but he's settled into a routine. He plays tennis with Izzy in the mornings. He wears clothes with embroidered nautical themes. Mom's done a rose garden, and tomato plants, and she's filled the whole garage with potted bulbs. Dad even helps her sometimes. It's sweet, seeing them together, weeding side by side. They planted a vegetable garden, and it's just sprouting. He's pretty impressed with himself."

"That's good," Arthur said. "I wouldn't have expected him to be so amenable to a move."

"To be honest, Adelia's the one I feel for most. She's the one who seems really out of place at the beach. She comes back here during the week to work, and when she drives back out, she prowls around in her cardigans, irritated about getting sand in her shoes."

Arthur laughed. "And Elizabeth?"

"She joined a performance art group. Every week she destroys a different household appliance with a crowbar."

"Every week?"

"I know, it's crazy. But the crazier thing is, my dad loves it. He's her biggest fan. He goes to every performance and comes home raving."

"He was always proud of you guys."

Diana caught her breath and looked down at his feet. He was wearing old gray sneakers, the same kind he used to wear as a kid. "Too proud, sometimes," she said. "More proud than we deserved." She could feel him watching her, but she was suddenly too ashamed to look up at his face.

"So why are you still here?" he asked.

"I'm rebuilding the carriage house," she said. "I got my certification. Finally. Apparently, I've found my voice in renovation. I'm 'most expressive in moments of nostalgia for the abandoned past,' as my adviser poetically put it. It turns out I'm incapable of letting things go." She glanced up at his face long enough to see that he was looking away, his expression so distant that it was impossible to deduce what he was thinking. She felt a lump rise in her throat. "Anyway, I finished the plans, so I'm just waiting for the permit. The contractor's meeting me here at noon."

"That's great, Diana," he said. His tone was wistful, as if coming from somewhere far away. "I can't say I'm surprised. But that's really impressive, and I'm happy for you."

She watched his profile. He was squinting off into the space where the carriage house would go up. He seemed thoughtful and sad. Their childhood had fallen so far behind them, and now they were adults, standing in the same driveway, divorced from their previous selves. She remembered with sudden clarity William at the kitchen table, muttering, "He says you've changed so much he hardly recognized you." After the night in the hospital, when she fell asleep on Arthur's familiar shoulder, she had somehow imagined that the time dividing them had closed. That their lives had intersected again, if not romantically, still meaningfully. One disastrous night and she had imagined there was significance between them again. Now she felt herself sinking. "I'm not sure why I'm so stuck on it," she murmured. "I can't think about anything else but rebuilding that carriage house, just as it was, before we ruined it. It's crazy. Even my dad seems to have forgotten about it now."

"Well, it's lucky you won't give up on it, isn't it?" There was an edge to his voice that seemed to surprise him. He turned abruptly to look at her, as if he wished he could catch what he'd said before it reached her. She could feel the heat of a flush creeping into her outdated face and couldn't think of anything to say in response.

"I'm happy Isabelle's better," he said through the terrible silence. His words had the sound of conclusion. "I've been worried about her."

Diana nodded. He had stayed with her that night in the hospital until he knew the surgery went fine and the emergency was over. He stayed for Isabelle's sake, not hers. Only the stupidly nostalgic side of her could have imagined an intersection in the lines of their lives after all these fragmented years.

"I'll see you, okay?" he said, touching her elbow lightly.

"Okay," she said, and when he had disappeared into Anita's house, she was left in the driveway with all the things she might have said years ago, before so much time had passed that saying them would be a useless mistake.

Chapter 22

Adelia's number was 131. She had been waiting in the Permits and Licensing Department of the County Commissioner's Office for an hour and a half for her number to be called, her eyes trained on the TV monitor that summoned the citizens of Bronwyn County to their reckoning. The bag that contained her application—thick with copies of Diana's plans—sat on the floor between her navy ballet flats. When she first sat down, the chosen number was 61; Adelia watched as a handsome young man with a cell phone attached to his belt headed toward doorway number 8. She considered taking out the work she had brought from the office, but her mind was racing, and it was difficult not to be distracted by the progression of the numbers.

It was possible that she might lose him. He had gone off to the shore with Margaux at Adelia's own urging, and the experience had not forced him to acknowledge how badly he wanted to return. At first, when she hatched the plan, she thought, *Let him go off with her. Let him live in the place where she lives, that place she occupies beyond human relation. He'll want to return as soon as he's arrived.* But he was happy at the shore, and Adelia was alone again, as she had been in the apartment in Brooklyn. But this time she had no dream of William to keep her company. In Brooklyn he'd hovered just beyond her grasp; now she'd come back to him. She'd gotten so close that she'd lain with him in his bed, her cheek on his chest, feeling the body that had eluded her so long.

The blinking number moved from 73 to 74, 74 to 75, 75 to 76. If she couldn't bring him back, he'd be gone forever. For ten years she lived close to him, and that was nearly enough. Then she stepped across the threshold into his house, but by that point he was already leaving, following Margaux to the place Margaux had been hoping to go. The chance that she might lose him forever rattled around in Adelia's diaphragm. She was having trouble breathing fully. She got up and walked over to the water fountain, which emitted a dribble so pathetic that her lips brushed the metal spigot as she drank. Over her bent head, the number switched from 98 to 99. Adelia tensed in expectation of some grand resetting that might happen at 100, an apocalyptic shift: 100 turned to 101. She returned to her seat. She sat down and adjusted her skirt, crossing her legs at the ankles. The hem of her skirt—navy blue and pleated—reached the middle of her knees. This was the kind of outfit she'd worn since she was twelve. And now she was in her fifties. Adelia had passed over from her youth without realizing. She'd finally gotten William, only to watch him leave. She closed her eyes and remembered him dancing with Margaux under the mosaic light of that disco ball, his eyes so soft and far away. Adelia had wondered if it was cruel of her to want to yank him back to the world that she lived in. But could she follow him there? Could she cling to him at the beach, watching while he gardened with Margaux, hovering off to one side while they danced under glimmering lights? When she opened her eyes, she looked down at her hands: she had been clutching her own palms so hard, there were eight red crescents left by her nails. Her own ferocity surprised her; determined Adelia had always held on to things too hard.

She watched the neon number move from 128 to 129, 129 to 130, 130 to 132. She blinked. What happened to 131? She waited. 133. Her lips parted; this wasn't right. She waited again. 134. Her mouth was wide open; had they skipped her number entirely? 134 shifted to 135. Adelia Lively stood and looked around at the crowd of passive waiters; had no one else witnessed this event? An elderly man was collecting himself to appear before his maker. Quickly, mercilessly, Adelia hurried to beat him to teller number 3. She flew across the room, soundless, an avenging angel in her pleated skirt and ballet flats. From behind a sheet of glass, the teller looked up from his computer and folded his hands on the desk, awaiting her arrival. His glasses were thick and he peered vulnerably at her, moleish and overexposed, one of those people who could never survive in the wild.

"Excuse me, sir, but my number wasn't called." Adelia told him, taking a seat, leaning toward him.

"Oh, dear," the mole man said. There were pictures of a red-haired woman framed behind him, evidence of a life outside the Permit and Licensing Department. "Your number wasn't called?" He pushed his glasses up the bridge of his nose.

"No, I was skipped." Even as she said it, Adelia perceived the weight of what she had said. She was skipped. She had been skipped over, never pulled up into proper adulthood. The hand that passed over young women and selected some of them to become mothers had hovered over her head and then moved on so that she lived her life alone, waiting, hoping for the hand to return.

"This is my teller," the old man whined from behind her. "This is *my* teller."

"Can you just wait a minute?" Adelia asked without turning around.

"Would you look at that," said the man behind the glass plate, who was squinting at his computer. "You *were* skipped, weren't you?"

"This is my teller!" the man insisted.

"Just wait!" Adelia said.

The mole man flinched; his little red mouth seemed far too sensitive for a fight. His allegiances were torn between the old man and Adelia. "Ma'am, if you could just step aside while I help this gentleman, then I'll get to you right after him."

"I will not wait any longer! My number was before his!"

"Please lower your voice."

"I will not move," she whispered angrily.

The teller blanched. Adelia could tell that his red-haired wife would have performed better in this circumstance; without her, the shortsighted mole man was lost aboveground. He swallowed, then appealed to the man behind Adelia. "Sir, would you mind waiting for just a minute?"

"This is my teller," the old man said again, but he had already given up the fight.

"Fine. I'll be with you in a minute. How can I help you?" The teller shifted his attention back to Adelia.

"I need a B-3 building permit."

"Name?"

"Adelia Lively, Esquire. I am the owner's legal representative."

"ID?" She handed him her license. "You've filled out the application?" Yes, Adelia Lively always filled the appropriate applications. "And the plumber and electrician also filled out their sections? You can give them to me now, with copies of the plans."

Adelia slid these through the crack beneath the teller's glass. He flipped through the pages. "Adair Architecture," he muttered. "Intern, Diana Adair. And who is the supervising architect?"

Adelia stared him down. "William Adair." She refused to blink. He certainly had not agreed to supervise, but now was not the time for moral quibbling. The teller paused, agonizingly, then continued flipping through the application. He seemed satisfied. Effective Adelia, stuck on a fading idea, had hired the appropriate contractors, forged a note to attain the architect's seal, checked with neighborhood association bylaws. The appropriate forms had most definitely been filled out.

Finally, laying aside the paperwork, the teller squinted at his computer, his mouth working. "We're running at about a week for processing right now, assuming everything checks out fine. You should get it in the mail in a week." A receipt printed behind him in fits and starts. Adelia stared, counting, numbers ticking away in her mind. For one week Adelia would wait in Breacon while William withdrew. One week, and then Diana would be ready to build. The contractors were waiting with their largest team. One week and two months for the house to go up. When it was almost up—not before then, she couldn't stand too much more time in the rental house, watching William while he watched his wife—she'd go back down to collect him. Two months, and Adelia would ask for one more leave of absence from her skeptical boss, who never once imagined she would be so irresponsible this late in her illustriously competent career. One week and two months, and she'd try one last time to retrieve the man she loved from the place he'd withdrawn to and bring him back to the place where she remained.

"You should get it in a week, two at the latest," the teller said again, eyeing the old man hovering behind her.

"What if I don't?" Adelia asked. "I've been skipped in the past."

"If you don't receive the form, you should call this number," he said, sliding a piece of paper through the slot in his glass pane.

Adelia took it. She stood with dignity and shouldered her purse. "You should keep better track of your numbers," she said, then ceded her place at the glass.

Chapter 23

After a week Arthur still hadn't come by. He was there, next door, but he stayed hidden in the squat house with its orange shutters. There was that to worry about, as well as the fact that William still refused to talk about the building plan. But the permit came through, and Diana's second meeting with the contractor went well enough that she was able to relegate these facts to the edge of her mind, clearing a space for the carriage house to rise up in its completed form. The contractor assured her that he would be able to use the salvaged beams, the glass doorknobs, and the slabs of cement. She asked that the new wood be cedar; he agreed. They turned to her blueprint, and her heart stopped while he inspected it, as she waited for the flaws that he would find. "We can start on the foundation tomorrow," he said. She held the cool, smooth cylinder of the rolled blueprint in her palm while she accompanied him back out to his truck.

In the evening, she walked to the grocery store under oaks and maples heavy with late-summer foliage. She bought herself milk and cereal, and supplies to make spaghetti for dinner. As she walked home, the plastic bag bumped against her calf. Her thoughts were collected, organized around the lines of the new structure, until she passed the Schmidts' house. She thought of knocking on the door. She could ask him to have dinner with her. She could make him spaghetti, and they could share a bottle of wine. Then she reminded herself to be less of a child. Their lives had progressed. It was enough that she remembered how to draw, and that she had made a blueprint that would eventually come to life before her eyes. She kept walking, and the bag bumped, and the air was thick with the smell of fading summer.

While she ate her pasta, she leafed through a coffee table book of great architecture, taken from a shelf in her father's basement office. Afterward, she washed her dishes and put them in the sink. She took the book up to bed with her. It was difficult to fall asleep. The air was hot, and even when she opened the windows, it was as though the branches of the trees were sweeping hotter air into the room. She kicked off her covers and lay there, looking up at the ceiling, listening to the bullfrogs croaking from the pond. Since she'd started the new plans, she hadn't struggled as much with falling asleep. She had allowed herself to concoct elaborate fantasies as she drowsed off: building a great structure, regaining Arthur's affection, resuming her old sureness. But tonight her mind was spare. The part of her that had been filled with dreams was empty, replaced by a hollow sensation. She set her mind to imagining the inside of the carriage house before it burned. She visualized the pointed angle of the roof and the pattern of cedar beams that crossed the air, cutting it into bordered triangles. She smelled its old wood, felt the round coolness of the glass doorknobs in her palm. At some point, she fell asleep to the sound of the bullfrogs and the swaying arms of the trees.

In the morning, she woke up early but it had already gotten hot. In her pajamas, she sat at her desk and unrolled the blueprint again. She checked each detail. When she was satisfied once more with its mathematical precisions, she changed into shorts and a striped T-shirt. Adelia had bought her leather sandals at a store in Rock Harbor; she slid these on her feet. She considered herself in the mirror while she brushed her hair. She was tan, and she knew she looked better than she had when she first came home in June. Somehow, in the rush to finish her plans, she'd forgotten about her own figure. Now she was surprised to notice it in the mirror: her arms seemed stronger and more capable. She shrugged, watching her shoulders rise and fall with easy mechanical motion. So this was the form she would fill. She bent and splashed water on her face, then pulled her hair back into a ponytail. At the kitchen table, she studied the architecture book while she ate her cereal. When she was done, she rinsed her bowl out in the sink, then walked over to the Schmidts'.

When she rang the doorbell first, no one came. She rang again. When the door opened inward, it was Anita who appeared. She was wearing a pink bathrobe, and her thin hair was cropped close to her head. There were circles under her eyes. Diana remembered that she hadn't checked how early it was.

"I'm sorry to bother you, Mrs. Schmidt," Diana said.

"It's too late for that now, isn't it?"

"I was hoping to speak to Arthur."

"He left," she said. Behind her, the shades in the living room were drawn, and the furniture looked gloomy. "He went to Poughkeepsie to check on a distributor."

"I see," Diana heard herself saying.

"I believe it was a brewery. After that he's going back to the city. He can't stay here forever." Diana focused on Mrs. Schmidt's feet, her toes gnarled around the thong of her fuzzy pink flip-flops. She could feel Mrs. Schmidt considering her. "He waited longer than I thought he'd wait," the old woman continued. "He was worried about your sister. The one who burned the house down. But she's fine, and I'm fine, too, so he left this morning."

"Ah," Diana said. She didn't move.

"How is that sister of yours who burned the house down?"

"She's better, thanks."

"That one I admire. When I saw it burning, I told Arthur, 'I'll bet it was that little one. That little one's got guts.'"

"She's been through a lot," Diana said.

"But she's a fighter. I've always admired a fighter. Your father, prick though he may be, is also a fighter."

"Yes, he is."

"Tell him to come back soon."

"I will." Diana tried to smile. "I should go now, Mrs. Schmidt."

"Go, then."

Diana walked down the flagstone path to the driveway, then abruptly turned back. "Mrs. Schmidt," she called. The old woman was still there, watching Diana's retreat from the shelter of her large pink robe. "Will you tell Arthur that the house will be finished next month?"

"You're building it again?" Mrs. Schmidt asked. She looked surprised by the news.

"We're starting today."

"On your property?"

"Yes. Just as it was."

Mrs. Schmidt folded both pink arms over her chest. She surveyed Diana, chin tilted up.

"Will you tell him, please, that I won't give up on it?" Diana said.

"Sure," she said. "I'll tell him."

"Thanks," Diana said, but Mrs. Schmidt was already shutting the door.

Chapter 24

After Labor Day, only William, Isabelle, and Margaux stayed at the beach. Elizabeth drove up on Wednesday evenings to practice with her theater group, but she went back to Breacon after dinner. When she brought the girls to visit on weekends, they were preoccupied with school friends and spiral binders and seemed eager to get back to the suburbs. House by house, the town of Rock Harbor emptied. The tennis pro from the Grubby Tub went back to Montclair; even the Russian maids returned to their sources of origin. Once again, Louise was left behind while the rest of the world moved on. She wandered around the downtown area, a person forgotten. As September progressed, the leaves started to change, but they did so less dramatically than the leaves in Breacon had. Fall in Rock Harbor was less of a seasonal shift than it was a general draining out. Sand swept up from the beach and spread itself across the streets. The Grubby Tub became a ghost bar. Louise watched her tan fading a little bit each day and was filled with a muted version of despair that manifested itself as a constant desire to drive to CVS, where she wandered among fluorescent aisles searching for a perfect product. She purchased a vast array of lip glosses; none of them suited her. On September 26, she received a text message from Bradley that read simply: "I am a married man." She didn't reply.

In general, Louise felt less sad than far away. She had been wandering around the world since she graduated from high school and went to work in London for a year that turned into a decade. By this point, Louise had gotten very far from her point of origin. Occasionally, when she and Margaux walked through the empty grocery store, pretending to look for something, Louise missed her mother in Melbourne. Sometimes she sat on the back porch while William and Margaux gardened together, and she wondered if her own mother and father were wordlessly sharing toast at the kitchen table where Louise was once a little girl. There was a silent physical closeness between William and Margaux that reminded Louise of the kitchen in Melbourne with its cabbagey smell and the tea towels printed with lemons, and there was a defeatedness to William's posture when he allowed the screen door to bang shut behind him that made her think of her own father coming home from work.

Outside of these singular moments, Louise could barely remember what it was like to wake up next to a person, let alone the smell of the kitchen in Melbourne, or the precise print of those tea towels. In late September, Arlene threatened to come down for a weekend visit, but Louise evaded her. The idea of drinking shots with Arlene while attempting to attract pathetically lonely men so that afterward hilarious stories could be told had somehow, somewhere along the way, become nauseating to Louise.

On October 4, Adelia showed up at the rental house. William waited for her on the front porch without making any movement to meet her. After she lugged her suitcase up the stairs to the porch, they stood close together, as though deciding whether to kiss or shake hands. William offered to take her bag, but Adelia shooed him away. Inside, Izzy was eating a microwave pizza and barely looked up from her magazine to acknowledge Adelia's entrance. Later that afternoon, William and Izzy ate their dinner early in order to go out for a nighttime tennis game under the lights, so at dinnertime Adelia made herself a salad and ate it alone at the kitchen table. Louise avoided her. There was something unsettling about her distress, as if it might be contagious. Still, Louise kept an ear out for any unusual activity through her cracked bedroom door. Adelia set up camp in the downstairs bedroom; in the morning, it was evident she was going to stay.

After this unmomentous arrival, Louise and Adelia started sitting together on the back porch, watching Margaux and William garden. To sit with a woman like Adelia, watching William through the shadow of the screen, feeling Adelia's late-life loss, was enough to send you into perambulations through the aisles of CVS for the rest of eternity. In CVS, the endlessness of helpful products soothed Louise. There were solutions for everything: for calluses and corns, blocked sinuses and acid reflux, acne and rosacea, overthick eyebrows and ingrown hairs. There were other regulars at the Rock Harbor CVS, most of them with obvious problems, and Louise allowed herself to wonder about their stories while she perused the spectrum of scented candles. She browsed the anti-inflammatories and felt relieved to know that there were whole aisles set aside for the achievement of physical numbness.

After her trips to CVS, she returned to the Adair house temporarily immune to the depression that came with witnessing a family's collapse. Her desire to write the great Australian-American novel of the century began to fade, but that was fine. She was only twenty-seven years old. There was plenty of time. For now there was some comfort in wandering silently in an emptied town, watching Adelia watch William, surprising herself with the depths of her own melancholy. There was also comfort in escaping into Margaux's journals. To open their pages reminded Louise of a closet she used to love sitting in as a child. She could have huddled in that closet forever, feeling the weight of empty coats draping her shoulders. There was a long fur coat that her mother had inherited from her mum, which fell over Louise's shoulders so heavily that she felt as if she'd wriggled into the emptied body of a bear. There were rustling windbreakers, the smell of cured leather, and rubber galoshes that Louise could fit her bare feet into and imagine she was waiting out a terrible flood. She held her breath in that closet while her parents fought and made up outside, or her brother played with his friends, or the dog whined in his loneliness. And when she opened the door and walked out into the bald light of the outside world—no one having noticed how long she was gone—there was always the same disappointment at having to reveal herself once again. When she read Margaux's journals, she experienced the same feeling of sitting in another person's long fur coat. She saved them for late at night, when the rest of the family was sleeping and she had the kitchen to herself, so that she could disappear most easily into the closet of Margaux's words.

August 1996

Each time I see Isabelle, it's for the very first time. I know this isn't true, because there are pictures of us all through the house, because she is my daughter, because I gave birth to her and William is her father. I have their names written on a piece of paper on my desk: Elizabeth, Diana, and Isabelle. But I am always struck by the same surprise: who is this girl, with her long dark hair and her thin arms? She seems so perfect that I want to touch her. I have to keep my distance to avoid doing this; it would frighten her if I did. She carries tennis rackets with her. She is the child of William and Adelia. But she gives me long looks, as if asking for something secret I can't remember. And I can only notice that she's pretty. It's surprising every time how pretty she is.

Just now she came up to my door and looked at me as though there was something she needed me to explain. She was wearing coral shorts and a sleeveless denim shirt tied at the waist. She stood in my doorway, waiting for me to explain, and I had no idea what it was that I was supposed to say. "Is it just erased in the end?" she asked, pulling all of the air. "Is it all just erased?" She seemed terribly upset, so I shook my head. "No, no, it's there," I told her. "It's definitely there, forever." I thought this would comfort her, but she only looked more lost. I wanted to be close to her, but I knew I'd misunderstood. I needed the distance to see her and remember her. "Do you want it to be erased?" I asked her. She only covered her face with her hands.

It wasn't the right thing to say. If I could remember who I am to her—why she looks at me with her expectant eyes—I might have helped. But she's new to me each time I see her.

Having read this in the darkness of the abandoned kitchen, lit only by the narrow beam of a single lamp, Louise was washed with new light. She looked up to see Adelia standing at the doorway, ringed with white rays from behind. She flicked on the overhead lights, and it became clear that she was staring at the book in Louise's hand.

"What's that?" she asked.

"My journal," said Louise. She had never struggled with lying.

Adelia stared. Her face was jagged. "Why are you reading your own journal?" Louise was about to explain the merits of reading one's own journal when Adelia lunged, quick as a descending falcon, and grabbed it out of Louise's hands. Louise tried to hold on, but the surprise of the attack was so total that she had little time to prepare an adequate defense. And then Adelia was reading the page. She turned to its cover. She looked up at Louise. "This is Margaux's."

"She gave me her permission to read them."

"And you took it?"

"She gave me her permission," Louise repeated, hating the whine in her voice.

"Stay here," Adelia said, then left Louise in the light-flooded kitchen, strangely calm while she waited for the moment of her judgment.

When William returned with Adelia, he held the journal in one hand and looked at Louise in such a manner that she immediately glanced away and attempted to forget. "You will leave tomorrow. We'll arrange your pay through the agency," he said. "My wife"—at this point Louise thought she could see Adelia shudder—"is a woman who values her privacy. You've violated that. These should have been left undisturbed."

There were things that Louise could have asked. *What about you, who didn't let her go to a home when she wanted to? And what about Adelia, who came to live in her house? Didn't that get in the way of her precious privacy?* But Louise couldn't stir herself to fight. Why did it matter if she stayed in yet another temporary home for yet another temporary year? It was time for her to leave. She'd miss the journals, but it was time to move on.

All night she packed her bags. She'd acquired so many toiletries that it was impossible to fit them all. In the end she dumped a trash bag the size of a baby, full of unused lipsticks and hand creams, into the bin outside. When she came back in the house, Adelia was sitting at the kitchen table, wearing her white nightgown, waiting for Louise. She was not going to permit any final shenanigans. For old time's sake, Louise left the door to her room open a crack. She was not the only one being watched. When she was done packing, she gathered all of Margaux's journals—even the one with the guilty stain—and carried them with her when she tiptoed upstairs to Margaux's room, followed by otherworldly Adelia. "What are you doing?" Adelia whispered at the top of the stairs. Her whisper was violent. "Giving these back," Louise told her. "Quickly," Adelia said, pursing her lips.

In her room, Margaux was asleep. The profile of her resting face was so familiar that it gave Louise a stab of regret. She leaned over Margaux's bed. "Goodbye," she whispered, placing the journals at the foot. Empty-handed, she watched Margaux sleep, aware of Adelia's presence in the doorway. Margaux's eyelids fluttered but didn't open. "Bye now," Louise said one more time, and she was somehow very sad to have to leave without a response, without any recognition of all they'd accidentally shared.

On her own, back in the writer's den in which she had made very little writerly progress, Louise couldn't sleep. She kept thinking of how casually she had said goodbye to her mother in Melbourne when she first left for London. More casually than she'd just said goodbye to a woman who never wanted to know her. She couldn't stop remembering how easily she'd walked away, how she'd failed to return for nine whole years. At the time, she thought of her parents as depressing. They had a dismal way of dragging themselves through the door when they arrived from the outside world, toting their groceries or their thermoses. It seemed so defeated and bland. She couldn't imagine living such an unimpressive life. The Great Louise Herself. One of the most powerful girls in her school, with her quick wit and her shapely calves. These ridiculous things gave her so much confidence that she was willing to wave goodbye to her mother at the hedge. Her mother was holding a tea towel in one hand and waving with the other as Louise's cab pulled past the corner and out onto the street.

For some reason, while she lay awake, this image remained stuck in Louise's head. It was impossible to sleep. In the end she stayed up reading a gossip magazine until the light outside was grayish and the first bus was due to arrive. Then she shouldered her bags.

On the front porch, Isabelle was waiting in a rocking chair, holding a mug of hot chocolate. She was draped in a velour blanket to ward off the chill that had crept into the air since summer ended. "Where are you going?" she asked.

"Your father fired me. I'm leaving."

"But where will you go?"

Louise shook her head. She had no idea; she hadn't gotten that far. She could stay with Arlene in Breacon until she settled on new plans, but Arlene's apartment seemed bleak from where she stood at this point. "Back home to Melbourne, I guess," she said, and she was surprised because she hadn't admitted this until now. She wondered where her mother would be sitting when she walked back in the door, whether she had spent the last eight years with the ghost of her daughter, or whether her mother had simply waved goodbye at the hedge and then shut the door behind her. Just then the bus rounded the corner at the end of the street. Louise gestured toward it. Isabelle saw it, smiled at Louise, then waved and wordlessly let her leave them behind.

Chapter 25

Diana oversaw construction, alone on Little Lane, for the months of September and October. The speed at which the house went up was amazing to her. It was like watching a creature come alive. A conjured being composed of beams and panels and cement. At the end of the day, she walked to the grocery store for dinner makings, and after dinner she wandered through the frame of the house. It was different each evening, more complicated and complete. She started eating her dinner there, carrying a card table and a desk lamp out and sitting in the company of the frame's even lines while clouds passed the empty space above her. One night it rained, a quick, heavy rain, and when she went out to the house afterward, the wood was so fragrant that she pressed her nose against it and closed her eyes.

On the second Friday in October, the roof went up. She watched from the patio as it become complete, shingles covering the open beams that had crisscrossed the crowns of maple trees when she sat beneath them in the afternoons. Shingle by shingle the house enclosed itself, battening down. Afterward, she brought the builders beer and thanked them for all their work.

She sat with them on the lawn, strewn with fallen maple leaves, until it was time for them to clear out. Alone except for the finished house, she packed up the car to return to the beach.

When she walked in the door, Isabelle was curled in the overstuffed armchair, studying her anatomy book. She looked up and smiled. "Hey, Di's back," she said to no one in particular.

Diana kissed her little sister on the head. The book in her lap was open to a picture of the heart, with its purple and red highway system of twisting aorta, ventricle, and vena cava.

"I missed you," Isabelle said.

"Me, too, Izzy." There was a deep brown scar on her collarbone where the bone had snapped in half and broken the skin; Izzy reached up and touched it absently as she continued to study the anatomy book.

William was out in the backyard with Margaux, clipping tomato plants. For a minute, Diana watched them from the screened-in porch. It was funny to see her father in his gardening gloves, glancing back at his wife for advice. Margaux sat on her heels, eclipsed by her large straw hat. Occasionally she pointed, and William adjusted his efforts. They worked in such suspended harmony that Diana hesitated before interrupting them. When she did move out to join them, the screen door clattered behind her.

"You're back," William said.

"I am."

"You've gotten some sun," he said. "Your looks are improved." Satisfied, he resumed weeding the flower bed.

When Diana went back inside, she found Adelia glaring into the refrigerator as though she could cause something missing to appear simply by virtue of staring hard enough.

"Adelia."

She spun around, bumping the refrigerator shut with her angular shoulder. "You're back, Di. How is it? How did it go?"

Diana took a deep breath. "It's so beautiful," she said. Relief flooded Adelia's face. "It still needs paint and plumbing. But Adelia, it's the best thing I've ever done."

"Oh, Di! I'm so proud of you." Adelia moved across the kitchen to hug her. Her embrace was bony and sharp. "I'm so proud of you, I could tear you apart." Diana, grateful, pressed her palms hard against Adelia's shoulder blades.

Chapter 26

Isabelle playing tennis was a thing to see. Lifting the ball between her racket and her shoe, crooking her leg like a shore bird. Strolling from side to side between points, twirling the racket on her finger. Concentrating. She was tan from spending her days outside, and she had put on enough weight since the operation to look healthy again. She was very tall. It was a good thing he had married a woman with Margaux's height. His girls were tall. Wide-shouldered, with real wingspan. Perfect for tennis. She was wearing a white T-shirt with the sleeves rolled up around her shoulders, and a Nike tennis skirt that she must have gotten at Smith's. Shopping at Smith's Sports on Main Street was something Isabelle never would have done in the past. She had always looked down on things that young girls like to do, such as shopping at places like Smith's Sports. And now she was chewing gum while she bounced the ball on her strings, playing tennis with her dad and rolling up the sleeves of her T-shirt to avoid a tennis tan.

Somehow the accident had caused her to take several steps back. That was how William described it to himself. It had caused her to reconsider the speed at which she had headed off, and to move at a more appropriate pace. The shift was enormous but invisible. The only remaining evidence of the accident was the scar on her collarbone. Otherwise, she was the same girl, and yet it was as though her body were occupied with a different version of herself.

He liked this version. This was a strange thing to admit, since this version was the result of a terrible accident. But the truth was that William liked this iteration of his daughter, who enjoyed playing tennis with him, picking up the ball like she used to, with her leg effortlessly crooked. When she prepared to return his serve, she swayed low, squinting across the net, and when she moved, there was an easy fluidity that his other girls had lacked. Diana was tenacious and her vision was better than that of any kid he'd ever seen, professional or not. She set her heart on winning something and didn't give up, at least not back then. Izzy wasn't so determined. She would never be as good as Di, mostly because she had taken too many crucial years off. Those years could not be gotten back. They were lost. Moreover, she had none of the killer instinct that Elizabeth had inherited from him. He would have liked to see her acquire a bit of Lizzie's grit, that glint in her eye when she was battering a kitchen appliance. But to see Isabelle's side-to-side movement, effortless and naturally economical, was to be convinced that she had been born to play this sport. With another year of hard training, she could play at college. Not D-1, but maybe doubles at an Ivy League school, as William had done. She could follow in his footsteps, the fourth Adair, including Henry, to play tennis at an Ivy. It was different now, of course. The girls on the Princeton team were basically pros. William did not find those girls attractive. Their legs were overly muscled, and it would be a shame for Isabelle to look like that.

But maybe she could play JV. It would give her a nice community. He liked to imagine her strolling over green lawns, friends by her side and a racket slung over her shoulder.

William was glad she wasn't going to college yet. She wasn't quite strong enough. It was a documented fact that her immunity was low because of the removed spleen, but also she emerged from the hospital fragile in ways that couldn't be attributed just to anatomy. It was as if she were a child again, looking to her father for strength. Not that you would know it, to see her play! Powerfully, she returned the ground strokes he fed to her backhand. She was best in a pattern of ground strokes, when she wasn't trying to win the point. Just spinning out shots like bright thread. She had the most technically perfect backswing that William had ever seen. She was admittedly slower than Diana had been. There was a long loping rhythm to her movement that wasn't ideal. But Isabelle was Isabelle, and she was still his, if only momentarily. She was still there with him, playing tennis every morning, rolling her sleeves and calling to him over the net.

She jogged to the service line. Once, twice, three times she bounced the ball in front of her tan knee. She tossed it up, up, watching it rise above her with the slightest frown between her eyebrows. And then, all in one fluid movement, she unfurled her body, arm and racket continuous like a long silver blade, turning. It was such a lovely serve that William had to remind himself to return, and he was off balance so that only his stronger forehand kept him in the point.

"Good get, Daddy," Isabelle called over to him when the point was over. Everything was going so well with her that William was tempted to drive her back to the club to play a match in front of Jack Weld, so that he would see how undefeated the Adairs remained. He would see Isabelle's perfect backswing, and William would mention that she was deferring college for a year because she wanted to work in the hospital, and that he was hoping she'd apply to Princeton. But William was not so far away from the night of the accident that he was unaware of the subterranean thing that had existed on Little Lane. Though he didn't understand it, it woke him up sometimes in the middle of the night. Then he lay beneath its shape. All he had to do was picture Isabelle's face after the dinner party, with those shadows etched into it, her dark arms floating above her white dress, drinking that bottle of wine before telling him she'd talk to Weld about the carriage house.

To imagine that was enough to make him recoil in shame, even when he was lying in bed at night and even though he didn't entirely understand the cause for his recoiling. He felt it with certainty. It had been there, and it was disturbing enough for him to want to stay far away from that street. He could forfeit his grudge against Jack Weld, if only for the benefit of his kids. He could just let it go. What's done was done; none of the old territory was reclaimable. And it was enough for him that Izzy was here, playing tennis with him, her brown legs creaturely, bouncing the ball once, twice, three times before she tossed it up to the sun.

Afterward, they walked home together along the cracked sidewalk, past Pam's Pancake House and the playground and the rows of houses that had been painted ridiculous sherbety colors. When they got home, Isabelle would make him a sandwich and they would eat together on the screened-in porch. He would not allow himself to imagine anything else, anything greater, than this right now. If it could be like this back on Little Lane, that might be different. If they could keep this closeness there, regardless of Jack Weld, despite the burned-down carriage house. But still. William reminded himself not to wish for too much, lest some of his wishes come true.

"Do you want chicken salad or tuna fish?" Izzy asked him from the kitchen.

"Surprise me," he told her, which made her smile. He watched her opening a can of tuna, mixing it with mayonnaise and red pepper flakes so that he would feel it in his nose even if he couldn't smell it. When the bread popped out of the toaster, she laid it on one of the sailboat plates and sliced a tomato from Margaux's garden, deep red and shot through with purple streaks. She salted the tomato slices, glancing up at him to catch him watching her, smiling in response.

"Izzy?" he asked while her hands moved deftly over the toast. "Do you want to go back to Little Lane? Or would you rather stay here?"

Her hands paused on the counter, but she didn't answer immediately.

"Because, you know," he said, excitement building in him, "if we went back there, we'd be closer to Lizzie and the kids. Mom could get another helper, and you could play tennis with better people at the country club. It would be great for your game."

She didn't look at him, but she lifted her left hand, holding the butter knife, up to her collarbone. She rubbed her scar with her thumb. Looking down at the half-done sandwich, she shook her head. No. Watching her, William felt as thirsty as he had ever felt in his life. His hands, by his sides, twitched to hold a glass of something to drink.

"We don't have to. We could just stay."

She was nodding already, first at the sandwich, then at him. He wanted her to say something. "*Say* something," he was tempted to demand. "Say something stable and strong, like a young woman who is prepared for the world." But he held himself back, because this time with her was a gift he had not expected. Because he'd lost her once, years before he'd been prepared to let her go.

"Sure," he said. "Sure, Izzy, that's fine. Mom and I are happy here. You can drive to the hospital. And you can study from here, and we'll find you more people to play with." He took a glass tumbler from the cabinet and poured himself water from the tap. Over its brim, he watched her moving between the refrigerator and the plate. She finished their sandwiches, and they sat together on the porch, facing the garden that Margaux had planted.

Margaux's garden, rebuilt. Since they fired Louise, she hadn't once wandered away. She stayed close. It couldn't last, of course, but William had the feeling that here, in this rented house, the three of them could stay close. For a while William and Isabelle were quiet together, eating their sandwiches, and then she stopped with a potato chip in one hand and looked at him. "Do you mind, Daddy? If we stay?"

"Of course not, Izzy-belle."

"I'm sorry," she said.

"Don't be. We're all happier here." And they were. He missed things only in theory. The walk to the club, the yard, the kitchen island, the Osage orange trees that he passed on his way to the train. These things he missed in theory, but in actuality, they seemed like aspects of a life he'd seen in a film. The kind of film that makes you nostalgic for places you've never been. Sometimes he woke up in the middle of the night and was engulfed by the strangeness of his new bedroom at the shore. The sound of gulls and the rustling ocean drifted in through his window, unsettling him in its foreignness. Those mornings he woke so thirsty that he stumbled to the bathroom to drink water from the tap only to find he had mistaken something else for thirst. A strangeness that sat in his mind like a boulder, too massive to be divided and composed, understandable only as a tightening in his throat that most closely resembled thirst. Then he sat on the cool porcelain edge of the tub to compose himself, the pre-dawn gloom lit by an overhead light, listening to the strange sounds of gulls.

These were the moments when he wanted to go home. After these nights it was a joy to spend time with Margaux in the garden, even if she barely spoke to him, because it was her hands that had planted the yellowwoods, when they were still wrapped in their burlap bags, in the yard on Little Lane. When William could not recall the smell of the Osage orange trees on Clubhouse Road, he felt so distant from himself that Margaux seemed close, and he sometimes reached out and touched the brim of her large straw hat and felt reassured that she was more present than most of the world.

In the end there was no need to go back to Little Lane. Its old urgencies and demands were strange to him. How could he have cared so much about a carriage house? How could he have imagined that his family's history was more real than pictures in a textbook? It had been too much for his family to bear. Things were better here at the beach. The days passed more happily. Here, there was tennis with Isabelle in the mornings. There was the perfection of her looping backswing. There were Elizabeth's performances, and time with Margaux in the garden. All of this was complicated, of course, by Adelia's unexpected return. She prowled the rental house, wishing for more, casting doubt on their new routines in a way that made William want to banish her to Breacon. So that he could occupy his beach life in peace. So that she would not waste more time wishing for him to go back. Soon she would pack up the Acura, and he would miss her and be glad she was gone. Then there would be less question of leaving, less hopeless desire for long-lost pinnacles. There would be Margaux's tough little roses and the smell of salt in the air, the surprise sometimes of the ocean through a gap between two houses. It was not too terribly little to live these days pleasantly, knowing that his girls would be fine, playing tennis in the mornings and eating lunch on the porch, remembering a world he saw once in a nearly forgotten film.

Chapter 27

On Monday morning, Diana went back to Little Lane to oversee the painting. Picking colors was difficult, since the paint on the original carriage house had been discolored by the time she was old enough to remember it, and the only pictures of the house that she could find in the attic were washed with the lemony tint that creeps over aging photographs. She knew that the sides were originally white, but within the spectrum of sixty whites to which the representative at Benjamin Moore introduced her, she was adrift. In the end, she asked Adelia to come down and help.

"It was almost glossy," Adelia reported, splaying out color sticks. "Like a house in a magazine picture."

Diana moved toward the glossier shades. She pointed at Glacier White, Ice Mist, Paper White, and Snow.

"Yes," Adelia said, tapping the wall with her fingernail. "It was Snow. I think it was Snow."

They went home with a carload of Snow, and in the afternoon the painters arrived. One hour into the job, however, Diana could see that the color wasn't right. It blazed in its whiteness, as though someone had transplanted a glacier to the mellowing light of Margaux's October garden. It was too bright. Even Adelia understood; she'd been biting her lip all morning, watching the glint of it spread across the wooden lines of the house.

"It looks too new," Diana said, standing by Adelia's shoulder.

"Yes," Adelia agreed. "It's not right. It's not right at all."

Back at Benjamin Moore, they faced the expanse of the color wall again. They considered Paper White. They considered Wedding Veil and Chantilly Lace, Gardenia and Baby's Breath, then turned to Rice Paper and Parchment. Adelia could remember the color's freshness, the crisp cool of it against the sweep of summer trees. She remembered an American flag snapping from the pole, patriotic and new. Diana remembered the way the building had been sinking into the ground on one side. She remembered the bare flagpole, reaching its iron arm out of the loft window, dripping with icicles in the winter. She remembered cocoons that nestled in the eaves, far whiter in their spun solitude than the peeling paint outside. In the end, they settled on Rice Paper and drove back to Little Lane in silence, consulting memories of a carriage house that existed as a different entity in each of their minds.

By the time they got back to Little Lane, Diana was eager to test their color choice, so she couldn't help feeling irritated when Elaine Weld called out to them in the driveway. She was hurrying over to catch them, clutching an armload of catalogs and an apple. Diana and Adelia waited for her to approach.

"The house looks lovely," she said. "You've done such a good job."

Diana smiled politely. Adelia was staring past Elaine Weld's left ear. A frosty silence opened between them, and Elaine angled herself more sharply toward Diana.

"We've missed your dad this summer. Has he had a good time at the beach?"

Adelia's face tensed.

"It's been fine," Diana said. "Izzy's enjoying herself."

"And how is sweet Isabelle?" Elaine asked. "We've been so worried about her. Abby called from Amherst the other day to ask if we'd heard about her health."

"She's better," Diana said. "She's out of her cast, and there haven't been complications since the surgery. She's doing well."

"Oh, thank God. We were all so concerned. My husband acted as if it were his own daughter in the hospital."

"Your husband is an asshole," said Adelia.

Elaine stared for a moment, taken aback. "I'm sorry, what did you say?"

"I said your husband is an asshole."

"I don't appreciate that," Elaine said, coloring.

"No, I'm sure you don't," Adelia said. She crossed her arms over her chest and finally looked Elaine in the eye. "Listen, Elaine, I'd love to chat until the sun goes down, but we're very busy right now."

"You threw rocks at those builders, didn't you," Elaine said. Her hands were clenched into fists. "You were the one who threw those rocks. My husband said so, but I told him he should be more generous. I told him that you were a good person at heart." Adelia had turned her back on Elaine's outrage and was busying herself unloading cans of Rice Paper paint, but Elaine hadn't finished with her. "*I* told him that we should have pity on *all* of you," Elaine continued, her voice rising to a new pitch. "I told him that even though William was on an ego trip, we should feel sorry for him because his wife was sick. And I said that women our age grew up in a frustrating time and that your meanness was disguised unhappiness. And even though Isabelle was always a bad seed, I reminded myself that she was only Abby's age, and I pitied her because she had *you* instead of a mother."

Adelia was already moving up the walk, carrying two plastic bags of Rice Paper, but at this point she turned around and her eyes were electric. "And your husband, did he pity her? Just how much did he pity her?"

Diana could feel Elaine trembling under the strength of Adelia's gaze.

"Grow up, Elaine," Adelia said. "You've lived your entire life as a child." She took her burden of paint and headed into the house.

Elaine's face was drained of its color. Diana was tempted to apologize for Adelia, but she did not. "We've got to get back to work," she said instead. There was some comfort in standing up for Adelia. Though Elaine refused to look at her, Diana lingered a moment longer, unapologetic, then followed Adelia into the house.

That night Diana and Adelia set up the card table inside the carriage house. They made plates of ravioli and carried them out to eat in the newly hewn, cedary space. Through the open window frames, they could hear the last bullfrogs croaking. Since the incident in the driveway, Adelia's eyes had softened as she watched the new shade of paint spread across the front of the house. Now she held a glass of white wine in one hand and closed her eyes, inhaling the cedar. "It's perfect, Diana," she said.

Diana looked out the side windows to the Schmidts' house. Two bedroom lights were on, the shades half drawn. It was like an island just off the shore on which occasional glittering lights signaled the presence of living inhabitants. "I love it in here," she said.

"You remembered it so well."

"As soon as I started, it came back to me. Complete. I couldn't remember it at all, and then as soon as I put my pencil to paper, the whole thing was there."

They ate their ravioli in silence until Adelia looked out the window. Diana followed her eyes to the half-drawn windows down the street, still glowing against the darkness. "Do you miss him?" Adelia asked. "The way he was before?" Diana nodded. Parts of Arthur that she'd forgotten over the years had also come back to her while she drew the carriage house. The downward slope of his voice, the way his eyelids were heavy over his eyes. For years, the fact that she had once been loved by him had been nothing more than a hollow idea, and only when she started to draw could she remember how it felt. The memory altered her, even though she knew that time was over. She had told his grandmother that she was finishing their carriage house, and he hadn't come back. He had stayed in Breacon long enough to know that Isabelle was fine, and then he'd left. He had a life of his own. Diana would have liked to explain to Adelia that she was strong enough to survive that. She didn't need Arthur as she once had, now that she could remember how to draw as she used to.

"I miss him, too," Adelia said, breaking the silence. Surprised, Diana turned back to Adelia. "You should have seen him playing tennis," she said. "Or at a dinner party, wearing a green sweater, telling a story that made everyone laugh." Diana began to understand. Adelia wasn't looking at the Schmidts' house anymore; instead, she had angled herself back to the Adair house, three-storied and haughty against the darkening sky. She was talking about William, not Arthur, as he was before the stroke. "I remember when he would tell me about your tournaments. I've never seen a father so proud. You could hear it even in the way he said your name. He could do that. I still remember the way he used to call my name when he walked into my house, so that the whole empty place was suddenly full."

"But that's him," Diana said. "He's still that person."

"He is, isn't he?" Adelia asked, then amended her tone to sound more certain. "Of course he is."

"He's the same as he always was," Diana said, although he wasn't, none of them was, and here they were in the carriage house wishing they could just go home, except that they were already there.

Chapter 28

Because it was a Saturday and she had no practice with the performance art group, and because there was a chill in the air that made the girls huddle closer to her, flushed with an excitement they couldn't explain, Elizabeth decided to make an Autumnal Feast. She felt alive, as she always did when she brought the girls to Rock Harbor for the weekend. Somehow, away from Breacon, her mood lifted and she remembered all the possibility in her life. She was sitting on the front stoop of the shore house, scraping the seeds out of a pumpkin so she could roast it for soup, when Arthur drove up. As she scooped seeds and shook them into a metal bowl, each wet spoonful landed with a *whap*. Her toes, warm in gray wool tights, flexed and unflexed around the edge of the stoop. She was wearing a poplin dress under a gray cardigan, and she was thinking to herself that she must have cut a picture of real domestic bliss, sitting there, scooping her pumpkin. Like the kind of woman who doesn't experience such a thing as divorce. Just an attractive woman in a poplin dress, scooping seeds out of a gourd. She was happy. As Arthur parked and got out of his car, she saw herself through his eyes and thought that only now had she become herself. Later this evening she would drive to the junkyard with Jeanine from the Performance Art Group, and they would sift through discarded domestic appliances. She and Jeanine would talk about what it meant to be a woman, so that when she came home to kiss her children on their damp fragrant foreheads, she would feel as though she were returning to a secret corner of her life, kept safe by her trips to the junkyard with Jeanine. Sheltered, even if she had no husband to kiss her own forehead after she had gone to sleep. It occurred to Elizabeth, as she gripped the pumpkin between her knees to scrape out the last remaining seeds, that now that she had gotten to this point, it was likely that there would be a man in her life, and probably soon. How could someone stroll by and see her in her poplin dress, the late-October sunlight soft across her face, and *not* want to make her his own?

So Elizabeth was feeling composed and sure of herself when Arthur walked up the step, his slouch slight now, his eyes still a little hooded. Despite her confidence, as Arthur approached, she found herself becoming slightly disoriented by his presence, which dredged up memories of those awful final days on Little Lane. She thought of that soured dinner party with Adelia's briny chicken, and she vaguely remembered Adelia saying, "I think Arthur's charmed by Isabelle." She remembered that Isabelle had been drinking with him before she stupidly went out in the Jeep, and so as he approached, she straightened her shoulders and gave him a look that said, *We have moved on beyond Little Lane, and we are happy here without you.*

"Hi, Elizabeth," he said.

She offered him her most regal smile. He stood in front of her, confident in the way of successful men. She realized that he was looking past her into the house, probably for a glimpse of Isabelle, and Elizabeth felt invisible. "She's not here," Elizabeth told him, recovering herself.

"Do you know when she'll be back?"

"I'm not sure. She's playing tennis with our father."

He didn't move. She had never particularly warmed to him. His success in the restaurant business had momentarily impressed her, but she had her doubts about his substance. As a kid, he seemed unimpressed by her family to the point of disrespect. He came to Little Lane wearing sneakers with holes in the toes, and Elizabeth's own sister had fallen in love with him, and he had spent a good deal of his time in the Adair house. Despite all this, he always glazed over when they showed him the clippings about their tournaments, or told him about when William was a kid on the same street, walking over the same golf course to the same club. Those stories were who they *were,* and if Arthur had no interest in them, Elizabeth wasn't sure how he could have *known* Diana. Or how he could possibly care about Isabelle, except to assuage his own guilty conscience over drinking with someone who was only eighteen before letting her burn down a historical monument and then drive off in the Jeep.

"Look, Arthur," she said without standing, one hand on the pumpkin for support. She was taking care of her sister, tending to her family. She was proud of her ability to be strong in this role. "I'll let her know you came by. But I have to tell you that she's been doing very well this summer, and I think it's best if she doesn't spend too much time in the past. What's done is done. She's moving on. She has a sense of purpose now. I don't want to see her lingering over things that are over and finished."

"Sure," Arthur said. "Of course." With some triumph, Elizabeth thought she could detect a deepening of his slouch. "That's good," he tried again, then broke off. "I'm glad she's done well this summer."

"Yes," Elizabeth said. "It is good. We're proud of her."

He was studying Margaux's shrub roses, and he didn't respond immediately. When he did, his voice was steadier. "Please tell her I came by," he said. "I won't bother you again, but will you tell her I went back to Little Lane and I saw everything she's done? It's beautiful. Could you tell her that for me?"

Elizabeth watched him go. She was perplexed about what exactly Isabelle had done in Breacon other than burning down the carriage house. She experienced a moment of doubt about whether she had understood anything he had been talking about, and she was irritated by the way this doubt clouded her autumnal mood. Arthur hadn't once asked about her. She wondered why people on Little Lane were so narcissistic that they never thought to show interest in *her* life, as though they assumed, now that she had kids, she was boring and plain and content to live in the shadow of a husband somewhere, projecting former glory onto her children. She remembered again, as Arthur drove off, that on Sunday night she would have to chauffeur the girls back to Breacon, and the ascent that she experienced in herself at the shore would once again come under attack by suburban mediocrity. There she would fall into an uncomfortable nap until she could return to the beach, and that would be the pattern of her life as long as the girls were in school. Even as she comprehended this, she detected the faintest smell of winter in the air, wafting from inland to the beach. A slight uptake in the wind and a clamping down of the light. Elizabeth took the emptied pumpkin and went inside to the kitchen. Heaving her whole weight into the task, she cut it into segments that she could lay in a pan, and as she did that, Diana and Adelia came in from their trip to Breacon to deal with the painting of the carriage house. Feeling their entrance behind her, Elizabeth was suddenly terribly angry that she had been left to deal with Arthur's visit on her own.

"Well, we found the right shade," Adelia said. Diana beamed. They were so busy with their triumphs that they didn't notice how hard she was working, on her own, without anyone to help.

"That's wonderful," she said, chopping an onion.

"You can't believe how many colors they offer. It's confounding, trying to find the differences between a thousand different variations of white."

"I'm glad you found the right one," Elizabeth said, but she was not glad, and it made her no more glad when Isabelle and William came in with their deep tans, flushed from exercise and carrying their discarded sweaters. She remembered once more that it was only she who would have to go back to Breacon on Monday in order to live her life and raise her children, and the rest of them would continue to live in a beachy dreamland where people did not get divorced and sick people never declined. She felt bitterly alone, the only one who had to go home, which may have been what prompted her not to keep Arthur's visit from Isabelle, as she had planned to do.

"Izzy," she said, "Arthur Schmidt stopped by to see you. He told me to tell you hello."

There was a halting of activity and a spreading silence. William sighed and lowered himself onto the couch to bend over the jigsaw puzzle with which he had become morbidly involved since coming to the beach.

"He probably wanted to be sure that you're better, since the accident and the carriage house fire," she said, emphasizing "carriage house fire." Even as she did, she felt uneasy in the awareness of her ill intentions.

"What did he say?" Isabelle asked. She was standing with her tennis bag sloping over her scarred shoulder.

"He said that he's glad you're doing better. I said you've moved on and none of us are lingering in the past. He said he was happy for you."

Diana sat down abruptly. Isabelle unshouldered her tennis bag and sat down opposite William, watching him work. Adelia was staring with her uncomfortably protruding eyes. There was the sound of William dragging puzzle pieces across the glass coffee table.

"The soup will be ready in an hour," Elizabeth said, trying to change the subject. She looked over at the vase of sunflowers that she had placed at the center of the table back when she was excited about the idea of making an Autumnal Feast to celebrate her family.

"He didn't want to stay for dinner?" Isabelle asked weakly, as though she didn't know what else to say to break the awkward silence.

"No, he was just checking on you. He said he was leaving again, and he only wanted to stop by." Elizabeth looked around at the room. Everyone was strangely quiet. She felt confused. She had *defended* them against an intrusion from the early summer, and they were acting as though she'd lost a crucial battle. Were they worried for Diana? Diana, who was so triumphant about her success with the carriage house that surely she was no longer nostalgic for a slouchy kid she dated when she was just eighteen? Elizabeth looked around. Other than the sounds of William's puzzle pieces, they were completely silent. Adelia and Diana hadn't moved. Why were they so hideously mute? What strange new weight had settled on them all? She wanted to reach out and shake them. "Why are you all so quiet?" she asked. "It's not as though the pope stopped by."

Without answering, Adelia swooped in and grabbed the colander of peas that Elizabeth had placed in the sink. "I'll make these," she said severely, and Elizabeth knew she would boil them into oblivion. She felt helpless as she watched Adelia dumping the peas into the water she had prepared for the soup, aware that she had miscalculated her announcement about Arthur but not entirely sure how. She had the sinking feeling that they might all stand there forever, suspended in the rental kitchen, having each individually missed each other's point and therefore doomed to a lifetime of paralysis.

"Why are you all so quiet tonight?" she asked again. No one said anything. "This is our last weekend here for a while, and I'd rather, when the girls come in from the yard, if you could act as though you're not all slaughtered seals."

No one said anything. William did not look up from his puzzle. That goddamned puzzle and his renewed closeness with Margaux were infuriating to Elizabeth, as if he had given up on his vitality and decided to prematurely age along with his wife. She wanted to go get her crowbar and bash it over the coffee table, sending fragments of glass and puzzle flying into the oppressive air. "Is no one going to say anything? We're going back tomorrow, and you're all just going to sit there and ruin the weekend we have left?"

"You don't have to go back, Lizzie," William said. "You could stay here, and the girls could go to school. You can keep acting with the company."

"We're not going back to Breacon?" came Lucy's voice from the door. "Wait, we're not going back to Breacon?" She was hovering on the verge of tears.

"No, honey pie, we're going back," Elizabeth said, lifting Lucy up. She had gotten too heavy to pick up easily, but Elizabeth wanted to be holding something close to her in the midst of this strange, unfriendly living room. "We're going back, but Granddaddy and Grandmama and Izzy are staying here for a while."

"Why aren't they coming with us?" Lucy asked, and Elizabeth wanted to tell her that it was because they were the only grown-ups in the family, but she noticed that Lucy hadn't cursed once in her distress, and somehow that disturbed her, so she said, "How the fuck do I know?" Lucy's eyes widened. "Huh, honey pie?" Elizabeth asked. "How the fuck do I know?"

Lucy grinned. It had been right to say that. She opened in Elizabeth's arms. "How the fuck-fishing damn-balls do we know?" she asked Elizabeth, and Elizabeth buried her face in Lucy's neck.

"You shouldn't let her curse like that," Adelia said, but Elizabeth didn't care. She wanted her girls to be tough and she wanted them to be happy and she wanted them not to care what Adelia thought or why Isabelle looked so lost or why Diana sat so heavily in her chair. Leave them their complicated weakness. Elizabeth wanted her girls to be strong.

"We're going back on Monday," Elizabeth said. "So you can go to shit-school."

And then Lucy was laughing, and her neck smelled like dirt, and she was heavy in Elizabeth's arms, but Elizabeth had gotten strong from a summer of bashing things in with her crowbar, so she carried Lucy out of the kitchen to the yard, where she let her drop like a wheelbarrow onto the earth. Lucy used her hands to lead Elizabeth over to where Caroline was testing the pH of the vegetable garden soil, and the three of them sat together low and close to the solid earth for one more weekend before they went back home.

Chapter 29

On the first Monday of November, Diana arrived to take William back to Little Lane so he could see the finished carriage house. They asked Isabelle if she wanted to come, but she politely declined; her presence would have cast a shadow over the occasion. Awkwardly, Adelia asked Margaux if she'd like to come, but Margaux only tilted her head, perplexed. "Where are you going?" she asked. "Have I been there before?" Isabelle watched her confusion carefully.

In the end, they took only William, leaving Isabelle to keep an eye on her mother. When the house had emptied, Isabelle went up to her room and chose a purple-and-pink-striped towel for sunbathing. It was strangely warm for November. It would be the last day of the year that she could sit out, and she wanted to cling to it. She wore her blue plastic sunglasses and alternated between her stomach and her back when the exposed side got too chilly. With cold fingers, she flipped the pages of her anatomy book, focusing on the red-purple chambers of the heart. She started close to the house, but as the sun fell, she had to move away in order to escape the growing shadow. The anatomy book gave her the comfortable sensation of having an important dream to strive after, but one that nevertheless was glossed over and distant. She switched onto her stomach and felt the press of the towel against her belly. Her shoulder blades were warm; she allowed her shins to sway from side to side. The next time she picked up the towel to move it out of the house's shadow, she noticed Margaux puttering around in the garden, and the knowledge that she and Margaux were alone together was mildly pleasant, like sun on her skin. She turned the page to examine the spleen, which she was missing. Because of this, her immunity would always be low. People in the Renaissance blamed the spleen for vitriolic behavior. Without hers, Isabelle was not entirely human but was an altered creature who harbored no resentment or rage. She focused on its minute parts with the dispassionate eye of someone studying a disease she would never acquire. After the spleen, she moved to the liver, which was depicted in bulges of yellow and brown. In a while, she had to move her towel again. The one patch of sun remaining in the yard was a rhombus extending over Margaux's vegetable garden. Isabelle took herself there. When she lay down, she found herself face-to-face with her mother's pale calf. She smelled it. It had very little scent. She propped herself up on her forearms and looked at her mother, whose face was engulfed by her hat.

"So it's just you and me," Isabelle said.

Margaux sat back and looked down at her. "Why are you still here?" she asked.

"I don't like it on Little Lane," Isabelle told her. "I think you can understand that."

Margaux watched her uneasily.

"You know, I thought of you a lot," Isabelle went on. "When I was by myself in that hospital room, and I felt like my chest was collapsing. You want to know what I was thinking? I was thinking that, by being there, in the hospital, I was losing an important fight. Like I was going down for the count. I kept trying to think how I could get back in the ring again, but then I thought, What if I just give up? What if I skip it altogether and pretend I was never in there to start with?" Isabelle stated these questions without expecting her mother to answer. She was used to conversing with her mother's silences. "At first," she continued, "the idea of it scared me, but then I got it. That's what you did. You built a family and then you erased it. And look at you now. You seem happy enough, right? I started thinking, Maybe Mom is wiser than I understood. Maybe she's been showing us all this time that there are choices to be made." Margaux shook her head and resumed her weeding. There was a slight twitch under her left eye. It looked uncomfortable, but Isabelle continued prodding anyway. "I thought, What if Mom knew that we get one period of grace, and then we spend the rest of our lives wishing we could go back? So why don't I just go back now? I'd never thought of it as a *choice*."

"So you are not going back," Margaux said, and the vein was twitching visibly. She shook clumps of earth off the white roots of the weeds, then threw them aside. "I'm sorry, but I don't understand. What about your father and your mother? They won't want to leave you here alone."

Isabelle looked at her. *Your mother wouldn't leave you here alone*. "Are you pretending, Mom?" she asked. "I won't tell. It can be our secret."

Margaux looked very odd with that vein twitching and one of her eyes slightly wider than the other. "You can't just stay here," she said. "They can't just let you stay here like this."

Watching her, Isabelle did feel some pity, but despite her missing spleen there was also a thin line of unavoidable meanness that laced the edges of her mind. "No, I'm fairly certain that William will let me stay here for as long as we both shall live."

Margaux was silent again. She was focusing on a row of carrots.

"Did you know how bad it was for me when you got sick?" Isabelle asked. Margaux didn't say anything. "Did you know what was happening? Did you feel me getting lost?"

"This is all very silly," Margaux murmured, and then she started picking at the soil with a gardening tool that looked like a giant's curved fork.

"I don't know if you knew," Isabelle allowed her. "I'm really not sure. If you did, I wish you had done something to help me out. No one seemed to notice." Margaux continued jabbing the soil with her fork. "But I just don't know if you knew," she sighed. She pushed her plastic sunglasses up on her head. The light was flat enough that there was no need for extra shadow. "Anyway, I'd like to stay with you for a while. I'd like some time with you. I promise I won't be here forever. After a while I'll go on with my life. I'd only like to stay here now."

The rhombus of light was shrinking around them. It seemed to be taking her mother with it, so that her cheeks were growing more drawn and she was fading into the shadow under her hat. "You cannot stay here with me. You have a life to live."

"Just for a while, Mom. We can talk about all the things you missed."

"I don't know you," said Margaux, the pitch of her voice rising. She was resorting to her most dramatic strategies.

"Listen, Mom, it's okay with me if you're pretending," Isabelle answered. "I'm not blaming you for leaving me behind. But I'd like to know now, after everything, if you just couldn't stand to remember or if you really forgot." Margaux stared back in silence, and in an instant the shadow clicked shut around them, so they were locked there together in an iron light, staring at each other. Margaux's eye vein was throbbing terribly, and Isabelle thought of leaving her alone, but she wanted to know for sure now that she thought she could understand. She had gotten this far, after all. And so she and her mother watched each other. Isabelle wasn't going anywhere. But her mother was stubborn, too. She was more stubborn than Isabelle could have guessed. She didn't answer, so they sat there together in that locked light, and it was only after a long time that Isabelle understood Margaux wasn't ever going to respond. She was picking up her gardening gloves and her spade and her large torturous fork. Wordlessly, she was standing and brushing the soil off of her clothes, and she was marching back inside the house, so that Isabelle was alone with her anatomy book, on her pink and purple towel, in a dark air by a dark ocean that beat its fists against the unanswering shore.

Chapter 30

William was quiet during the car ride home. He had resisted coming at all: the previous night, when Adelia let him know it was time, he told her in no uncertain terms that he no longer cared about the carriage house. "But you care about your daughter, and she's worked hard on this," Adelia told him. "Why can't we just let it go?" he asked, and Adelia felt so desolate that she stayed awake all night. Every time she closed her eyes, she had the sense that the world around her would disappear if she didn't remain alert, so she would open her eyes again and blink at the ceiling fan. She had fought for the carriage house. She had fought with all the strength in her reserves, because she believed in everything that it stood for. It was their habitat. To live on her own forever without knowing that habitat existed was more than Adelia could bear.

And so she was silent as they returned from exile to the house on Little Lane. If William couldn't remember that this was his home, she would be lost. The only thing he said for the duration of the ride was, "What have the neighbors been saying about it?" and Adelia answered, "Who cares about the damn neighbors?"

When they pulled into the driveway and got out of the car, Adelia allowed Diana to walk beside William. Diana had worked so hard. So much was riding on this for her as well. Adelia watched them walking together, and it was almost too much. Such an arc they had traveled. When Diana was younger, Adelia had enjoyed imagining the exceptional woman she would become. She had enjoyed watching William report the news of Diana's recent victories with that unabashed triumph in his eyes. Both of them had changed. Diana's success with the carriage house had revived her spirits, but Adelia suspected that it was a fragile recovery; Diana looked as though someone had slapped her when Elizabeth announced that Arthur had come for Isabelle. Adelia doubted that she could withstand another major disappointment, and William was so unwieldy beside her, glancing back so often toward Adelia with that cross look on his face, that Adelia worried he would fail to rise to the occasion. When they came around the side of the house and the new building rose into view, Diana and William stopped. Adelia caught up with them and searched William's face. He gazed at it coolly, his expression unchanged.

"So there it is," he said at last.

"It's the same, isn't it?" Diana asked. Her words hovered in the air.

"The design is similar," William replied. They moved closer to the house. Adelia and Diana hung back and allowed him to approach on his own. He raised one finger to the paint. He tested the wall with his weight. He looked up the corner of the house to the roof, then backed up to them. "It's well designed, Diana," he said. "It's fine. But it's not the same." He glanced at Adelia, knowing she would be angry, but still bullheaded in his conviction. "It's not what you want to hear, but the truth is that it's not the same. It's a house made with different wood. Thomas Hardy said the spirit of the building is in the stones, and he drafted enough cathedral renovations to know what he was talking about. It's true. This is a different house than the one my grandfather built. The paint is different, the shingles and the windowpanes. I can't feel the same about it."

"Oh, William, just wait before you say that," Adelia said, taking his arm and clutching it. "Just wait before you say such a terrible thing." She led him inside, and she could feel herself gripping too hard, wanting to hurt him so that he would feel the importance of this moment. They pushed through the door; Diana followed. There, inside the empty space of the house that Diana had built, Adelia pointed out the ways that Diana had tried. "See, William, the doorknobs are the same," she said, pointing out the little prismatic knobs. "They were saved from the fire." A flatness had settled over Diana's face, and Adelia could feel herself growing frantic. "And the floor panels, William, do you see them? Those are the same. That is the same cement your grandfather poured." William looked down at his beach shoes. Where was her William? It was essential that he arrive here from whatever distance he had retreated to. She took his arm again. "Come here, William." She dragged him over to the wall and pulled a chair from the card table in the corner. "Stand on this." He obeyed simply because it was the easiest thing to do. "Look up, do you see that beam? It's the same cedar. Touch it." William reached up. It was the movement that he made when he tossed a tennis ball to serve, one arm reached high, his face tilted up with a slight frown. He touched the beam. He stood like that a long time without saying anything, and then Adelia realized there were tears streaming down his face. Diana could see it, too, and she leaned hard against the wall.

"It's fine, Dad, don't worry," Diana said. "We tried, but it's okay."

"No, William," Adelia said, "it is not okay! William Adair, what is the matter with you?" It was not okay at all that he would not even try to remember himself in this place. "Your daughter has built this house for you, and it's the same as your damn carriage house, and what could possibly be the matter now?"

"Don't worry, Adelia," Diana said. "It's fine. I promise, it's fine."

"I'd like to go inside," William said, getting down from his chair clumsily, like an old, defeated man. "I'd like to go inside for a minute."

"Oh, for Christ's sake, William!" Adelia cried, but he was heading out the door toward the house, and Diana seemed rooted in place, so Adelia followed him. "For Christ's sake, she built that house for you!" she said. He kept moving. "She saved those beams from the original. The cement panels are exactly the same; she lugged them over one by one, your daughter did, for you."

He slid open the screen door. Inside, he sat down on a stool at the kitchen island and put his head in his hands. "I could smell it," he said.

Adelia stopped in her tracks. "What did you say?"

"I could smell the cedar," he said. "The way it used to smell. When we were kids and we played in there, when my brother was alive, when the house was ours."

"You smelled it." Adelia moved to his side. She touched his shoulder and he looked up at her.

"The doctor said it was impossible," he said.

"Maybe," she said. "Maybe, but things change."

"I swear to you, Adelia. I swear I smelled it. It smelled like it used to when we played up there in the fall. Like long-gone summers were trapped in the loft, bottled by cedar. I swear to you that I smelled that."

"You really did?" she asked.

"I swear on my life," he repeated, looking directly at her.

"Swear it on my life," she told him.

"I do," he said. And then he pulled her closer, and her fingertips were on his collarbone, and she could feel the warmth of his face against her own.

Chapter 31

Diana felt nothing after they left. For a while she leaned against the wall, looking out the window at the Schmidts' house. The house where Arthur once lived. Even this she felt nothing about. Even the fact that he had come to the beach looking for Isabelle and Elizabeth had sent him away. Twice in the course of one conversation, when Elizabeth told them in the living room, Diana was taught how far she and Arthur were from each other. Her response to even that lesson was muted. After an initial breathlessness, she felt nothing. She would spend the rest of her life feeling nothing about the fact that he was no longer hers. A wave of exhaustion swept over her, and she wanted to get off her feet. She climbed the new, sure stairs to the loft, empty now, and lay down on the fresh cedar floor. Light filtered through the window in the owl's nest above her. She lay still, listening to the occasional faint creaking of the settling house, until she heard the sound of the door opening and footsteps on the stairs. She opened her eyes in time to see Arthur's head rising over the rim of the loft.

He stopped when he saw her. "Sorry, Di, I didn't know you were up here."

She sat up. "No, it's okay. I was just resting for a second."

"I wanted to come over and see this one last time before I drove back to New York." His face seemed pale in contrast to the dark circles under his eyes.

"What do you think?" she asked.

He scanned the new loft, the new owl's nest, the new beams. Diana remembered that his shadowed eyes had made him seem serious, even as a teenager. She used to love the way his eyes narrowed around an idea, holding it close for consideration. "It's perfect," he said finally. "You remembered it perfectly."

"Thanks, Arthur," she said. "While it was going up, I imagined you seeing it. I kept thinking of your face."

He didn't say anything, and she regretted her effusiveness. He had come for a last look at a building that was briefly part of his life. What was it in her that grabbed for him so desperately as soon as he came close?

"Could you wait here a second?" he said, and retreated down the stairs. She had the horrible thought that he might not return, that he had told her to wait so he could escape from her excessive hope. Time lengthened. Her heart sank. When she heard the door opening again, she didn't dare believe it was him, but the top of his head appeared, then his shoulders. He was holding a green blanket.

"Here," he said, spreading it out on the floor. "Remember?"

She joined him on the blanket, sitting with her knees drawn up to her chest. She couldn't bring herself to meet his eyes, so she trained her vision on the pattern of beams that crossed the air in front of them. She hesitated to speak, feeling oddly frightened, as if to say something would be stepping out into empty space. "Elizabeth said you came to the beach house," she said at last. "That you came to see Isabelle, and she sent you away."

"She said I came to see Isabelle?"

Diana focused hard on the details of the owl's nest, each scallop of each shingle.

"I came to see you. My grandmother said you were finishing the house, and you wanted me to know. I assumed . . ." He trailed off, and she waited for him to continue. "When Elizabeth told me you were doing better, I figured she was probably right. You seemed so happy when I saw you in the driveway, getting ready to start building. I thought maybe it was best if I left without dredging up what happened a decade ago."

"It wasn't a decade ago," Diana said. "It isn't even behind me. All this time I've stayed still while everyone else moved on with their lives. I kept thinking I'd move eventually, but I stayed still, waiting for you."

"You didn't, though. Look at this place. Look at what you've done."

She looked around. The gambrels of the ceiling, the heft of the beams, the rectangular frames of the windows. She could draw them out in front of her. "It was our house," she said.

"I've been trying to forget this," he said. He, too, was tracing the details of the loft with his eyes. "It's not easy, now, to come back here."

"Let's just stay for a minute," Diana said.

They sat together on the green blanket, light from the owl's nest streaming over them, then lay back, facing the dark cedar ceiling. When she closed her eyes, she could feel warmth across her eyelids; when she opened them, the side of his face was a shadow surrounded by brightness. They stayed there so long, the daylight started to ebb, and when the wide blade of it had narrowed to a single line and darkness dropped over them, they moved closer on the blanket. There was his shoulder, his elbow, his knee. The bridge of his nose and the shallow under his eye. The heavy cylindrical curve at the back of his head. These were his geometries, shapes she had nearly forgotten. The architecture of a love she lived in once. She assembled lost lines slowly, gathering his surfaces. He allowed her to approach. She could feel her fingertips on the curve of his ear, her palm on the plane of his jaw. Her heart beat in the cage of her ribs, then against the warmth of his chest. They lay together for a long time, and it was even longer before she remembered that this was a new house, in a new yard, and they would have to start over again.

Acknowledgments

All my thanks go to my family, for helping me write this book and every other story I've written: Colby, for reading it first, and for many advisory walks around Hemphill Park; my father, for showing me the importance of books; and my mother, for teaching me to love characters of all possible types, and for never giving up on my grammar.

I am indebted to my agents, Kerry Glencorse and Susanna Lea, who have been tireless champions; to Nan Graham, who guided the book into its final form with keen editorial insight and all possible care; to Kara Watson, whose thoughtful counsel has been indispensable to the book; and to the rest of the team at Scribner for all of their generous help. Thank you, also, to Venetia Butterfield and the team at Viking UK for their invaluable support.

Many other people deserve thanks for helping me at every stage of the book: Rebecca Beegle, for all her wise council; Ivy Pochoda, for allowing me to copy her in so many ways; Jen Lame, with whom I completed my first book-length endeavors in high school; Ben Heller, for helpful conversations about what a good book should do; Gary Sernovitz, who is the kind of writer I'd like to be; Tom Darling, for showing up in Wyoming at just the right time; Philipp Meyer, for galvanizing and instructional biweekly summits; Anna Margaret Hollyman, for all her encouragement; Louisa Thomas, for exchanging stories with me since college; and Divya Srinivasan, for coming to my aid at every critical moment. Many thanks go to The Rubber Repertory, whose *Biography of Physical Sensation* inspired "A Diary of My Life in Sensation." Every English teacher I've had deserves all my gratitude, but in particular Helen Vendler, who first told me that I was a writer.

Finally, I am grateful to Ben, who makes everything seem possible.